The
Choreography
of Ghosts

Andrew Mosley

ANDREW MOSLEY

To Sam,
With love
from Andy

First edition printed and published in the United Kingdom 2025.

A CIP catalogue record of this book is available from the British Library.

ISBN (Paperback): 978-1-0369-0691-7
Imprint: Independently published
Typesetting design: Matthew J Bird

For further information about this book, please contact the author:
https://www.andrew-mosley.co.uk/

The
Choreography
of Ghosts

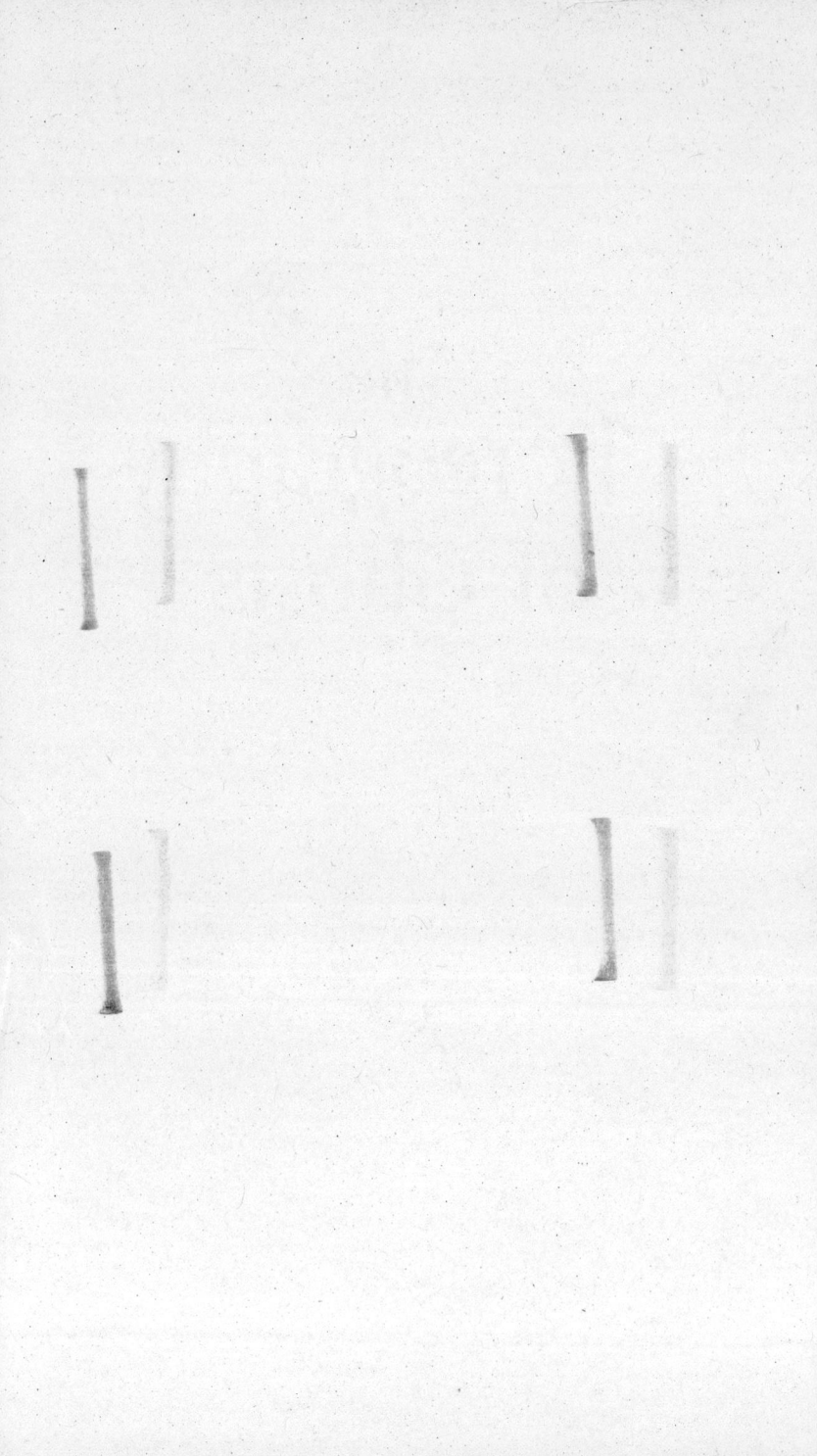

For anyone who was ever lost and those who were never found, travellers and seekers, and for Jude, The Patron Saint of Lost Causes.

I

One Last Dance?

Our stories always end in silence, but they never begin that way. Tinkling piano keys and the ringing of finely cut crystal glasses, constantly clinked as an accompaniment to excited voices and exaggerated exclamation, filled Michael Morrison's mind; a swelling cacophony from another time that induced a violent full-bodied shiver.

Eyes closed, the breathtaking symphonies of history's greatest composers and the words of its most distinguished authors were instantly muted, buried under the debris and dust of the derelict library in which he stood. The alcohol-inspired amorous intentions of peacocking dancers whispered conspiratorially into the eager ears of supposedly temporary partners were slowly quelled. The party was over and it had barely started.

This grim scenario would have been incomprehensible to Morrison when Marianna first elevated him from the darkness he trawled and now he must rise again. What had happened would help him. He knew that now, though it was a conclusion he had previously been unable to comprehend.

Too many hours had been lost staring up at the house, this house, straining to understand the happenings of that night that went so wrong – he did not know then just how much worse it would become – and trying in vain to make sense of the subsequent events that would destroy the Bianchi family.

Soon after the party it hit him that he could never have been Marianna's saviour, not that she had told him she needed rescuing, or from what. Could not tell him, perhaps. When she nervously ventured somewhere near to doing so, his reaction was self-centred and spiteful.

Finally, the courage to return here had emerged within him, brought about by the occurrences of his second Christmas in Padria, this town in which he had arrived friendless and alone but now felt more at home and alive in than he ever did in England.

The relative calm of the walk from his apartment had provided a welcome buffer from the constant hauntings of his confused mind and was only disturbed as he neared the long ascent to the house.

As he made his way across the harbour the landlady of The Star of the Sea had hailed him, shouting: "Michael, are you really going there? Is that wise? Are you sure you will be okay? Please, please be careful. Come back for me if you need help."

He had waved, half-crossing the cobbles.

"I need to do this Gabriella and I need to do it alone, otherwise I will never move on. It's difficult, so difficult, but it will be okay, we will be okay, I promise you."

He was unsure why he added the last part as he was in no way convinced he would ever be able to fully commit to another relationship and there had not been any solid indication of anything other than friendship from her, which he was fine with.

"Call in tonight, we could have a drink, talk about it or maybe catch a film or something afterwards," she called.

"Do they show them with subtitles at the cinema in Padria?" Morrison had asked, manufacturing a slight smile.

"Ha, very good, they don't, but if you intend to stick around, you could always try learning the language."

She beamed fondly at him, revealing almost perfect white teeth, and Morrison, heartened by her support, nodded his affirmation.

He waved again and walked on past the fishing boats, the seasonally unemployed tourist vessels resting after a summer and autumn of day trips to the nearby islands, the restaurants and bars quiet after a busy festive period, their owners taking a well-earned break before New Year's Eve.

The reassuring smell of a sea-washed pebble beach momentarily transported him back to a childhood of holidays on the east and west coasts of northern England, but at the bottom of the slope that led to the mansion he was struck by the enormity of the task ahead.

Breath shallow and increasingly fast, he took his first steps on that pathway - a pathway walked so many times by Marianna but only once before by him - since his move to Padria.

The house was now in full view, the once pristine ochre paintwork dirtied and graffitied, windows broken, the fencing erected to prevent entry torn down.

Roberto Rossi, in hushed tones, had warned him the place had fallen into disrepair, so what he saw should not have come as a surprise, but his body had retreated into something akin to minor shock.

In blue deck shoes, flimsy and unwise, he stepped tentatively over a discarded piece of wire mesh and entered what was once the garden, now strewn with litter, piles of ash from fires, empty beer cans and smashed bottles. Iron gates stood alone, allowing and denying access to nowhere. A small number of goats, maybe five or six, wandered nonchalantly and carefree near the cliff edge, seemingly oblivious to him.

A sturdy grey vehicle, built for negotiating rough terrain, was parked close to the entrance and halted his progress. Was it the one he had seen on the street leading to Stefano Bianchi's new house when he had gone to confront him?

He was almost certain Bianchi would be back here now, inside this fractured house that once gave shelter to his fractured family, but was he alive or dead?

Swallowing hard, he walked towards the gap where the heavy oak door once hung but now just hinges remained, leaving it possible to simply step over the threshold.

Shaking, scared but not terrified as he stood alone in the now silent palace of pain, the commotion of that lavish but calculated celebration of something still somewhat unclear took up residence in his head.

A stifling concoction of dampness, dust, dirt, the musty stench that gradually fills then envelops a house abandoned, had smothered the overbearing aroma of the polished furniture and the expensive perfumes of the guests he had inhaled on his only previous visit. His nose twitched and he rubbed it vigorously.

He surveyed the wreckage. The library that had transfixed him, the mirrored dance hall, the hubris-filled balcony, the red-carpeted corridors running away from the grand reception area now little more than sprawling dumping grounds filled with the discarded remains of the unappreciated possessions of the Bianchis.

When he closed his eyes, the racket subsided, but he did not gain peace. Voices in his head; he heard Bianchi, he heard Marianna, loud, competing, arguing maybe. He heard them but he could not make sense of anything they said.

Breath rapid, he clutched his side, the nagging pain he had thus far ignored letting him know it wasn't leaving him.

Blowing heavily, still not recovered from the trudge up the hill, he assessed the situation. He was no killer, not in the physical sense. Nevertheless, during his brief involvement in the lives of the Bianchis one death had become two and now possibly three, and if the note in his shaking hand delivered what it suggested then he must accept his share of the blame.

For eighteen months he had carried out his own private inquest into Marianna's death, but only recently summoned up the courage to actively seek answers, maybe find some form of closure before he could move on and begin to live again with any sense of purpose.

Finally, after five hundred days of deliberation, a cowardly avoidance even, here he was, and as he looked into the house everything he saw was in black and white. All colour had been drained from his world just as it had in that bleak period of introspection spent walking his cursed and crumbling hometown.

What was once a showpiece was now barely a shell that housed little more than the ghosts of a family extinguished, a family that never did dance as one, yet was somehow orchestrating Morrison's moves, choreographing what he considered could well be his final dance.

Recollections of his last visit, compounded by rising anxiety having received Bianchi's note from Rossi, sped across his mind like a film reel; the people they had seen on the approach to the house, the women in long expensive dresses, adorned with statement jewellery, advertising their wealth in order to leave no-one in doubt as to their position in society.

He thought of Marianna's silk dress of shimmering black with red around the hem and the trepidation he felt, the acid building in his stomach as they exchanged apprehensive glances. He remembered her father as he entered the building - he looked nothing like her, sounded nothing like her, behaved nothing like her - his smug image reflected in a picture he picked up during the party, a photograph of a family physically together yet mentally so far apart.

The sharp winter sun pierced the wreck of a building, yellowing the swirling dust and temporarily blinding Morrison, and as the sounds of that dreadful night faded and died, for almost a minute he saw nothing.

***

Clusters of people were moving in rhythm to what Morrison understood to be traditional Italian folk music, but which sounded to him to be of Greek or Turkish origin. Some had dressed for the occasion - the pre-launch of a dance school which was to open in the new year - in long flared skirts of deep red and black, frilly white shirts and shawls to afford protection against the chill. Others had arrived as if they had simply happened upon the event while venturing out for a leisurely post-Christmas pre-New Year stroll, perhaps punctuated by a drink or two in one of the busier than usual bars in the Piazza San Marco.

Morrison considered the music an acceptable addition to the usual sounds of the square and infinitely more satisfactory than the tacky pop which, with a fair wind, he could occasionally catch emanating from the sports bar on the main route into the tourist area of Padria.

Tiredness overcame him as the walk back to his apartment from the Bianchi house had taken longer than he had estimated, the discomfort caused by the griping in his stomach forcing him to pause on several occasions, staring out to sea to appear as if he was merely taking in the view over to Pompeii. The thought that he should trouble a doctor only briefly occurred. There was no time for that. Not yet.

The cumbersome package he was now carrying added to his burden as he affected smiles at passers-by still infused with seasonal cheer.

Stressed and exhausted, he had rested on the bench on which he had been sitting with Marianna when she had first mentioned the party, shuddering as it struck him that not so long ago both their bodies would have made an impression on the seat and now only one of them was able to do so.

The painful memories, combined with the dying afternoon sun's still sharp reflection from the surface of the water, caused him to screw up and close his eyes.

He could never have foreseen during that carefree night they had spent in Padria that it would so swiftly turn unbearably and irretrievably awkward between them and that he would immediately be plunged back into the crippling self-pity from which he had only just emerged. Was that Marianna's fault or was the real issue that she was not the person he wanted her to be?

A fragmented version of the final words Marianna said before he left her for the last time, turned away and did not look back remained with him. Maybe they always would.

Nervously pushing her silky, dark, almost black hair away from her face and then once again as it cascaded back down, eventually grabbing a fistful, twisting and tightening it into a coil, she stuttered in her attempt to find the right words, which he now heard as: "Today you know my life is one of deceit. I lied to you because at first I thought nothing would come of us, but then I grew to love you and that is why I show you the truth Michael, even though I realise you can never understand and I know it will be the finish of us. I needed you to know. I could not lie to you anymore."

Her face narrowed, cloaked in despair, her brown eyes, maybe through fear, wider than he had seen them before, so deep they were almost black holes, unable to meet his - and she had always met his eye.

He couldn't figure out her exact emotion; was it crushing sadness, guilt, recognition of defeat, anger with him or another, fear or the realisation that an end had been reached?

Morrison looked hard at her for a few seconds, her body shaking inside that beautiful dress as they embraced for the final time. His hurt and disappointment had shown in the terse, clipped response he offered to her words, before looking down at the ground, turning on his heel and leaving, quickening his pace to hasten his exit from that house and the lives of the wretched people within it.

The first words they exchanged once more occupied his thoughts. As he looked up at the clear blue sky he remembered it had been raining lightly on the morning their worlds collided.

He, an author suddenly without words uncomfortably delivering a university seminar aimed at giving the six or seven students sitting casually in a semi-circle a confidence-boosting opportunity to express an opinion in front of their peers. Her, a mature student, engaging, exuding intelligence, enthusiasm and an unconventional beauty and spirit. A spirit he could not possibly have known had already been broken.

As an opening gambit he had asked the group to talk about the best work they had ever read. Without hesitation she had replied: "A Tale of Two Cities by Charles Dickens because of the history, the mystery, the

13

injustice, the graphic detail in which the collapse of a belief system, a people, is described."

Marianna's answer, delivered confidently and eloquently, was markedly and excitingly different to those given by the others who talked about how reading Harry Potter had stirred a latent interest in the written word or muttered something pretentious about Tolstoy or Dostoevsky. They seemed affected, trying to look, dress, talk and think how they believed a stereotypical student should, whereas her style and the content she added to the discussion appeared both natural and effortless.

Her response greatly interested him, though what she said next should have intrigued him, concerned him even, but he was lost to her words by then, distracted by this beguiling Italian woman in that small tutorial group. Would he have even noticed her in a larger gathering?

He was mesmerised by her warm smile, her mouth twisting and turning in tune with her emotions as she spoke, her hands never still, the pupils in her eyes flashing from light to dark, and the slightly unnatural pattern of her speech. English was not her first language, so maybe a vital clue in what she said had eluded him.

Leaning forward, her elbows on the desk, her focus not moving from him, she had added: "I will not insult you by quoting the brilliant first line of the novel, but I would say that the whole thing affirmed my belief that 'repression is the only lasting philosophy' as the Marquis said, Mr Morrison, Sir."

He wished he had asked why this was her opinion, but he didn't. He didn't ask enough questions. Strange for a former journalist, a writer. Maybe he didn't want to know. Knowing often ruined a situation or resulted in anti-climax. However, very soon he would find the answer that would bring this sentence into all-too-sharp relief.

Stirred from his memories by the sound of children screaming and laughing, once more for good luck, and lord he needed it, he had tapped the part of the bench on which she once sat, tensed and relaxed the muscles in his face, glanced over towards the steps by the side of the marina and headed on in the opposite direction.

Back in his apartment, the dancing in the square had only briefly distracted Morrison. The strong clinical fragrance of shaving cream which lingered on his fingers from early morning surprised him as he covered his eyes with his hands to shut out the happiness in front of him and returned to debating his role in the destruction of this family he barely knew.

Subconsciously brushing over his hot brow with the back of his hand he once more scanned the scribbled message Roberto Rossi had translated for him, offering up a casual "If he's not dead, kill him" as he handed it over.

The note, in black biro, read: "Go to the house and you will find what you desire, what you need. Now we are together once more, Sofia, Marianna and me, and if God should forgive me and bless me with the opportunity I shall do all in the power he affords me to undo the horror I created. Stefano Bianchi."

His attention turned to the picture of Marianna he kept in his wallet, the only photograph that evidenced their one short visit to Padria together.

Taken before she had informed him of the party, she looked relaxed and happy, like the dancers now performing outside, but should something in her huge eyes have told him the smile was merely a mask for the deep anguish she had held within herself for so long?

It struck him as odd that he could not accurately recall her; how she looked, her contours, her scent, her touch. Only her eyes and smile remained fully with him. How had the delicate details of her features slipped away so quickly, so easily? How had he allowed that to happen?

He grimaced once more at the realisation there was so much of her life she had felt unable to share with him.

He stared at the huge amount of money - he hadn't even counted it - beside him and ran his hands over the black dress that he had laid out on the table. The dress that had belonged to Marianna.

What was he supposed to do with it? He couldn't keep it, could he? He surely couldn't keep the money either. What about the large, framed picture which had been secured within the pile of cash? What did Bianchi mean by leaving it for him? Was he proving a point?

His lack of sympathy at the death of a man he had only recently shared a whisky with repulsed him. His reluctance to hand over the contents of the package appalled him. Then again, to whom? He had not fully considered the moral and legal arguments surrounding his unexpected acquisition. He would deal with that later.

Outside, the end of a particularly lively song was greeted by whooping, cheering and clapping, and by the time Morrison slowly slid his hands away from his eyes, the depth of the lines ingrained on his palms reminding him of his advancing age, the dancers had, as one, become motionless. Once more, silence.

2

A New Start

"Hey, what the hell do you think you're doing?" shouted Morrison. Searching for the keys to his apartment, he had witnessed the outer door at the bottom of the stairs open and a spiky-faced, slender man, face ablaze with anger, hurl a cat into the street with an accompanying volley of abuse.

"The cat is a bloody idiot. Sleeping, eating, drinking, pissing, shitting, messing the place up. He is a lazy good for nothing arsehole," screamed the man, who was sloppily dressed in ill-fitting jeans, held up by braces, and a creased t-shirt with a large hole in the shoulder.

"He's a cat. What do you want him to do? You can't treat him like that. Your attitude horrifies me. I've a good mind to report you to the police," said Morrison, now as agitated as the owner of the unfortunate animal.

He loved spending time with the cats around the quiet lanes just off San Marco, mostly ginger and cream, dozing away from the direct heat, and he wasn't putting up with this type of behaviour.

"What's it got to do with you? My attitude horrifies you, does it, you pompous self-righteous English imbecile? What I do in my building is my own business, but do whatever you want. Go on, report me to the police."

The man accompanied his rant with an obscene salute known to Morrison as the bras d'honneur.

"There's only one imbecile here and it's not me or the cat," said Morrison, his voice louder, red-faced, fury increasing, jabbing his index finger in the direction of the man.

"If you're so bothered about it why don't you have the fucking thing, you interfering know it all?"

"I will have the fucking thing if you don't want him. Bring him here and I will take him."

Morrison, muttering to himself, slammed the door behind him and stormed up the stairs.

Stomach acid rising, he was irritated now, with himself, with everything, the argument ruining the contentment he had felt as he walked that warm August afternoon, a new-found spring in his step, observing life in San Marco and on the esplanade that separated the town from its volcanic sandy beach.

Unsettled, he rested his elbows on the windowsill, his hands cradling his head, gazed out and pondered. Did Marianna ever sit in this square eating her lunch, enjoying a drink with her friends? Did she come here with other lovers?

Did ever-decreasing fragments of her voice and smell linger in the atmosphere, tiny imprints of her footwear in the warm stone? Did she arrange meetings here and tell of the horrors of her home life? Did her mother come here before her? Would people have recognised her and whispered that, yes, that was her, "one of the bloody Bianchis? They think they own the place."

He imagined her, effortlessly stylish, always gracious and polite, greeting those she knew and those she didn't as she stepped along the alleyways and across the squares of Padria. He considered this area was not too far from her home, yet not within sight or sound, enough distance away to gift her precious hours free from the confines of a life and status that should have made her the envy of all she came into contact with, but instead had trapped her and left her to perish alone.

He smiled as he recalled how she had helped him see life differently through her compassion, encouragement, belief, love and enthusiasm for everyone and everything that surrounded her.

Then he squirmed as he remembered the night when, after a few glasses of wine, he had told her he sometimes considered ending it all, he had tried before and would maybe do so again. In the morning he felt weak, weak and stupid, but he remembered she had shown him that despondency was not the only future and the words that had lit up his novels would return, and that he should write again only when he was ready.

But Marianna left him, in a way twice, and he thought now that their wonderful three months together had ironically made his situation worse. If they had not met he would never have had false hope and buoyancy brought back into his life. She had wrapped herself around his weary wrecked wintered heart, protected it from all that hurt, freed it up to beat in time with hers, squeezing it tighter and tighter and then, just before breaking point, abandoned it to slowly and forlornly beat on.

A pain, like an out of tune guitar string twanging in his abdomen, reminded him the agony was physical too. He took a tablet, his third of the day.

He noted that Franco's had its usual cluster of customers, including the moustachioed man perhaps in his early fifties who dropped in between two and three most afternoons except Thursdays and, depending on its availability, occupied the same seat facing the seemingly endless snake of vehicles heading into and out of town. Ensuring the umbrella protected his balding pate from the burning sun, he would order a double espresso, which he would drink in around ten minutes before proffering a €2 coin to the waiter, Pino, and leaving to make his way to somewhere Morrison did not know.

The mostly loquacious Pino never appeared to speak to this man, both somehow sensing a reluctance in the other to engage. The sign of a good host, Morrison thought, the ability to know when to attempt conversation and when to remain silent.

Locals ate saltimbocca and snacked on meatballs stuffed with mozzarella, arancini, small bowls of pasta and various breads with homemade hummus. Tourists, stopping to take selfies by the fountain or making their way from the ornate church, gorged on too early in the day margherita pizzas and patatine fritte, already quenching thirsts with lagers and local wines.

A family of four ordered espressos, doubles, huge colas with ice, two chose pastries, the boy and the mum, the man happy with his beer, the younger woman watching her figure, even on holiday. A teenage boy in a wheelchair was being fed by his family and occasionally someone would tap him on the shoulder and whisper words of encouragement or comfort. Morrison wondered what had happened to him and if it had been recent.

A tiny man and a suitably small black and white dog joined a group of men, all in their sixties or seventies, to smoke and while away some time debating the issues of the day without actually buying anything. This appeared not to concern the amiable Franco, who busied himself cooking and popping out to chat to passers-by with an easy charm that had undoubtedly won him much custom over the years.

Pino, Franco's son, fussed over a well-dressed young man - clearly giving him more attention than the moustachioed chap - perhaps in his early to mid-thirties. Morrison had seen him before and presumed them to be friends, noting Pino patting the man on the shoulder and laughing with him as he danced round the tables balancing impressive amounts of glasses and stacks of plates on trays.

He enjoyed watching the movement of those in the square, giving thought as to who these people were, why they were here, what the back stories of their lives might be and occasionally jotting down a brief description of the characters he saw and the areas they inhabited.

Today though he could not muster the faintest degree of concentration and each time he began to write Marianna appeared, Marianna spoke to him and Marianna touched him. The vision did not look like

Marianna, for she seemed to be slowly disappearing from his view, but he knew it was her.

He was disturbed by a knock on his door and as he opened it he heard the one across the corridor slam.

There in front of him, in a transporter atop a tray full of litter, was a somewhat disgruntled looking cat - ginger with thin white stripes down the length of its body and a large white patch on its chest - alongside several bowls and boxes containing sachets of food. Next to it was some paperwork which, after unpacking his new acquisition, he discovered were veterinary records for his apparently six-years-old new friend, Romeo Rossi.

Morrison would later visit the vet at the address given to register himself as the new owner, but for now decided to feed the cat and head out to purchase him some toys.

"We'll rub along just fine here," he said to Romeo, who was already stretched out on the settee, seemingly unfazed by his new surroundings or that he had apparently moved in with another human, who was currently rubbing his ears, receiving loud, sonorous purrs in return.

Having scribbled a few words thanking the owner for providing him with Romeo's possessions and asking him some simple questions, he pushed the note under the door of the apartment opposite and headed to a nearby pet shop.

He returned barely twenty minutes later with a scratching post, several balls and catnip mice, and found a folded scrap of paper pushed beneath his own door informing him that Romeo was a healthy cat and in addition to detailing his favourite foods there was a sentence of apology.

Morrison learned that the man had been lonely since the death of his wife and adopted Romeo six months ago, believing he would provide him with company, but his impatience and frustration had meant he did not always treat his pet or, indeed, other people, with the respect they deserved.

He felt a surge of unexpected affection for his adversary, resolving to return their relationship to its previous state of minimal and non-confrontational contact and not to mention the incident that had resulted in him sharing his living space with a cat.

Despite his softening towards Romeo's previous owner - who he estimated to be around sixty five and living alone judging by the lack of noise from his apartment save for the low hum of the television or radio and the odd blast of classical music - he was suddenly overcome by a strange feeling that this man would not simply slip out of his life.

Questioning why he had never previously heard Romeo and why the man, presumably a Mr Rossi, given the cat's name, had been less friendly than almost everyone else he had encountered since his move to Padria, he shrugged and concluded that maybe he simply preferred to be alone.

He could understand that.

As he lost himself in thought, Morrison considered how he had grown fond of Franco and Pino. Franco, a jolly, generous chap, overweight but with the healthy look of someone who had lived a happy life in the sun, revealed little of his life at first, possibly assuming Morrison was a tourist who would visit once or twice then disappear back to wherever he had come from. Gradually he warmed as Morrison called in for food, wine or coffee at first just once a week, then, as he settled in Padria, most days.

He favoured sitting alone and, while friendly to anyone who attempted to exchange pleasantries, was careful not to become too involved. That basis for a relationship at first extended to Franco, but trust and bonding developed between the men, and after a time the same with Pino.

Observing from a distance was a strategy he had employed throughout his adult life and his move here had enabled him to continue to live this way. He intended to keep his circle of friends small and select, to avoid meeting or getting to know those whose destructive minds - Mr Rossi? - would add to his natural leanings towards the negative, but despite himself he was becoming acquainted with an increasing number of people in San Marco.

In general the Padrians were kind to him, invariably speaking in English and interested in his background. In most of the bars and shops he had visited during his time here, owners and waiters, their words accompanied by frowns or smiles of resignation, talked of changing times.

They told him which stores used to be in and around the square, about the invasion of mobile phone shops and supermercatos, how custom these days was different, not just local, British or German, but from across the world, from America to China, Japan to Russia. They informed him how the tourist season had extended due to climate change, which helped business, but also of how unruly teenagers playing football, singing, dancing, shouting and generally hanging around making nuisances of themselves until late was becoming an increasing problem.

"They spoil it for everyone," Franco's friend Tommaso, who also ran a bar in the square, had told him, before laughing and adding: "But maybe that is just my view because I am getting old. I would be the same if I could still dance or kick a ball. Wouldn't we all?"

Others reminisced about their past, cooking, waiting tables or playing music on cruise ships, farming, producing fruits and vegetables, making wine and selling it for a low but still profit-making price as good standard vino della casa in local bars.

Morrison loved chatting with them, learning of their history, Padria's history and writing down what they had told him should the urge and desire to write seriously again ever return to this disillusioned author of two published novels.

Many aspects of living in a different country had worried him, but his concerns were largely without grounds. His lack of Italian had not proved problematic. Most locals spoke English and were happy to do so and the written word was either familiar or made obvious by an accompanying gesture or sign.

Occasionally he would be told to slow his speech, but this had been the case in England, and he was learning to take more care in the way he spoke, his Yorkshire accent noticeably fading the longer he remained in

Padria. He would not drive here, so difficulties on the chaotic roads were also avoided.

Little reminded him of home and even when it did he appreciated the likes of the sudden downpours of rain in late May, early June and September and, as the huge drops spread on the pavements and roads, how they captured the perfumes of the flowers, fruits and trees, combining to generate the aroma of an Italian season. How this happened he did not know, being largely ignorant of the rules of science and nature, but he loved the sensation produced when the natural elements collided with the materials of modern life in this way.

He suffered no homesickness and felt he was gradually leaving behind the dark moods, the malaise, the anger that had taken over his every waking hour and rendered him unable to write, to love, to live any more.

His move, he must concede, had reduced him to a day-to-day existence without any real purpose - well, except for the obvious, of course - but this he appreciated and even enjoyed.

So much so that when relaxed, as he had been prior to the confrontation with the man across the corridor, he relished losing himself in thought while gazing out across the square, on which canopies protected bar-goers from the heat of the sun, the breeze of an evening and the occasional torrential cloudburst.

He loved it too when strings of fairy lights threaded between the trees reflected in the cobbles below as day turned to night, providing the area with a magical shimmering half-light that sprung shadows on and off the walls of centuries-old buildings.

Enough of that though, instead of watching the world go by he decided he would actually join in and make the short journey past the small shop where he regularly purchased wine, the popular newspaper La Stampa, which he would attempt to read in order to improve his perfunctory knowledge of the Italian language, and perhaps some sweets or chocolate.

He would offer a "good day" and "how are you, Luigi?", always in English at the insistence of the portly proprietor, cross the busy road and head to a table on the periphery of the oppressive heat outside Franco's bar.

"Espresso, Mr Morrison? Perhaps a small snack? A glass of wine?"

"An espresso is fine for now Pino. A tiny bit early for wine for me today. Maybe a glass or two later."

"As you wish Mr Morrison."

Morrison took pleasure from the hustle and bustle; barking dogs, motorists furiously beeping in remonstration at another's supposed blunder, smiling, chatting visitors wandering aimlessly, happy to be free of whatever life they had left behind for a brief week or two, and the locals going about their unremarkable daily business.

He was strangely calmed by the morning symphony - reprised in the early evening - of speeding cars, clattering exhausts, hammered horns, shoes striking pavements and excited chatter as people went their separate ways to places of work, the houses of friends or family and later returned home again.

The area was beginning to inspire and captivate him, though it was not a central hub. It was away from the tourist traps and many walking the streets in Padria came to a certain point and assumed they had reached the end of the road.

The street of shops that provided for the residents actually served as a link between the central area and the outer San Marco district, which consisted of a main street, a network of ancient alleyways that had kept their charm despite the gradual encroachment of modern life, and the piazza with its basilica, the signature building situated at the far end as the roads narrowed and headed away from the sea and into the hills.

Sometimes, while quietly enjoying his drink at Franco's, Morrison would concentrate on the art people made through their movement around the square, which by its very shape gifted them a natural frame within which to work, its appearance ever evolving as the characters shifted around, in and out of the canvas. He wondered if the strokes made with the brushes that were our hands and feet degraded or improved the picture.

He kept his thoughts to himself, aware of how pretentious they may appear, leaving him open to ridicule. He certainly wouldn't be sharing them with Romeo's former owner.

Bursts of positivity had him fleetingly believing that in moving here he had broken free, but he knew in his heart he did not yet truly feel that. The debilitating stomach pains, though much reduced over the past few months, would remind him that all was not yet well. That would take time.

He had managed to rid himself of the almost obsessive urge, the need, the desire even, to compel himself to write every day, to create, to produce something tangible to prove to himself he could still do it. And, of course, to somehow justify his existence.

Marianna had helped him do that. Taught him that it didn't matter, that he didn't have to incessantly plumb the depths of his soul, to purge himself each day for little or no satisfaction. He realised his mental state had severely deteriorated through endlessly exploring and obsessing over lost causes.

"Leave it Michael until you feel able to correctly judge life once more, to accurately measure it, make the right decisions and then start again. There is no rush. You have all the time in the world," she had implored him, softly clasping his fingers between her thumb and index finger, all the while seeking acceptance in those world-weary eyes.

Finally, he heeded her advice and no longer considered himself to be Michael Morrison the novelist; the novelist he had told her was slowly dying. He was now just plain old Michael Morrison, the very same from which he wrote to escape in the first place. Only his new lifestyle gave him the option to become Michael Morrison the novelist once again, should he ever wish to.

He readily acknowledged - if only to himself - that any conversation in Padria had not touched upon the real reason, the unresolved part of his life, Marianna's life and Marianna's death that had brought him to Italy and ultimately provided a route to his potential salvation.

He would tell them eventually, his new friends, show them his photograph of her and they would study it before shaking their heads. No, they did not know her.

Likewise, there had been no mention of his two books; his long-awaited success with *The Patron Saint of Lost Causes* and abject failure with the unappreciated follow-up *Walks Through Weeping Cities*, a work he believed to be his best but of which the savagely critical reviews had sucked away his desire to write.

When Franco and Pino first questioned him about his move to Padria he merely answered: "I did not want to get to old age and realise I would die without experiencing other countries, unfamiliar lifestyles, different people. That is all. Nothing more. You never know, maybe I will move again. Tibet has always fascinated me. For now, though, Padria is my home."

Closing his eyes, he tilted his head towards the sky and again drifted back to the first time he saw her. Maybe he would never shift that memory and why would he want to?

The warm spring rain that Bradford morning had encouraged him to slowly run the last few hundred metres into the college.

After asking the students to introduce themselves, he was immediately struck by the way she stared straight into his eyes when she said her name and added that she was pleased to meet him. The way she spoke, her soft, lilting voice, Italian, obviously, but such good English, as advanced if not better than the rest and they were all from the north of England.

The way she dressed; casual but smart, slim dark blue jeans, brown leather loafers, white t-shirt with a dove-grey cardigan draped around her shoulders, dark hair tied back into a neat ponytail, small gold studs in her ears, understated yet noticeable. Ah, maybe he could still conjure up her image after all.

Her mystery; why was she here? Her eagerness to learn; she was older than the rest, possibly a student who had missed out on further education when she was younger, maybe got married, had kids and returned to education as she felt somehow unfulfilled.

But oh, it was so far from that, as he would later discover.

He thought again of the moment he walked away from her. Too wrapped up in his own feelings, so much so that he never looked back. He should have returned that night. Just to get answers. Just to make sure. Just to make sure of something, anything, everything. But he didn't. He walked away. Just walked away. And as before he had met her, for a long time after he struggled to do little else but look back.

"Your espresso Mr Morrison." A bowing Pino disturbed him from his melancholic solitude.

"Grazie, Pino. Sorry, I was lost in thought for a while there."

"Ha, it happens to all of us my friend and maybe it does us good to dream. Prego, Mr Morrison."

Pino, whose intermittent over-politeness pushed him into the realm of the stereotypical waiter, laughed when Morrison told him about his new acquisition and the confrontation with the cat's antagonistic and somewhat prickly former owner, who he said was not such a bad person once you got to know him.

"You must understand he did not used to be this way."

"No, it is because of the death of his wife. He has been lonely since then. He told me," Morrison said.

"Ah, yes," Pino said, hesitating, biting lightly on his bottom lip and raising his hand to clasp his chin, before adding: "That is true, but there is so much more to Roberto Rossi than loneliness and a bad temper. He has money and on the face of it no worries, but in the past he made bad decisions and paid a heavy price for them. When he can trust you and you him, if that is ever possible, then maybe he will tell you."

Morrison nodded, wondering what he meant, but decided not to pursue his line of questioning regarding the man he now knew to be Roberto Rossi as, with almost a grimace on his face, Pino turned away and started to clear a table.

Michael Morrison again lifted his head to the skies and closed his eyes. He felt almost content with life and remembered he had been attracted to

Padria at first sight when he arrived here with Marianna one sunny early June afternoon around two years ago.

This little town by the sea, where he had sought seclusion from a life sometimes lived in the spotlight, but more often within its darker rim, won him over with its manageable size, the pleasantness of the locals, friendly but unobtrusive, the beautiful views on the leisurely stroll to and around the harbour, the delicious summer aromas from the abundance of colourful flowers and the lemon trees as he paraded along the narrow streets.

Morrison thought of the bus driver, as he returned to Padria - this time alone, without Marianna - informing him he would soon be living in the best place on earth.

"Paradise sir, a beautiful paradise."

"As all paradises must surely be," Morrison had replied. He laughed, noting his moment of happiness as a feeling so rare it had become unfamiliar to him.

3

There's Some Explaining To Be Done...

Now, despite the evidence already presented to the contrary, should you believe Michael Morrison to be a man of whimsy and impulse, this is where you become enlightened to the fact his move to Padria was hardly born of haste or chance.

Rather, it occurred due to a strange combination of circumstances involving an unlikely religious dalliance, romance, tragedy and the overcoming of a bizarre fear of a small insect.

He had felt nothing in some of the most incredible churches and cathedrals in the world. Then on a weekend writing retreat on an island off the south-west coast where he walked up and down cliffs and saw little in the way of life except birds he didn't recognise, he felt more freedom than at any other point in his life. Just him and the untamed sea, the leaping waves colliding with granite, water gradually winning the battle for territory.

A man could go missing here and who would know? Who would care? The thought of disappearing crossed his mind, but he walked on for hours until darkness fell and he could almost walk no more.

Next morning, a lighthouse, a graveyard and a church. The lighthouse, decommissioned, imposing, was locked, which was disappointing. The small, well-kept graveyard housed several generations of no more than twenty to thirty families, all no doubt subsequently having fled the island as survival grew harder. The names on the stones had gravitas and drama - Trevithick, Penhaligan, Tremayne - they belonged to their time, whenever that was.

The church's austere exterior lent it a cold dignity. Go on, have a look, he told himself. There's no reason to be scared, yet surely it was fear that drew people to such places. Could he see the light here? Was there even any light to be seen?

The weather-beaten splintered wooden door opened with ease. He surveyed the scene, careful not to go too far in, and apart from himself - and possibly the great Almighty - it appeared the building was empty.

Rather than the intense beacon of enlightenment, the vision he almost craved, there was a starkness, an emptiness. This was a basic, barren church designed to make worshippers humble, to curb their hubris and crush their desire for promiscuity and intoxication, which in the days when it could boast a sizeable congregation was everything anyone might possibly enjoy.

It was cold, astonishingly so. He almost felt the church was angry at being deserted, left alone, abandoned to rot.

Fourteen rows of wooden benches suggested a capacity of around one hundred and eighty parishioners, possibly reached at the peak of its popularity, and Morrison wondered if any of the islanders now long resident in the graveyard had dared risk the wrath of God and his preacher by going missing on a Sunday. Bibles were still placed, presumably for tourists should they feel the need to step inside this foreboding house for some guidance.

A dustiness, a musty smell infused with the distinctive aroma of polish, caused his nose to twitch, a muscle memory of the air he breathed on his few visits to church as a child.

A bright winter sun, kinder than searing, bounced off the windows, disturbing his vision and thought. Chest tightening, he shielded his eyes and turned to walk away. But something made him look back and stare directly into the light which, instead of blinding him, seemed to pierce right through to his brain, clearing the film that had covered his eyes and long dimmed any view of a desirable future.

The feeling, the effect, a quickening heartbeat accompanied by a slight nausea, stayed with him, growing deeper each occasion he revisited it.

Back in Bradford he could not shift the images from his mind, imagining congregations of times past, weddings, funerals, Christenings. What he had seen and felt that cold January day in that remote island church was not immediately apparent to him - it took many months to reveal itself as a message that he must again welcome passages of light into his life.

In time it served to reverse his aversion to houses of God though not his beliefs and he would regularly make a point of going inside a cathedral or church when exploring an unfamiliar city or town. He was uncertain what it was that drew him in, but something about them that had unnerved him now stirred and inspired him.

After his time on the island, he experienced renewed energy and a burning desire to create. He wrote with a fervour, naming his story's protagonist Jude after The Patron Saint of Desperate and Lost Causes, Jude Thaddeus, better known to some, though not by Morrison at the time, as Jude the Apostle - his character one of the forgotten seeing the light and taking up the fight on behalf of those deemed to be beyond hope or redemption in a city that mirrored their plight.

The place was beset by sickness, so were its people and so was Jude. Down on his luck and living on the streets he may have been, but Jude wasn't the wastrel those who passed him by without so much as a cursory glance believed him to be. He persevered, won followers, disciples, and together they endeavoured to improve the fortunes of a city forsaken and, like those of Michael Morrison, those fortunes would be reversed thanks to *The Patron Saint of Lost Causes*, who would come to represent a guiding light through the darkness.

The writing of the book and the hope for the world he envisioned through Jude invigorated Morrison and, as his creation rose from the streets, he felt himself rise too.

His confidence, demeanour and attitude became enhanced as he threw himself into his work, living inside the head of this person who now dominated his every waking hour, this person who devoted his time to bettering the lives of others. The pain disappeared, the tiredness relented, his breathing became more relaxed. His work made him happier, proud almost, but not quite.

All had turned out well for the character but not so for the writer. He knew his new-found contentment wouldn't last; it couldn't last. For if the publication of *The Patron Saint of Lost Causes* had taken Morrison up life's hill, the reaction to his second novel, *Walks Through Weeping Cities*, sent him sliding down its unforgiving slope at some speed.

But there had been light before and maybe there could be again.

Indeed, there would be again. As next came romance which, as we all know, can do funny things to a person. He had gradually discarded the lessons he learned from that visit to the island church and again allowed the light to dim, to flicker on and off, off and on, and eventually almost die, but Marianna protected what little remained of his flame, gave him purpose and an order to his life.

Yet no sooner had her sunlight bathed him in its golden glow than death, her death, ensured its appearance would be no more than fleeting. And yes, like love, tragedy can also make a person behave in curious ways.

It was imperative he made sense of what had occurred. Where had she gone and why? Where had her knowledge, her spirit, her empathy, disappeared to? Surely it doesn't just all evaporate when we die. Where was her light?

It was his duty to discover why she had put it out and conversely kept his burning. She had given him a reason to keep his fire alight and he must use it to honour her. But how? It was all too confusing, still raw, his mind too cluttered, too clouded to see a way through.

Finally came the incident with the moth which once more inspired him to look for light instead of clutching at darkness. The instant it died he understood its urgent need to cling to the feeble artificial illumination that seeped out from the single sixty-watt bulb in the living room of his flat. Its dizzy flight, unfathomable habit of night-time freefalling and apparent random nature of its destination had brought about immediate panic on its arrival, and he had been chosen to either put out its light or facilitate its safe removal.

He took the latter option, but an irrational fear meant his efforts began with indecision and concluded in minor tragedy. Close up, shaking hand poised ready to clamp a glass around the wall-bound insect, the moth appeared more beautiful than he could ever have imagined and Morrison realised his anxieties were based not on an intense dislike but on a failure to comprehend the reason behind its existence and its behaviour.

He stared at it, wondering what it was feeling, if indeed it felt at all, for what must have been several minutes. Then he placed the container within six inches of its surprisingly sturdy body and drew away, apprehensive of sudden movement on its part or of accidentally crushing the insect.

Eventually he steadied his hand then jerked the glass forward onto the wall, encapsulating his target. He had expected the moth to throw itself around, to attempt to escape its trap, but it remained perfectly and serenely still. No sound, no movement.

He slipped a thin piece of paper between the glass and the wall and carefully carried his temporary prisoner out of the flat, down the stairs and onto the scruffy untended scrap of garden, where he lifted the glass and retreated.

When he returned he saw the moth had remained on the paper, motionless, dead. He had put out its light for ever.

Morrison fixed a prolonged gaze on the newly lifeless creature, its dull, at first sight almost colourless body and wings covered in scales. He noticed two intense blue and black eye spots set against a pinkish background on its hind wings. Captivating really.

Braver, he pulled its forewings - folded roof-like over its body - forward and saw its eyes were now deadened, no longer able or needed to scare off potential predators, its antennae down. A curiosity to him, maybe two to three inches wing tip to wing tip, he took a picture and after searching a website concluded it to be of the Eyed Hawk variety.

Does the moth head to the light to facilitate its dance or is it trapped by the brightness? Its mission surely always ends in disappointment; a window to crash against, a dim bulb in a terrible room, a fire to scorch its wings and a moon out of reach, its flight spent way before its intended terminus.

Morrison determined he would never again be afraid of the moth and its quest for light. He would also search for a new life, a new light. He was aware he would eventually have to fight his way through the dark and take the risk of getting burnt, but that was for later.

***

We see him as he leaves the dead insect to walk this weeping city one last time, his mind in turmoil as he patrols the streets and considers: did any of the people here think like he did?

Did they not desire to walk in other lands, better lands? Did they wonder about springtime in St Petersburg or Prague? Did they dream of walking among Amsterdam's tulip fields, spending the breath-sapping early months of the year in Sydney or late summer-early autumn on the Amalfi coast, where he had been with Marianna? Did they imagine gazing across Red Square to the Kremlin from beautiful St Basil's Cathedral or strolling along the cool shaded side streets of the lesser-visited Venetian islands and asking themselves what they had done to deserve living in this place? He asked himself this every day, but he never answered.

Head down, avoiding eye contact with anyone, he seeks self-justification for his wasted years, but does not find it.

As time passes the reasons behind what we have done are often lost and his brief period of success had seen Morrison embracing a different world, mixing with the arrogant and pretentious, spending too much money in expensive wine bars and drinking clubs, all the while knowing it was not really for him. It couldn't last, he lost all self-respect, so he returned to what he had before, except now he was safe in the knowledge that, should he desire, he could just walk away.

Dressed all in black, he crosses over to Centenary Square and stares at the grand, defiant, almost boastful features of the one hundred and fifty-year-old Gothic city hall, which stood for so much good but oversaw far more damage as greed and corruption inevitably overcame whatever laudable intentions the aldermen and good burghers may have had. Here civic pride was born and here it appeared to die, yet this beautiful building still commands the right to stand guard over this once wool capital of the world, now a capital of poverty and decline.

Will he turn and walk uphill towards the Arndale Centre? "Christmas time in Bradford, the lights are bright in Bradford, the price is right in Bradford, the Kirkgate Arndale Centre for all the family" ran the television advert back in the 1980s. We see Morrison smile as he remembers the jingle, but it doesn't tempt him there. Not today.

Instead, he goes the other way and gazes at the listed buildings of neo-classical architecture and wonders how a city that once held international industrial exhibitions ended up like this. Communities built with vision, love and care, beautiful parks, theatres, mills the size of whole villages, printing presses pounding the words of the country's journalists on to paper, yet so much emptiness. The more a place grows the more there is to lose, he supposes.

He knows he could have left when the money from his writing came in and his circumstances changed, but he chose to stay or, more accurately, made no decision at all, a brief taste here and there of the flash of the capital city aside, and now as he looks around he grimaces, realising he is not too different from this city.

Ah, now he's looking up above the bars and boarded-up shops; long-gone insurance companies, banks, drapers, clubs exclusive to those working in certain industries, the words The Liberal Rooms carved into quality stone, sturdy if unspectacular northern buildings garnished with Germanic finishing, now gone to flats, storage or disuse, the music from the clubs below bouncing off walls and ceilings that encased spaces whose intended purposes have been lost forever.

He's visualising gatherings around sturdy boardroom tables - people sipping port behind well-made curtains, quality products manufactured in this city by workers proud to do a job for their proud bosses who pulled the strings in these proud parts - discussing the important matters of the day. What deceit, what crime conjured up in those rooms then, as sometimes now. What do the ghosts here think? What must they think?

Moving on to Grosvenor Street, the scene of a million Saturday night sins, he recalled some words he had written in his unloved second novel: "Here on this street today and every bloody day there's blood in the water, blood in the alcohol, blood on the dancefloor, and outside there's blood in the puddles, blood in the snow, blood every bloody where you bloody well go. Slash, cut, burn, buildings razed, bodies buried, skeletons in cupboards. This city could bleed to death but the people dancing and shouting in its bars wouldn't even notice and if they did they wouldn't let it ruin a night out. They would find something else to do that."

Music forms the rhythm of Morrison's slowing march as it leaps off pavements unfortunate enough to sit outside these pubs, in which every night starts with good intention but will, for someone, end badly. This wasn't a street of music that would inspire creativity. This was the Boogie Street of Leonard Cohen's creation, an escalator of temptation for everyone trapped here at this moment - and Morrison was, as always, among it or, at best, just minutes away. He might hate this place, but he did not want to forget it. It should never be forgotten. Forgiven? He was not so sure about that.

More bitter, harsh words written after another of his walks: "Streetlight, you could have been in Paris shining on the Eiffel, in Pisa the tower, London on the Thames, New York the Statue of Liberty, Sydney, well, take your pick - the bridge or the Opera House - but no, you ended up here and so did I. You, shining above me, separated only by the rain and the chaotic armies of insects attracted to you.

"Poor you, poor me, poor bloody city, its poor bloody whores, the poor bloody men who use them, the bloody violence, the bloody grime, the bloody stench of failure, corruption, failed plans, a bloody past but no bloody future beyond badly-planned estates with their badly-planned families, people trying hard in places called the Beacon - wherever there's a Beacon, a Hope Project, an Eden Garden, a Paradise Row, a help centre called The Light that wants to make you shine, you know you're down on your luck and the only way isn't up, baby."

He bites his bottom lip as he runs through those sentences he knows by heart. He was in a bad place when he wrote those words. He had forgotten the love, the joy in people making the best out of the situation they had been dealt.

He jolts, then laughs as a large woman - out on the town which buzzed with the potential spit of violence around every corner - starting a drinking session which would at some point undoubtedly take a turn for the worse, shouts over to her friend: "I'm stressed right out. I've had mi lashes done, mi nails done, mi 'air done, bin on t'sunbed, and I just thought fuck it, I need a drink."

"You do reyt love, you deserve it," her companion replies.

Back in his flat the song he plays reflects the decline in his life he facilitated when he switched its light back off, the singer lamenting her partner's choice to always sit underneath the crack in the roof where the rain pours through. It was where he always sat too - but not for much longer now.

He's sitting, thinking about how it all went wrong. He had wanted to go dark with his follow-up to *The Patron Saint of Lost Causes*. He felt dark but he went further than he had intended, and reviewers did not warm to its descriptions of madness born from life in a depraved and deprived city in which people shared scraps of pasties and chips with pigeons in empty shopping centres.

They said it didn't work, too cynical, depressing, nasty. So he tried poetry but it was bleak and bitter, though his publisher had already agreed to a small collection, which had subsequently been released on the quiet, probably more in the hope it would sell on the back of his other work before his popularity waned rather than through any admiration of his dubious efforts.

Doubts over his talent existed long before any of his writing was published, and they returned, became entrenched until he fell out of love with words. Fell out of love with life. He had nothing more to give and sighs now at the realisation he will be afforded a status similar to that of music's one-hit wonder. There will be no *Michael Morrison's Greatest Works* for sale in all good discount bookstores near you.

Then he briefly smiles as he remembers how he fell in love with Marianna and his whole life changed again. But now that was gone, she was gone, and the poetry and prose were absent from his life once more.

The only positive option, Morrison thinks, is to save himself, to go too, but not in the way he had told Marianna he would go on that night he revealed his true self, the night she saved him from that true self. It was obvious where he had to go and what he needed to do.

Michael Morrison may have choreographed the moth's last movements, and maybe those of Marianna - such a sacrifice with what aim in mind? - but his own dance was not yet over, and he knew exactly where it must recommence.

He would pack his bags and go where the streetlights don't need to shine because it's never truly dark. His time in this weeping city, where the light in that island church, which he had allowed into his soul, his spirit, his mind and body, like Marianna's light and that of the moth he had carefully tipped off the paper and into a clutch of weeds that had broken through the cracks of his concrete pathway, was almost spent.

So just do it. Don't delay a moment longer. Just go. And he will. Impulsively, he Googles a website advertising rental property in Padria and a flutter of positivity overtakes him. A clear-headedness, an increasing heartbeat. He is on his way.

4

A Heart Still Faintly Beating

"Looking good this evening, Mr Morrison. Very slick, very... mmm... how do you say it... sooo-ave. You are going somewhere special? Seeing someone special maybe?"

He had pondered whether he was too old for the slim-fitting dark denim jeans, pale pink thin cotton jumper and deck shoes he had yet again chosen to wear.

Back home as he packed for his new life he had put all his black clothes, except a decent pair of designer jeans that had cost a considerable sum, into two bin liners which he took to a charity shop. From here on, he told himself, there would be no dark and he would embrace colour with the same enthusiasm in which he intended to embrace his new life. Easier said than done.

At 5ft 10ins and of slight build, he was still in reasonable shape, certainly slimmer than most men his age and, after initially assuming Franco was having a friendly joke at his expense, he waved across at him with more enthusiasm than he had greeted another person in a long time, thanked him for the compliment and shouted back with a grin: "If you've got it, flaunt it Franco, that's what they say, don't they?"

Morrison enjoyed Franco's company, the cheery chef often making a beeline for him as he finished the last orders of the day, bringing over any bits of food surplus to requirement in the kitchen, often clutching a large Italian beer and pointing to it, adding: "My treat to myself Mr Morrison, for still being alive at the end of the day."

Franco, his gentle voice prone to high-pitched rises at the end of the sentences he spoke in disjointed English learned from a career dealing with tourists, seemed interested in Morrison, his views on Padria and on a wide range of subjects from football to politics, the differences between their countries and what he thought of the locals.

His unforced friendly nature had helped Morrison settle and adjust to the pace of his new life with ease; rising late with no sudden jolt from a startling alarm, a leisurely late morning stroll, a daily paper to read alongside a lunchtime snack and drink in a piazza-side café, perhaps a brief afternoon siesta snoozing on the sofa with Romeo, followed by a couple of glasses of wine of an evening.

In his short time here, this routine had won him favour and friendship as he got to know, to various degrees, the people who owned and worked in the cafés and bars and some of those who frequented them. As such, he had quickly become familiar with and fond of the town, its features, its people, its changing temperature and atmosphere as the seasons shifted.

The horrors that inhabited his head and which his still cluttered mind was preventing him from confronting, were gradually clearing and Morrison knew he could not and would not need to put off the main reason he had come to Padria for much longer.

The clear blue sky attracted his gaze, and he inhaled the fresh air that fused with the fragrances from the foliage surrounding the square and realised he was already stronger and healthier, physically and mentally, than he had been when taking in the smells, sights and sounds of the streets in England. This, despite the combined fumes of the thousands of vehicles undertaking the daily crawl along the main route between the tourist centre and San Marco, which, unlike its bigger neighbour, had retained much of the charm of the simple yet graceful architecture shaped by its eighteenth century economic development.

"Not much changes here, Mr Morrison. Then maybe everything changes if you know what I mean. It's just that it happens so slowly you don't notice. Like how you don't observe the change in a person you see every day, then you see pictures years apart and all is different," Franco had explained to him with a casual shrug of his ample shoulders.

Coffee and café chains had opened in the main town, but only one such here. Its arrival caused a degree of consternation and Franco knew the locals who used it, many of whom had objected at the time the plans had been revealed. Some couldn't look him in the eye. In reality though, because of the sort of person he was he had held on to the large majority of his custom and didn't bear any grudges.

A bar further up the square, by the basilica, was now advertising its opening night, boasting of fine wines and dining.

"They come and go, Mr Morrison. They come here thinking they are different, that they offer something for the more discerning customer, but they have to shut up shop when they realise that yes, people will come for a treat once, twice, maybe three times a year, but not enough to make the business pay. Maybe these places work in the big town, but not here where they come because the rents are cheaper, but the people are poorer and cannot afford their prices on a regular basis."

To an extent the long-term existences of family businesses such as Franco's had kept the place true to its purpose and Morrison appreciated that.

As he walked away from Franco, he recalled the late afternoon towards the end of April when he arrived in Padria, a confused mess of sadness, nerves, hope and regret.

The spring sun served up a degree of warmth but there was a chill and light rain in the air, which had deterred many from venturing out, safe in the knowledge that months of hot weather were on the horizon.

The bus from outside the airport had cost €10 and the driver sold him a large bottled beer for an additional €4, something Morrison could not believe would ever occur in England. Oddly, in contrast, a sign at the front warned "Do not eat on board" as though that would cause more problems than drinking. It made him smile now as it had done then.

As the vehicle slowly made its way around the bay it had become apparent that tourism had hugely exacerbated the existing difficulties with the narrow, hilly roads not designed for large coaches and the volume of traffic restricted to the one available route.

Vesuvius, menacing, dark, brooding yet at this point calm, and every other clichéd metaphor Morrison could conjure up, loomed over villages and towns which now made their fortunes from the giant that once slayed them, visitors spilling out from buses to explore the ruined cities of Pompeii and Herculaneum, buying souvenirs and eating and drinking in the street-side cafés.

Churches dotted the high points of hills like all-seeing eyes, but Ave Marias deliberately situated on every sharp bend suggested they could never offer drivers enough protection from an even higher evil as they risked their lives every time they took to these treacherous roads.

The bus crawled past houses painted in ochre, terra cotta, green, grey, pink and yellow, some scruffy, dirty and dilapidated, others with windows gleaming in the early afternoon sun as they perched at a safe distance above the sea. He scribbled hasty notes of the diverse colours, the landscape and other observations he had made.

Silently, he took in the blue sky and sea, a ten, maybe fifteen-mile vista, and though apprehensive at his move abroad and nervous of the confrontation he knew he had to face, envied those whose every day began and ended with sights of such beauty. Now, maybe he would finally be able to share that experience.

The swell of optimism reminded him of the feeling he experienced while on a coach trip through Western Australia en route to Perth when passing went through a town called Esperance. Later, a long time later, he looked up the definition of the name and found it meant hope. He hoped this particular journey would bring esperance into his life. He already knew it was the right one to make.

The carabinieri, dressed in black, blue and red, yelling, pointing and waving their arms, amused him. The high-pitched rhythm of their sirens, he would discover, was an almost constant soundtrack to life here, accidents causing delays and impatient horn-honking drivers caught up in the jams condemned to another hour in yet another queue.

Other police stood, apparently directing traffic, aggressively blowing whistles as men and women trading fruit, vegetables, sorbets and coffee from the backs of brightly decorated Piaggio Ape 50s fought for their place on the roads with cars, delivery lorries, taxis, large tourist coaches, local buses, mopeds and motorbikes.

All this excited him and, as they drew to a standstill by the Piazza San Marco, he considered the possibility of Marianna travelling that same route, perhaps on that very same bus, maybe even on the same seat, but then concluded she probably did not use public transport.

He put his pen and notepad away – he considered jotting down observations and ideas a less conspicuous way of working than typing on a tablet when in public – and felt himself start to shake as he thought about his life-changing move, his apprehension pin-pricked by an emerging sense of purpose and the anticipation of huge, positive change.

He heaved his bags from the storage rack above, having travelled relatively light due to having had his essential possessions sent on ahead to the flat he had chosen to rent above the tabacchi in Piazza San Marco.

Walking on to the square, not fully concentrating on where he was going, he only just managed to avoid barging into an elderly woman hunched under a black umbrella. At his repeated and somewhat frantic "...sorry, sorry" he thought he heard her utter the words "bless you", which provoked a smile.

He noticed a bar with the name Tommaso's in white above the black door and spotted the nearby tabacchi he had been instructed to call in to. He crossed, passing by the side of a bar or restaurant with chairs and tables optimistically placed outside - he would soon know this to be Franco's - stretching towards the end of a set of unprepossessing three-storey buildings; small shops, doors shielding stairs leading to apartments above offices, a general store.

Evidence of the fuss and flamboyance of the Easter festivities had disappeared - aside from the tatty remains of bunting and the odd poster advertising events past, now peeling away from display boards - and the flowers were blooming in colours and numbers not normally seen in England until around late May, the foliage far more verdant and bountiful.

Inside the shop he blinked as his eyes adjusted to the sudden darkness, taking in its predictable array of newspapers, tobacco, cigarettes and pipes arranged neatly on wooden shelves and in cabinets, supplemented by a selection of confectionery, savoury snacks, a lottery machine, cold drinks, alcohol and a collection of small machines that appeared to represent some sort of postal service.

He found the slightly stale smell of pipe or cigar smoke that surrounded him not unpleasant, but briefly wondered if it would make its way up the walls and through the ceiling into his flat above.

He introduced himself to the small, chubby man in white shirt and black trousers, stocking the shelves and making his way between a small number of tables and chairs. The shopkeeper had anticipated his arrival and handed over the keys to the flat with little fuss other than a warm smile that spread over his fleshy face, a basic introduction - "Ciao, Luigi" - and to note that if he needed anything, information, provisions, help, he should just ask. He was in the shop every day but Monday, 8am to 9pm.

Morrison nodded several times, thanked him and walked, as instructed, down a small alleyway, unlocked the door and carried his bags up the two flights of stairs to the entrance of his flat, which he accessed through use of a second key.

The apartment, he found, was small but neat and contained all the essentials, as he had been informed it would. Pictures of beaches and coastal scenes were dotted around the walls, which were all painted white, creating a light mood, which Morrison thought would help him keep cool - and provide an illusion of space - should the heat of Italy become stifling.

The kitchen had everything he would require plus a fancy-looking Lavazza espresso machine, which he vowed to learn to use. A shuttered window looked over several apartments across and to the right of him, with a large, concealed garden area in between, containing fruit trees and vegetables; to his surprise he could see mandarins, pomegranates, oranges, aubergines, melons and peppers.

Empty cupboards lined the corridor, which stretched past a functional bathroom and concluded at the other end with the apartment's one bedroom which contained the usual items of furniture.

The sitting room area featured a second shuttered window, this time much wider and longer, and provided expansive views out on to the square and across to a restaurant with a sign identifying it as Franco's.

Morrison had found the place on the internet and secured its rental through an agent, who would also deal with the payment of bills. Luigi in the tabacchi was the named direct contact and any queries other than financial should be dealt with through him, he had been told.

Taking a seat at the dining table, he jotted down a brief list of basic questions regarding post, water and the fuse box, and later that evening pushed his note into the letterbox attached to the store. Luigi responded in similar fashion the next day, his answers written neatly in English - alongside a friendly note informing him that bus tickets could also be bought from the tabacchi - of a standard which surprised and impressed Morrison.

How much had changed since that day? He was now in a happy place, pleased he had made the move. Even the heat bothered him less now than during those initial exhausting walks in the summer months when the heady mix of tourists and the fumes from the vehicles that carried them stole the air from the central areas of the town.

He had quickly discovered he could escape this, as he had done today, by simply avoiding the town centre and walking to the harbour by following the sea wall.

If it was particularly hot he would occasionally break his walk by stopping for a half-bottle of the local wine he favoured at a small family-run boutique hotel that boasted a garden bar seating area across a road closed off to traffic. There he would gaze across the Bay of Naples, so blue, a blue interrupted only by the odd cloud, the near perfect peace only broken by the chugging of a fishing boat, the buzzing of insects, the whizz and whirr of gardening tools and the occasional cawing of gulls annoyed at whatever gulls get annoyed about.

The clouds floating above Vesuvius, Morrison thought, appropriately enough resembled an explosion, but all was still, the real explosions the bougainvillea, the red roses, the lantana, yellow here, and in the next section of garden, tutti-frutti.

Above him, with shuttered windows open, guests were taking photographs and videoing the bay, staring across at the settlements under the volcano and wondering if those living there worried all their days, their forebears forever nearby, immortalised in lava for all to see.

"You are changing Sir. Your skin is no longer as white as that of an Englishman. The sun, it turns you into a Mediterranean, an Italian, a Padrian even. That is a good thing," the waiter told him, looking serious.

Morrison was happy with that. Happy. Not a word he had used on a regular basis over the past couple of years. He could not recall feeling this relaxed since he was a child at home through the long summer holidays, and even then his over-fertile imagination put constraints on him that he had only recently realised were not really there.

"I am doing my best not to burn but it is hard when you are a pasty-faced Englishman who is still not used to weather of this kind," he told the waiter, with a smile and a shrug, holding out his hands in a gesture of helplessness.

Refreshed, a further twenty-minute walk took him to the narrow, cobbled thoroughfares filled with shops touting their souvenirs from morning until late at night, their owners often eschewing the traditional siesta that provided respite in the days when quality family time came before the relentless pursuit of holiday season money.

It was the same the world over, he thought with a smile as he once more recalled his childhood seaside breaks in the north of England and wondered how do the hotels, bed and breakfasts, cafés and bars in Bridlington, Scarborough, Blackpool and Morecambe survive these days without the Wakes Weeks' trains that used to deposit whole villages and towns during the summer factory shutdown?

Who buys the postcards in those places now? Who buys the buckets and spades, the "kiss me quick" hats, the tat from novelty shops, and who plays the slot machines like he and his father before him? Who forms the queues that lined up for the fairground rides, the candy floss, the fish and chips? Just ageing ghosts perhaps. But where will the ghosts of the future go? Too many for the fairground ghost trains left rusting in abandoned resorts, their final journeys long forgotten, that's for sure.

There were ghosts here too and he often thought of them - one in particular - as he negotiated the steep mediaeval cobbled decline to the old Greek harbour, where he felt time almost stood still, only the clear ringing of a bell on top of the tiny church giving notice of the passing of every fifteen minutes.

Attractive old lamps, once lighting the night with gas, but now solar-powered, would flicker into action in the mid-evening as the sun began to dip. A man sang opera too loudly in Italian outside the church, his cap filled with small coins chucked in by passers-by. Those populating the small patch of beach lowered the umbrellas that had protected them from the glare of the sun earlier in the day, as the flags and bunting hung outside flats and across paths fluttered in the breeze.

Renovation work and damage caused by invaders - tourists of a different nature, plundering rather than providing wealth, but both types stealing something of the soul of the place - had understandably changed the appearance of the area, but Morrison could still conjure up what he believed to be an accurate visualisation of its original state.

Maybe he would set a short story here, he thought, as he imagined events of yesteryear. Try a new genre? A murder mystery perhaps. There was certainly no shortage of possible venues in which to stage a character's grisly demise. He was pleased that his mind seemed able to accommodate the possibility of writing properly again with no concern regarding publication. He would simply write for his own satisfaction.

Morrison attained pleasure from leaning on the railings here and watching the sunsets over the harbour and their disappearance away to Capri, the blue skies over Vesuvius in the other direction. Tiny fishing boats, bigger vessels, ferries and cruisers went about their business under the almost vertical cliff, the town teetering above, and further away, huge cruisers moored up and disgorged passengers onto transfer vessels.

He took to watching the boats coming into the harbour and the bar and restaurant owners endeavouring to entice people in with offers of "a drink, beer, cappuccino, wine, something to eat perhaps, fresh fish caught today, pasta, pizza?" Morrison was sure the pushy men and women stationed at the entrance to each establishment put off more custom than they won with their thinly veiled harassment and statements of the absurdly obvious.

He considered how the area would originally have been little more than a simple fishing village before the tourists came and word got around that this was a place to see and be seen in, perhaps in the 1920s, after which they hacked into the cliffs and built hotels for the wealthy to eat, drink and sleep in while overlooking heart-stopping sheer drops into the harbour.

Looking up, he could see the coaches transferring large groups of middle-aged people, mostly English and American, to these costly establishments. After checking in they would be dragged around the busy streets on walking tours conducted by hot and bothered-looking guides, leading them to shops proffering fridge magnets, tea towels and the ubiquitous limoncello made from supposedly secret family recipes. They would then be herded into expensive fish restaurants with whose owners deals had been struck to sell basic tourist menus at over-inflated but tempting "special" prices.

At first, Morrison did not feel entirely safe when walking these narrow, winding roads as gesticulating drivers, in seemingly erratic fashion, sped under bridges, through archways, below lines of washing strung between apartments, past grimy windows protected by iron railings or, in more well-to-do areas, shuttered windows and large, sturdy, wooden doors.

He thought of Mrs Di Caprio, who had moved to be with family in Yorkshire after her husband Salvatore was killed by a speeding car in Naples. He felt now, especially as he tried to avoid the madness of the 7pm Monday rush hour traffic, that he understood more as to how this could have happened than he did when his mother informed him of the family's situation when he was a child of maybe ten or twelve and the Italian family were something of a curiosity in his neighbourhood.

"Do not worry Michael, it is perfectly safe," Marianna had told him, gripping his hand as they walked the streets here on that heavenly day they spent together that ended so badly.

"You will be fine. You will get used to it. Eventually you do not even notice."

She was right, he did get used to it. Not then though, only now as he walked alone.

A few months after his arrival he had spent considerable time observing the events of the feast of Sant'Anna at the end of July. Boats sailed in and moored in the old harbour, bobbing about as their inhabitants enjoyed local wines and pumpkins with fried fish while folk songs were played.

He spent time in a rustic bar called The Star of the Sea and watched as locals danced under the twinkling lights and fireworks exploded over the water, their reds, greens, whites and oranges lighting up the sea and the sheer cliff walls. He must have looked awkward, sitting alone, half reading a book, as the woman who ran the place would always take the time to ask if he was okay. If he felt awkward then, he no longer felt that way.

Today, as the sun began its descent, he stopped to observe the main town lighting up to the left of the old harbour and looked up into the hills, the winding roads built to take the well-heeled up to their villas, protected by churches and crosses from which they would regularly seek to gain forgiveness for the sins that brought them the wealth they claimed they truly did not covet. He knew all about that now.

One house up there would light up no more, just the odd lamp flickering on the approach to its once grand entrance. This was enough to let Morrison know that it - with all its history, lavish celebrations and tragedy - was still there, its candle almost out but its heart still faintly beating, its final breath and that of what remained of the family who once lived there, a family now well-known to him, surely not too far away.

He imagined Marianna here as a child, living above the bustle of the harbour, so close but yet so far away from the reality of most people's lives. He pulled the picture of her from his pocket, patted it and quickly returned it, feeling the familiar stab in his heart, the wrench in his gut.

"Oh Marianna, my Marianna," he muttered to himself as he turned away and continued his journey.

5

New Streets To Walk,
A Past To Confront

Walking the weeping streets he painstakingly documented in his novel had been for many years a daily routine for Michael Morrison and it was fair to say his habits had not significantly altered since his move to Padria.

He still spent his time wandering, observing and thinking. It was just, well, these streets seemed happier. He was happier too. He knew, however, that danger was always lurking. If nothing else, life had at the very least taught him that.

As he leaned back on his bench, their bench - yes, he was there again - hands on his head, eyes closed, he thought about the holiday, their one visit to Padria, that signalled the end of their relationship.

Three months, that's all it had been. Other relationships had lasted for years, so why had this brief liaison disturbed his emotions and shifted his equilibrium so terribly? Was it her life or was it her death? If she had still been alive would they have been together now? Would she still have meant so much to him? Meant more, maybe? Doubting this, he felt a surge of shame.

They had stayed in the town as part of their only trip abroad which took them to parts of Italy Morrison had never seen, which when he thought about it was everywhere aside from Rome and Venice. He had loved the rugged, craggy beauty of the Amalfi coast where Marianna had lived through her childhood, wandering Positano's tiny alleyways and visiting the stunning gardens at Ravello, but they had spent just one night together in Padria - Morrison another alone - in what turned out to be the defining time of their relationship.

The weather was warm but not too hot, a breeze but no chill. Hand in hand they walked the coast along to the old harbour, stopping at cafés and bars, talking and laughing, Marianna occasionally chatting with locals in Italian and ordering drink and food with a confidence Morrison could never hope to match, even in England, speaking in his own language.

He remembered exactly where they were when he took her picture - a simple snap, her almost unaware - the one he still carried around.

They ambled along the cobbled streets, busy with souvenir shops and tourists, enjoyed a bowl of delicious risotto and drank local wine in a cosy little restaurant down an unassuming-looking lane, the whereabouts of which Morrison could not recollect. He wondered if the restaurant was still operating. Would he go back if it was?

As he laboriously replayed the events of that day he took a deep breath and felt he almost caught the smell of the perfume she wore, the wafts of mandarin orange, jasmine blossom, fig and sandalwood he would inhale as they walked.

He smiled as he thought of her greeting people, saying "hello" as if they had taken on the appearance of a saint, heavily accentuating both syllables, her extended pronunciation creating the word "hay-low".

He had loved the way she grabbed and swung his arm in an almost child-like manner, tickled the palm of his hand with her fingernails, painted bright red that day, and the way she listened to him and laughed at the things he said, his English sense of humour unusual and quirky to her.

"You are so funny Michael. So different to most men," she said, smiling.

"You are the only one who thinks so, but I am happy with that," he had replied. And he had meant it.

That evening they made love in the small hotel room, before sleeping contentedly through the night and waking only to the landlady's call for breakfast. Morrison had rarely felt so rested yet energised, but he was not to know his sense of peace would soon be shattered.

After breakfast they had wandered for a while, but he sensed her mood was markedly different, less carefree. They came to a bench - the bench he now occupied - overlooking the sea. Little conversation passed between them and he began to feel uncomfortable, worried even, as Marianna, almost taciturn, visibly and audibly nervous, her posture stiff, picking at her fingernails, turned to him and announced they would be attending a party that evening and it would not be to his taste.

"A party?" Morrison said, screwing up his face as he stared at her, his voice deep, quiet, almost a whisper. He instantly knew this would not be a party he would attend with enthusiasm or remember with fondness.

"Whose party? Where? You never said anything about a party. Why didn't you mention it before?"

"Michael, Michael, I am sorry, I should have told you, but I just could not," she said, grabbing his arm again, this time more out of panic than excitement, and then pointing across the bay and skywards.

"My father's house, up there on the hill. That's where the party will take place."

Eyes still closed, he recalled exactly the conversation in which she told him about her father, her mother, and their lives in the mansion above Padria; a few hundred words that changed everything between them.

He sighed as he acknowledged that he would soon have to confront his past with Marianna. He had made the first move by coming back here, his confidence in this unfamiliar world ever growing, and he was edging towards the moment when he could truly move forward.

He opened his eyes and took in the view from the bench, which was located in a small, paved area, surrounded by fragrant flowers, many of which he didn't know the names of aside from those he remembered from Marianna's tuition.

Across the bay he could make out the lemon groves cascading down terraces towards the water and, as he watched people on ladders picking from the taller trees, something in what he had observed made him promise himself he would never waste the produce that others had worked the land so hard to grow.

Moving on, he found his mood lifting as he took in the details of his new life, smiling, nodding, and waving a casual hand at those travelling in the opposite direction. In the busier areas and around the harbour, vendors would set up citrus stalls to attract passing trade, the rich colours and smells clashing with the salty sea air and the grey and silver fish from the markets and open-air restaurants.

Morrison would sometimes stop and exchange brief greetings or pleasantries, perhaps buy a lemon or two with plans to add it to a late afternoon gin, or take a small glass of limoncello, which a genial elderly man called Gino sold from the back of an Ape 50, and he would drink while chatting with him for a few minutes.

"Made from the femminello, which produces its fruits two hundred kilometres to the south in the winter months, ripens in spring ready to be picked in the early summer. You will find no better in Padria, signore."

"Well, I haven't yet my friend," Morrison would reply, genuinely happy to talk to the man, who he thought must be in his late seventies, dressed casually for the hot weather in floppy cream-coloured hat, matching shorts and stripy t-shirt, and always smiling. On the face of it content with what appeared to be a simple life.

His interest in what the seller had to say would sometimes earn him a fuller glass for his money and in return he would give his grateful friend a little more cash, which he would at first refuse, before, on further persuasion, eventually accepting, Morrison parting to a: "Next time sir, you will have a free limoncello, the best one of the day."

Occasionally there were misunderstandings, with Gino struggling to find the right word to express himself and Morrison unable to help due to his lack of knowledge of any Italian save for the real basics. Usually, after a few awkward attempts, they would stumble through and successfully communicate, with Morrison apologising profusely for his ignorance.

Gino would normally shrug and say: "No problem my friend, we get there in the end, we always do."

One day he handed Morrison a business card and said: "How about learning a little bit of the language? My daughter Angelina, she is a teacher and she speaks very good English. You don't have to learn it all, but she could teach you enough to get by and you might just find it interesting. You never know."

Morrison studied the card, nodded and replied: "Thank you Gino. I might just give it a go. What harm could it do?"

Within months of his move he had become a regular, walking these streets that on first sight did not seem to weep, learning and remembering routes that would become favourites. He felt he now knew them to the extent he could refer to them as being familiar to him. Some of the people too.

If he turned left out of the square the roads were slightly steeper and, should he continue far enough, would lead him into quiet hillside villages. Nearer walks took him through tree-lined avenues heading towards the sea. People walked their dogs along these streets, some ran free, seemingly knowing where they were going, and men sat outside bars, smoking, chatting and enjoying beer rather cheaper than back in the square in which he lived and much less expensive than in the extortionate town bars.

His lighter moods saw him offering a cheery "hello" here and a "good day" there to other walkers as he took a carefree step to the left and a shuffle to the right, wherever his route took him.

On occasion he still felt fragile and his sunny disposition could easily be reversed. On at least one notice board on almost every street there were posters, words in black on a white background, with names of people on them.

He would often stop and read them, the small parts he could translate telling him these were announcements of forthcoming memorial services for the recently departed - Giuseppe Castellano, Gennaro Cacale, Adolfo Albany, Michelangelo Casola, Rosa Maresca, Carmela Marzuillo, and Gaetano and Fortunata Scotti. The name Marianna Bianchi would have appeared on one of these, he supposed. He wondered where her poster was now.

He would take time to admire the mosaic work on the Ave Marias watching over every corner of the treacherous roads - lit in the evenings - as well as above churches, on bridges and street signs.

There were churches everywhere, basilicas and campaniles, and in these buildings packed with drama and a sense of fear there were also Christs everywhere; Christs suspended in mid-air, Christs on crosses, worried Christs at The Last Supper, Christs in scenes surrounded by pain, sad Christs, lost Christs, despairing Christs, pleading Christs, Christs in robes of white, injured Christs, betrayed Christs, crucified Christs, Christs made from gleaming, shining gold, overlooking structures of marble, walled by chapels dedicated to the saints, the great and the good, all appealing for offerings to help with their upkeep.

Morrison loved and hated these places in equal measure, his occasional visits, he liked to believe, enriching his spirit and occasionally causing his mind to flash back to that church on the island all those years ago.

He was not a man often given to the consideration of providence, but these churches made him question his beliefs or lack of them. One particular picture caught his eye. A woman looking at the baby Jesus, seeing him for the first time. The look on her face, is it one of joy? He didn't think so, it didn't look like it was, though history in its current form tells us that it should be. To Morrison the look was one of despondency, worry, doubt, cynicism, resignation even. Did the depiction of her discovery of Jesus signify the end of her search? Maybe she had realised this was not what she wanted. Or was there still more to search for?

Do searches ever end for searchers, he wondered, searchers such as himself whose minds endlessly seek and are never satisfied with what they have discovered?

In a tiny but beautiful church on the edge of Padria, Morrison could not help but be moved by the sunlight shining through the domed roof and lighting up a crucified Christ, surely a sign, for those who believe in such, of better things to come.

He made an offering, lit three candles, bent his head and uttered some words - they would not qualify as a prayer and he did not intend them to - for his mother and father, and for Marianna: "I love you and I miss you. I will always love you and I will always miss you. I promise to try always to honour you and to never let you down."

His favourite so far, and a church he had already ventured into on several occasions, was the Basilica di Sant'Antonino, named after Sant Antonino Abate, a persecuted seventh century monk, who became a hermit and a bishop and was reputed to have rescued a child that had been swallowed by a sea monster on the shore and saved the town from naval invasions, revolution, plagues and demonic possession.

A genuine saint like Jude, thought Morrison, and he wondered had Marianna, who had told him of her lifelong devotion to her religion, prayed here, cried here and asked Sant Antonino for help? He realised he did not know where her funeral had taken place. Could it have been here?

He lost himself in imaginings of the service. Who would have attended? What would have been said? What hymns were sung? How would her father have behaved and would others there have blamed him for her death as Morrison did? He told himself that if that was the case, possession of every object in the sacristy would not save him.

The pleasant percussion of the ringing of the midday and 6pm bells from various churches - apart from the basilica in the square, he knew not where - would take him by surprise, bring his thoughts back to the present, and he resolved to ask if they were those of the Angelus, which he half-recalled may be rung as a call to prayer, though he conceded he may be mistaken.

For him they were a reminder of the passing of his days. Where had the morning gone? What had he done with his afternoon? How had his evening disappeared in a trice? He endeavoured to look upon this positively instead of berating himself as he would have done when walking the streets of Bradford in an alcohol-induced malaise. The search for a less congested lifestyle was, after all, part of the reason he had moved here.

As he began to map these streets of God he would admire the huge pomegranates, aubergines, lemons, limes, mandarins and oranges hanging from branches. Galleries of gardens, whose verdant green canvasses were splashed with reds, yellows and blues, nicotiana and more bougainvillea, lit up the more well-to-do streets, the small terraces in most other areas simply decorated with potted plants and flowers, while magnificent cypress trees looked over hotels and public gardens.

Then suddenly he would be here again. Here at the bench, their bench, as he was now, internally thanking Marianna for patiently teaching him the names of these plants, flowers and trees.

"Michael, stop," she had said, pulling on his arm and leading him through a gate into a walled garden which surrounded a paved square dotted with seats, before pointing excitedly at a small plaque.

"Look, look, this was all built for my grandmother, my mother's mother and it says 'For Alessia Ricci (1926-1984), who loved the colour and joy that gardens bring to all'. All for her, isn't it amazing?"

This was where he had taken that picture of Marianna and he could see her now opening her arm in an arc to indicate the vast display of colour in front of them. A lovely memory, yet it was also where they had rested on the bench and she had told him about the party.

He often found himself here, reminiscing, wondering what he could have done differently, mulling over his recent past.

The aroma of fresh breads and the perfumes of basil, oregano and thyme emanating from terra cotta pots on the windowsills of houses behind the gardens would occasionally rescue him from melancholy, bringing about an illusion of hunger and a desire to rest while enjoying a small snack to dip in oils and perhaps some cheese and a carafe of wine alongside.

"It's not even 1pm but so what," Morrison would tell himself, remembering he had no particular place to be, no time to be there and no-one to be with.

Once in a while he would linger in a bar longer than intended, perhaps read a book while enjoying a bottle of Lacryma Christi, which he learned translated as "the tears of Christ" and was named as a result of the myth that Christ shed his tears over Lucifer's fall from heaven on the land, thus giving divine inspiration to the vines of the area. It was a local wine, not cheap, not expensive, and it was made with grapes grown on the slopes he could now see, the drought thickening their skins.

If the weather was poor he would end his trip by catching the rattling Naples train on the Circumvesuviana line back to San Marco from Padria's main station, which was located just behind the town hall. The station itself would have been a plain affair but for the fact that barely an inch of it or the trains themselves had been missed by graffiti artists, whose creative work, Morrison would in time discover, spanned the entire line into Naples.

Whatever his activity entailed, there was rarely a day in which he did not arrive back in the square and visit Franco's.

At least once a week Tommaso, Franco, Luigi and Romeo's bad-tempered former owner Roberto Rossi would meet there for a drink and a chat. His relationship with Rossi began to improve, though not quite to what he would call friendship, and on occasion he would find himself in their collective company. It was a situation he had come to appreciate and one that would prevent him becoming lost in his own world, a world in which he did not always enjoy living.

On this particular day, on leaving the bench he went straight home and watched two dogs at play in the piazza, a man, a woman and child following, shouting at them and laughing, and wondered if they ever wished to live alone as he did.

Alone, but not lonely, though sometimes accompanied only by his regrets. One regret in particular. A regret that shut out the rest. He was not sure this mattered any more. Such was his life now. Such were his days.

As he collapsed into his chair, exhausted by the long walk in the heat, back came Marianna, back came the suadade, a state he knew so well but had not yet learned to live with. Would he ever?

He could not have known when they visited Padria that a life here with her, a life anywhere with her, would never have been possible.

6

And Everything Changes...

Architecture interested Morrison. He appreciated it and regretted not being committed enough to have studied it in any detail, merely picking up minor pieces of information along his travels and from reading magazine articles.

Similar to his knowledge of art, it enabled him to hold his own in a basic conversation but was not considerable enough to influence the way in which he viewed the world. He felt this reduced his scope when it came to writing in this area to the extent that he would avoid the subject altogether or at best skirt evasively around its edges.

However, he knew enough to be impressed by a place.

As he stood at the bottom of the hill, eyes following the narrow but long winding drive that led to a magnificent-looking house that could be described as a mansion, villa or maybe even a small palace, he realised there was a lot Marianna had not told him, maybe even kept or shielded him from. He had inquired as to the purpose of the party, but her rapid shoulder shrug and off-hand response served as a warning to ask no more.

It was a house with a statement. Its owners were looking down on that part of town and those who worked and spent time there. At the fishermen, the bar and restaurant owners, the tourists and locals, and across the seascape beyond the main hub of Padria over to San Marco, little San Marco, not worthy of such a glamorous building with the prize of the best vantage point for miles around.

"Wow," he said, eyes flashing up, down, left, right, slightly annoyed at his lack of ability to eruditely describe the scene in front of him.

"Just wow. Why did you not say? Why did you not say this was your house? This was where you grew up. This house shaped your life."

Marianna had been taciturn all day and still she said nothing, merely hunching her shoulders and squeezing his hand as they began to make their way up the gravelled pathway, in step with a number of other guests, some of whom had instructed cab drivers to take them all the way to the entrance.

Morrison offered a half-smile and she responded, but her motions exhibited tension and apprehension even when she did eventually speak.

"Michael, you must relax. There is plenty to tell, plenty to talk about. I promise you I will explain all, just not now. We just need to get through this first."

Her eyes darted from side to side, adding doubt to her words. He had not seen such nervousness in her before and never had a promise sounded so hollow. He barely reacted, internally chastising himself for not expressing support at a time when she clearly needed it.

The majority of women wore long expensive-looking dresses in deep jewel colours. While some took the minimalist option when it came to finery, others eschewed this to, Morrison believed, display their wealth, with gold, diamonds and various other gems he did not recognise adorning fingers and ears, sitting on top of painstakingly coiffed hair and around wrists and necks of various sizes and ages.

Marianna, Morrison thought, had with little effort achieved a look somewhere between the two. Her silk dress of shimmering black with red around the inside of the asymmetric hem and the heart-shaped neckline showing a hint of cleavage gave her a flamenco look. So vastly different to what she normally wore. As a student she couldn't have bought it herself. Her jewellery, tasteful and understated, yet surely not cheap, also clearly had not been purchased from the type of high street establishment she might frequent back in England.

Morrison did not believe he had seen any of these items before and wondered if she had bought them in the couple of hours they had spent apart the previous day.

He mentioned this and, in staccato tone, staring at her feet as she spoke, she waved her arms around in an uncharacteristically dramatic fashion and, grabbing at the hem of her dress, almost shouted at him: "These are not new. This is not new Michael. None of it is new. It comes from an old collection in the vault. All old, like everything we have."

"Vault? Vault? Who the hell has their own bank vault?" The words had left his mouth almost before they had entered his consciousness, anguish building inside him and visible both on his face and in his body language, confused and appalled at discovering an unexpected level of wealth he had simply never imagined, considered or suspected. Suspected? That surely wasn't the right word.

The word "collection" also seemed to him a strange one to use in this context, but looking at the house in front of them and the background she had obviously come from but never revealed, it suddenly appeared much less incongruous, so he left it alone. Marianna, in turn, said nothing else, staring straight ahead as she marched towards the house, her house.

Despite the time heading close to 7pm the June sun was reasonably high, perhaps still having another hour of life in its heat, and Morrison could feel the effects of its retreating warmth but not as strongly as some of the portlier partygoers struggling up the hill.

Turning to look at the small fishing boats and tourist cruisers buzzing around the harbour, which was beginning to fill up with people searching for seats in restaurants and bars, he wished he was down there milling around, watching the death of the day and the birth of the night rather than approaching with growing unease an evening he already knew, even without any possible ensuing drama, would at best prove awkward.

In a hastily hired plain black suit and tie over a white silk shirt, Morrison was beginning to feel somewhat underdressed. He wondered if the building, appearing increasingly large as they neared it, could be described as Italianate, Renaissance perhaps, or was that the same thing? Those, he thought, may be more classical styles, while this appeared more modern, built by a family that had enjoyed some success and wanted to let everyone know.

He knew such houses had gone out of fashion at some point and this looked like it may have been built with some instruction to an architect to create a modern version of a Tuscan villa, its walls not washed white but somewhere near ochre or perhaps cinnamon, a colour stationed somewhere between the sun, the moon and the scorched land. He scolded himself for not knowing more but could not bring himself to ask Marianna, who did not quite hold his hand, simply linking the tips of his fingers with hers.

Finally, they were at the door. Marianna introduced him to her father with barely a flicker of acknowledgement passing between the two or from the father to Morrison, other than a brief cold handshake as Mr Bianchi moved along the receiving line to greet other guests, laughing raucously as he slapped backs, kissed cheeks and embraced shoulders.

He tried to look Bianchi in the eyes, attempted to get the measure of the man. As he moved along he felt anxious as to what he was about to witness in this house with its not yet discovered chandelier-lit drawing room facing the sea, austere-looking library overlooking the beginnings of a pine forest, tall windows with plush deep seats, wrought iron balustraded balconies, terraces and winding staircases; seemingly endless rooms furnished with elaborate wardrobes and dressers, finished with intricate carvings.

Marianna, he observed, bore little resemblance to her father, a small, stocky man with a bald head and self-satisfied smile formed by thin lips slashed into a round face. His white suit did not become him and was too small, his shirt buttons pulled taut, revealing a portly stomach, black bow tie strangling his thick neck.

Was Morrison being harsh to think he looked like a man who did not deserve his wealth but did not recognise the fact, preferring to live with the belief that he was better than others and to use occasions such as this to prove his misconception?

A pianist was playing in the expansive reception area, where a huge chandelier hung, its gleaming droplets catching the light, surrounded by a pillared imperial staircase that spiralled up, via a small landing, to a gallery in which people were milling around with glasses of champagne taken from a team of waiters and waitresses doubtless drilled to leave no vessel empty for more than a few seconds. It was not so much ostentatious as trying to appear so.

Gulping down champagne, Morrison was stunned. He literally had no idea.

"Why, why didn't you tell me?" he managed to blurt out, his lips quivering as he spoke.

"Tell you what? What was I supposed to tell you? Will you please stop asking that? Stop saying that," Marianna stuttered, her fearful, almost tearful eyes like marbles, flitting round a room that sang of wealth.

Who were these people? Who was her father? Who, in fact, was Marianna?

"I didn't want to spoil the surprise," she said, eventually, almost casually, her breathing slower, giving the impression of having regained some composure.

"Come," she motioned, leading him up the right-hand staircase, offering hugs, smiles, "hellos" and "I will talk with you later" greetings - sometimes in English, mostly in Italian - waving and blowing kisses to people as they made their way up to and across the gallery. She motioned him into a dark wood-panelled corridor with a deep-set window in which she made to sit, patting the space next to her to indicate that Morrison should do the same.

"I did not tell you because people judge Michael, you would have judged, you will judge. I hoped you wouldn't, but I think you already have," she said.

"Spoilt little rich girl, never had to make her own way in the world, everything given to her on a plate, never had to do a day's work in her life.

"This, this charade is my father's annual excuse to show off the house. He says it is to celebrate Padria, its beauty and its talent, but no real Padrians will be here, just the usual web of connections that use each other for whatever they use each other for.

"I do not really know. He does not tell me. But what I do know is that you know what this really is, I know what it really is and yes, I am here because I have to be.

"I know what you think Michael, you forget I have read your book. You walked your streets and you found corruption and you think you find it here with my family. You could not accept that and neither could I. Not for you at least.

"Most people, they don't know the real story. They don't know about my father. They don't know why I moved away to England. Yes, I have riches available to me and I have an allowance, otherwise I would not be able to afford to live away, but I do not wish to live with or anywhere near my father. This has been the way for many, many years.

"I try to make my way in the world, but I do not settle, and I do not earn my own money in the way I would like. I must come back, asking my father, then asking again and again and I do not wish to do that, so I feel ashamed as I always do. Each time I become less and less.

"I lied to you, if it even was a lie, because at first I thought it would not matter, but then I grew to love you and that is why I show you the truth now, though I know you cannot ever understand and I also know it may be the finish of us. I needed you to know. I could not lie to you anymore, even though it would have been better for me to never tell you and to stay away from here for ever."

She stopped as a couple walked past, carrying drinks, smiling, seemingly unaware of the drama that was unfolding between Marianna and Morrison.

"This sort of life, this sort of place, is not you, I know. For me it is more difficult for it is what I grew up with, what everybody I know had. To not have this would have been shameful, yet of course I do understand that not everyone does.

"My father says those people are failures, but he does not understand, because the money for this place came from his father and his father before. He was gifted everything, just carried on the business and now a lot of it is gone because he lived the good life, the too good life, the grand life. He never put in the hard work and we have almost lost everything, just like my mother lost everything."

What Morrison saw before him suggested the phrase "lost everything" meant something completely different to Marianna than it did to him and doubtless thousands, millions of others.

Before he could form a response, and he did not know what he wanted to say or was supposed to say, a group of people spotted the couple in the window and rushed over.

"Marianna, Marianna, oh my God, so nice to see you. It's been so long. You look amazing."

Enthusiastic kisses were exchanged, and Morrison was introduced to a collection of what he was given to understand were long-standing friends of the family, excited, exclaiming loudly in Italian, hugging and embracing. This scenario would be repeated throughout the evening and Morrison thought he had rarely felt more alone in company.

It was almost impossible for him to join in the conversations, mainly due to the language barrier, but also because he was totally preoccupied with what he had just learned. This had distracted him so much that he felt as if he was not really there. He jumped as her touch jolted him back to reality and she pointed back down the corridor to indicate she was returning to the crowd on the balcony.

Morrison took several opportunities to wander off by himself.

"Explore the house," she had almost commanded, the occasional waiter filling up his glass and attempting to guide him towards the enormous selection of food laid out on long tables in a room behind the balcony, the odd party-goer inquiring as to his well-being as he traipsed the building alone.

He watched the people and wondered about them. He stared into their eyes and saw little other than perceived superiority and overwhelming superficiality.

He was reluctant to enter the dining room, preferring to stay away from what he viewed as the loud self-satisfied laughter of the rich - who else but the rich can truly laugh aloud? Not those in the world whose every laugh is followed by a jarring, if sometimes brief, reminder that the night out they are enjoying, the drink, the food, the holiday, comes at a price they may tomorrow not be able to afford. Tonight, those people will close their eyes and forget, forget who, what and where they are meant to be in the hope that none of it will ever return and they will stay stuck in the moment.

Wake up they will though. Real people always wake up to real life. Not these people here, laughing because tonight comes at no obvious cost.

His thoughts were darkening with every minute that passed, bitterness enveloping him, his hand gripping the glass ever tighter, and he knew with every fibre of his being that he would not be able to find it within himself to allow their relationship to come back from this. But come back from what exactly?

He sat again, repeatedly hearing Bianchi's booming, braying laugh greeting yet another group of guests. Framed inside a window ledge cushioned in velvet, he gazed once more across the harbour and down the hill from the house, fairy lights twinkling in the trees lining the pathway he had trodden in reverse with Marianna barely ninety minutes ago, and as he watched the dying sun slipping behind the hills in the distance he sighed deeply, shaking his head.

As the evening wore on, he found that the building's towers were linked by the lamp-lit corridors he walked alone and were simply decorated, mostly white and featuring works of art ranging from landscapes and family portraits to black and white photography of people in the gardens of the house and the scenery that surrounded it. He wondered who these people were. Why had they been chosen to occupy this wall space?

In some of the older pictures the subjects appeared stern or forlorn, but back then it wasn't the norm to smile for a photograph. Morrison thought about the potential causes of their sadness.

In one picture, obviously more than thirty years-old, he saw the immediate family: mum, dad and Marianna, aged around ten, standing by an outbuilding in the garden, their expressionless faces giving away nothing as to their feelings, the fading colour of the photo adding to its aura of despondency. Who took that? Who had believed that such a very ordinary scene was worth framing for posterity?

As he stared through a window he could see that same structure, blocking part of the view of the area in which the forest recommenced, its continuity broken by the clearing that hosted this building whose thick walls did not prevent whatever love there had ever been escaping from a house that did not feel like a home.

He sat for a while, shifting awkwardly, brooding, stewing, her words echoing in his ears, in the dark oak-panelled library filled with books that looked too old to have been bought by Marianna's father - hell, he didn't even know his name - and too well-ordered to have been recently read.

Bound copies, loose-leaf, possibly even some originals, hardbacks, softbacks, some with no backs at all, from Dostoevsky to Conrad and Tolstoy to Kafka, with a full case devoted to Italian authors.

Morrison stared at the shelves housing books by Dante, Machiavelli, Calvino, Umberto Eco, Manzoni's *The Betrothed*, Primo Levi's *If This Is A Man*, and thought how honoured he would have been to have owned a mere fraction of this outstanding collection.

He briefly considered how satisfying it would be to slip copies of his works into the English section, though they could hardly be called classics and that is what most of these here were, and anyway it appeared that no-one ever looked at these books so his novels would sit unnoticed and unloved until they disintegrated along with the rest.

There were thousands of vinyl records and CDs, plus musical scores of works by Rossini and Puccini, Vivaldi and Bellini, opera singers from Pavarotti to Bocelli and Caruso to Corelli.

Impressive right enough, but nothing new, nothing loved, nothing quirky, nothing collected by a person passionate about music or books, and certainly not by anyone currently living in this house. In fact, did anyone actually live here aside from Marianna's father?

A couple in the library smiled contentedly but did not speak as they crossed the room, in which a slight mustiness brought to mind the university libraries in which Morrison delivered occasional talks - he hated the formality of the word lecture - as his novels began to sell, talks such as the one in which he met Marianna.

He quivered as he recalled his almost debilitating nerves on those occasions, caused partly by a feeling of displacement, as if he had broken into a scene he should never be a part of, and partly by having to speak loudly in public to a group of people he believed were likely to be more intelligent than he and who possibly believed the same. Imposter syndrome seemed to be the irritatingly over-used phrase for it these days.

He remembered the libraries he visited as a child with perhaps less than a thousand books, but all read, loved and appreciated, yet there were tens of thousands here destined to be forever unopened.

Leaving the library, he continued down the corridor, daringly peeking into drawing rooms, a smoking room and a fair number of clearly unused but expensively furnished and elaborately decorated bedrooms. As he moved away from the main body of the house it became colder and he shivered and turned back, reluctantly heading again to the main hub of the party.

He spotted Marianna across a balcony and she waved him over, cheerier, doubtlessly enthused by a few glasses of champagne, grabbing his hand.

"Come see the ballroom Michael, we could dance together."

The floor was busy with people stamping to the strong rhythm of an Italian folk song, while at one end of the hall a group of entertainers conducted what he presumed to be a traditional sword dance.

Morrison, still unable to clearly express himself, exhaled loudly and declined her invitation to take part: "No, no Marianna, I wish I could, but it just doesn't feel right for me tonight. I am sorry."

He studied the movement accompanied by dramatic gestures and facial expressions, and wished his mood would enable him to give more of himself. He felt as if he was an invisible onlooker, floating above the scene.

It was not the first time he had felt this way and the sea of dancers in front of him blurred and gradually faded as he lost himself in the past. His first time at a disco, on his own, years before the music hooked him in. His brother is there chatting, dancing, laughing. He hadn't seen Michael though. Michael had seen him and fully intended latching on to him just so he had someone to talk to, but he didn't because he couldn't, couldn't because there were other people there, a crowd almost and he already felt uncomfortable and out of place.

He didn't have the personality, was shy, nervous, and certainly wasn't about to move towards the dance floor. In a red and white hooped polo shirt, tucked into Wrangler jeans, he didn't look like he belonged.

There were people there he knew, who lived nearby, went to the same school and he couldn't let them see him. He didn't wholly understand why, but he knew that couldn't happen.

The under-sixteens disco, every Friday night in the Institute Hall, and while the village youth danced away the evening he could generally be found in front of the television at home.

Not this Friday though. After badgering from his parents, he'd ventured out, made the effort, but he wouldn't do so again and not long after he'd paid his five pence entrance fee he took his leave and walked slowly back, the long way round, so it looked as if he had spent more time at the disco than he actually had. Back home, music played on his old radio and the singer declared that he had danced himself out of the womb and into the tomb.

Here people danced, but not Michael Morrison. What exactly was missing in his life that enabled others to move in circles but left him rooted to the spot, the dancers twisting and turning faster and faster until the song stopped, giving him a few moments of motionless unity with the crowd?

He was snapped back to the present by Marianna tugging at his arm, offering a false smile in response to his refusal to dance.

"It's not just tonight Marianna, this sort of thing never did feel right. My life was not choreographed to enable me to take part like others do."

There was a brief silence until she was mobbed by a group of women who marched her out and down the corridor with a command of: "You must, must say hello to Martina."

Morrison, ignored and uninvited, remained alone once more, watching the scenes unfold in front of him.

As the dancers swirled and twirled, hands placed lightly and not so lightly on partners' waists, Morrison observed them deliberately catching their shimmering reflections in one or more of the many mirrors that walled this spectacular room.

Some would be partners in real life, some just on the dance floor, others taking the opportunity for a quick waltz, foxtrot, shuffle, boogie or whatever - he didn't even know what these dances were - with another while their husband, wife, boyfriend or girlfriend were engaged elsewhere, some no doubt conducting affairs in full view, some complicit, some blissfully unaware.

Suits too tight, suits not right, suits bright, bellies bulging out, over and under cummerbunds, some with ties, some without, some with loud bow ties, some open-necked. Old money, new money and probably, in reality, no money, swirled, twirled and smiled, their drink-glazed eyes betraying their true states of feeling, from love to deception, joy to exasperation, happiness to desperation.

Bodies in sparkling long dresses, glittering short dresses, plain dresses, long and short, high cut, low cut, bright colours and pastels, looking good, being told they looked good, hands creeping above and below waists, moved in and out of rhythm, those with eyes on someone else's prize betraying their intentions, but not so much their intended victim would notice.

Diamond boys, diamond girls, diamond men and women in the chandelier-lit spotlight, every one of them attempting to catch the eye of another, silently acknowledging and accepting their collective lies. These people did not dance to the tune of another. They choreographed their own movements, their own lives.

The air of money, of overwhelming invincibility, was evident, but Morrison witnessed the telling signs of nerves, guilt and apprehension as he watched closer from the edge of proceedings. He perched on another red velvet-covered bench, under a sinister looking portrait of a grossly overweight man with a large, hooked nose, dressed in a jacket of bright red, staring into the distance. He wondered what the man was thinking.

Would any of the people here tonight eventually have their portrait painted staring into the distance, believing it depicted them considering their lives, their world, their success, but in reality was simply oily vanity brushed on to, sinking into and spreading over canvas.

The smarm dripped, the smugness dripped and the self-satisfaction dripped from all of them. Nothing good ever drips. Morrison could never fit in with these people. You can escape, but you can never escape yourself, he thought.

Eventually, after what felt like a lifetime but was probably no more than twenty minutes, Marianna returned, a downcast look on her face, her eyes wide, dark and disappointed, lifting her arms and slapping them down on the sides of her thighs in obvious annoyance, announcing rather too loudly that as he clearly wasn't enjoying the party he should just go back to the hotel.

"I understand you are upset and uncomfortable Michael, but you could have made more of an effort to join in. There are so many nice people here. Would that have been too much? In any case, you would have found out one day, so why not today? Today, you finally know my life is one of deceit, so there it is. I could not lie to you anymore."

Later, he wished he had responded. Told her their whole relationship, her taking jobs in restaurants to supplement her meagre lifestyle, trying to make her own way in the world, to better herself through study, had all been based on a lie, not just her life in Italy, as she had said.

He had never really known her, not the true Marianna. Yet Morrison, embarrassed, downcast but stubbornly unapologetic, offered merely a sombre nod of agreement.

They embraced with more feeling than he had expected and he left the room, turning briefly to watch her briskly walk into the dance hall.

Staring straight ahead, heart racing, he almost ran down the stairs, across the grand reception area, out of the building and the lives of the people within - none of whom had noticed him leave or acknowledged him - leaving no traces of himself in any of their memories. Except perhaps one person, two at most.

With tears forming, his mind a maelstrom of images, he rapidly descended the pathway he had earlier walked up with Marianna, head down, a solitary figure avoiding eye contact with anyone he passed as he headed down towards the harbour, its fairy lights blurring. He hurried along the seafront to the small hotel where just hours ago he had felt happier than he had in years, a happiness that he could not now countenance as ever returning.

Eventually Morrison opened the door of his hotel room, their hotel room, and locking it behind him, he shut out Marianna for ever.

He felt compelled, almost driven by some force over which he had no control, to pick up a pen and write down his feelings and observations of what had just happened to him.

After almost an hour of frantic scribbling, amid bouts of intense sobbing, he flung his notebook aside as he crashed on to the bed, collapsing his body, pulling his legs up and dropping his arms down around his knees as if to form a shield.

At some point he used the word "crushed".

7

Search, Find And Seize The Day

"Hey, Mr Morrison, I am so pleased to see you. I have something to say to you."

The shout from the normally reserved Pino, who looked genuinely concerned for his friend's well-being, was loud and out of character.

His language was more pronounced, inquisitive and structured than Franco's, learned from school and a lifetime of conversations with tourists who, until recent years, almost always conversed in English in public places. Like his father though, he spoke quietly, sometimes almost reducing his voice to a whisper as he did now after his holler across the restaurant's outdoor seating area.

"Mr Morrison, you worry me. Those streets you walk, are they really there? Are the people you meet real? You ask yourself these questions. How do you even think of them and why?

"You search and search, then after your books you find. You find here. You find this square, the food, the limoncello, the espresso, the beautiful people, the midday sun which you go out in but then from which, like life, you hide, the shade from the trees on the avenues, the views of the sea and the hills beyond and, when it rains, the smell of the water on the warm Tarmac that you talk about. So lovely.

"But oh my, oh gosh, you must analyse every little detail. Mr Morrison, you are a very clever man and your book is a gorgeous yet sad thing, but for now, please just enjoy your drink. You think you have spent your life searching for happiness, but really you have always looked away from the light. Enjoy, Mr Morrison, enjoy."

Pino laughed nervously and let out a long breath as he finished his impassioned monologue, the length of which Morrison had not previously heard from him.

In around thirty seconds Pino, sometimes chatty, on other occasions slightly reserved, depending on who he was talking to and the nature of the conversation, had succinctly summed up what people had tried to tell him all his life.

His mother had said he was cursed by the books he read while others could simply take enjoyment from them. His father had never understood him. Marianna had thought him sometimes depressive and depressing. He didn't know what he was and had spent far too long trying to find out.

Morrison had told Pino about his writing after being asked about his life previous to Padria and the next morning had handed him a copy of *Walks Through Weeping Cities*. He did not know why he chose this in preference to *The Patron Saint of Lost Causes*. Perhaps it was because he revelled in being the underdog and maybe its lesser position in the literary hierarchy gave him a get-out if Pino did not rate his work.

The opinions of friends mattered to him and all that evening he fretted over what Pino would think. Was he inviting ridicule? Would his novel make him a figure of fun? Would Pino share it with Franco and maybe the others who would then be in on the joke he had imagined? God forbid Rossi would get to hear of it.

Two days later, without a word, Pino, tall and spindly, dark hair parted and receding, slightly nervous, placed Morrison's mid-evening brandy on his chosen table and with it the book he had been given. Morrison stared into his drink and wondered, had Pino even read it? If he had, he had done so at some speed. What did he think? Was it so bad he could not find the words to express himself or was he simply too polite to say what he really felt?

Helped by the brandy, a drink he always found comforting, and then another, Morrison began to relax as a steady stream of customers headed in and out of Franco's - a buzz gradually forming from conversation and laughter - many entering with the intention of merely purchasing a snack or two, but being delayed by their children's insistence on raiding the ice cream freezer, cleverly placed under the canopy by the entrance, brought into the counter area every night come closing time and carried out again first thing in the morning. The freezer was a rare concession from Franco to modern commercialism in that it had been successfully proposed by an ice cream company, the money from sales split between Franco and the gelato producer.

Morrison considered the time some of the children took to choose a flavour would have seriously irritated him and smiled to himself at his imagined impatience.

Suddenly he was aware of Pino - always light on his feet with the ability to move ghost-like around the tables - and the fact that no one else was in their vicinity.

An obviously worried Pino offered his opinion and Morrison, moved by the younger man's open, honest, perceptive words and, possibly given the mix of wine earlier, combined with the strength of the second brandy, mustered a verbose, overly considered response that essentially confirmed exactly what Pino had been thinking.

"But what is the perfect life Pino? What is happiness? Is it the man selling groceries from the back of his little van, driving all day, every day, in the sun around beautiful coastal villages meeting people who want nothing more than to hand over their money in exchange for his lovely fresh produce and grateful warm smile?"

"Slower, Mr Morrison please, slower..." Pino was struggling to keep pace with Morrison, his speech, as always in English, quickening as he warmed to his theme.

"Ah, sorry Pino, I'm getting carried away, forgetting myself. Where was I? I was going to say perhaps it's the fisherman out on a boat surrounded by gently lapping waves, his catch eagerly awaited by the impatient fishmonger as he heads back ashore soaking up the early morning sun. But no, no. There is pressure, the lack of money, the possibility of a fruitless trip out to sea.

"It all hurts and gradually destroys you. The artist doing nothing more than painting to his heart's content, but for whom? Just for himself at the risk of dying impoverished and famished? Or working to the tastes of others, a life and talent unsatisfied and unfulfilled? You, serving customers day in, day out? Your father repeatedly cooking the same food and you serving it, making the same conversations with the same people, day after day?

"How do you, how do we, get up and face the day, the same day, every day, until something comes along and changes it, perhaps makes it worse even? To have the temperament to accept that what you have isn't perfect, but it's good, good enough, good enough to get by and be happy or perhaps happier than you might otherwise be?"

The drink had raised the volume of Morrison's voice and the overly sincere nature of his words had attracted eavesdroppers.

He stopped for a second, lowered his voice and continued: "Again, what is this perfect life and where is it? Who has it and where? I thought it was me here, Pino, but no. Nowhere ever, because, you know, your past never leaves you. A lovely day, reading, writing, drinking in the sun, but always, always the dark to haunt you and gradually chase you down, and well, we all end up in the same sort of grave as everyone who did or did not try, did or did not search or find. The same grave..."

"Please, please, no more, no more," Pino interrupted, bothered now, anxious, his hand raised to halt Morrison's flow. "You will be remembered. Of course you will, remembered for your words. If you write again you will be more remembered. Is that how you say? Why not? Why not write again?"

"Ah Pino, I sometimes ask myself that very same question, but really I do not know the answer. I do not know what happened to the best of my written words, those anger-filled, emotion-rooted sentences penned with heart beating rapidly. Like so much else they just seemed to walk away or was it I that walked away from them?

"Everything I tried afterwards seemed forced, wrong, ideas but not emotions, and my ambition, whatever that was, simply bled and died. There are so many books, so many songs, but most spend their lives ignored, unread and unheard."

The waiter nodded, furrowed a brow, sighed and head down, changing the subject slightly, asked if Morrison's parents had been writers.

Suppressing a smile and quieter now, realising the alcohol had caused him to embellish his feelings, to say what he would not normally in public, he said: "No, no, no. My father had not the remotest interest in words other than the sports pages of the daily papers. My mother was different, she was fascinated by the arts and hankered after a life with trips to the theatre, the opera, the ballet, surrounded by books, but it was not to be, it could not be."

He halted and lowered his head, and as he finished speaking he thought of the music, the books, the art in Marianna's father's house on the hill, unloved and unwanted, filling the shelves simply for show, and felt sad at the cruel irony of the situation.

Noting the change in Morrison's demeanour, Pino expressed a genuine interest in reading his other novel and asked if he still made money from sales of his work.

Morrison told him royalties had been boosted by inclusion of his novels on college and university syllabuses, particularly in France, Germany and, for what reason he did not know, across Scandinavia, and he supplemented his income by agreeing to sporadic requests to contribute articles or short stories to newspapers, magazines and literary journals.

"You see, Mr Morrison, always remembered. Young people read your words. People know you, respect you, want work from you and for some who buy your books or borrow them from libraries you bring joy - and as

I say earlier, you have ended up here with all this beauty surrounding you."

"You did, Pino. You did say. I needed to escape my surroundings and I have done that. At some point back in England I stopped looking forward, stopped searching altogether, closed the door, but it didn't slam shut. So, I came here in search of a path with an end worth the journey. And here I am, trying to seize the day as you must too. Seize the day Pino, seize the day before it is too late.

"The day I should have seized was lost when the sun as I sat on a bench with a good friend, a very good friend, seemed to strike me blind. I thought I was blind for good, but now I am beginning to see again. It's another story, another story for another time, not for now."

"But Michael..." Pino rarely used his first name. "It is a story I would like to know. Surely there must be other days to seize..."

"But does it matter Pino? What does matter? Only where we are now and that we didn't do too much damage to get here and what we did we outweighed with good."

Pino looked hard at Morrison and eventually, after an awkward silence, said: "But I know you don't really believe none of it matters. You are still looking, searching. Maybe you stopped, but I think there are things you still need to do in life, things we all need to do. You wouldn't have come here otherwise."

Morrison, again surprised at Pino's ability to read him, acknowledged he was correct.

"Yes, yes, I have still not completed the search, I did not want to complete it, was scared of doing so, but maybe, just maybe, I have not reached the end of the path with all its twists and turns."

Pino stood stock still, holding the tray of empty glasses he had picked up from a nearby table, maybe waiting for more from Morrison, who touched him on the shoulder, laughed and said: "Do not think me clever for offering all this to you Pino. It has taken me many years to come to these conclusions and I do not know if any of them are in any way right."

"But no, no, Mr Morrison, you are of course right. I say you think too much, search for things that do not need to be found, but you ask how we get up and face the same day, every day? I do not have the answer to that question. I would have liked to have studied, gone away to university, learned how to express myself, but I stay here and now maybe it is all too late. This is all I have ever done, all my father has ever done, and I cannot know if I am happy with that until I search and return, maybe fruitless.

"When I have done that only then will I know that this was always my destiny, what I was put on this earth for, born to do and maybe even want to do for the rest of my days. Or maybe, like you, I will search again with the knowledge that I may never know what I am looking for or realise when I have found it. But know this, you have given me plenty to think about Mr Morrison, plenty to consider, and I thank you for that."

Pino, aware he should be helping his father, made to head indoors but suddenly turned back.

"One last question Mr Morrison. Your background, your family, where you lived, could that be the reason for how you are, how you think?"

Morrison said it could not. It was a stable upbringing, there was little money, but enough to get by, and it was only his own interpretation of what had happened to him that had dragged him down.

"You should not blame your background either, Pino. Please don't do that. I have done that in the past and I did not mean to prompt this train of thought within you, but you must follow your desires and do what you must."

Pino held Morrison's gaze for a couple of seconds and said he had better help his father - who had on several occasions poked his head out of the kitchen as if to request assistance - which Morrison saw as an ideal opportunity to leave, patting his friend on the shoulder and offering a conspiratorial nod before heading for his flat.

A large brandy by his side, he sat in silence, just a table lamp lighting up his room, replaying his conversation with Pino.

He put on some music he considered to be of an appropriately sombre nature, the alcohol adding extra depth to the words about ports in heavy storms harbouring the blackest thoughts.

He finished his drink, turned off the music and then the light.

8

Separate Journeys To The Same Place

*D*earest Michael,
I miss you so much, you lovely, lovely man, but I know we cannot be together. I think I knew this before the party, but afterwards I was certain. I know now I cannot be with anyone, but I truly believe that you can. You must, must move on. I, however, must not, cannot.

Three months. Just three months, but it felt like so much longer. In a good way, of course.

I have tried so hard to be a different person from the one I am, one that does not recognise or take advantage of the wealth of my family, acquired through means I should not accept but do. You said I was not a part of it, but I am, and you could not live with that. I am forced, because I am weak, to use the money of my father, to take advantage of his money, to rely on it even.

Eventually my mother could no longer justify her life and her decision to live it with him and through him. I did not know, could not know, could not understand, I was only a child, her only child, when she took her life. This hit my father so very hard and as I got older I understood. I understood why my mother did what she did, but other escape routes were possible.

She left him, left this world, but she also left me. Left me with him, with a man I would grow to hate, but also to pity. What could he do to undo the wrongs he had done to others in building a life that perhaps even he did not want or at least did not understand? All that money, all those possessions, but oh so lonely and with such a terrible meanness of spirit.

So, I stayed, stayed with him, though in many ways, maybe every way, I feel exactly the same as my mother did. Everything I do is through him, because of him, because of his money. I go to England to escape, but I can only do this because he pays. I stay here in Padria, but I do so in his house, at his expense, but also in many other respects the expense is all my own.

You cannot imagine the days I have spent in tears, the nights I have spent in tears, alone in my big room in that big house, crying, wishing I was not alive, wishing the other people at my school did not hate me because of my father, wishing he was not alive, but scared what would happen if he was not.

The nights I spent in tears, wishing the other children, the ballet teachers, music tutors, horse riding instructors, did not hate me because of my father, who paid them to 'make something' of me, so he could show me off, show off more of his success. I did, of course, eventually understand. I had heard the stories, the whispers, knew who the men were who came to the house for the long meetings held in secret away from my mother and myself, and I knew what they did. Some of what they did.

Almost always in tears, wishing my mother was still here, yet pleased she is not, wishing she had taken me with her, but more than anything wishing that while she still had the strength she had taken us both somewhere far away from him. Just the two of us, anywhere but in that house, with him, on that hill, in Padria. But I knew in my heart, if she had, he would have hunted us down, had us found, wherever we were, and dragged us back just to keep up appearances, keep up the façade of a happy family.

The night before the party with you was the only time I ever stayed anywhere in Padria away from the house and it was the best night I spent in Padria, truly the only night I could say I felt free, living my own life, in my own town, with someone I thought I could love and who could love me.

Except I wasn't free. I knew about the party. I had told him I was in Padria. How could I not? He is my father after all. He was putting on this party for business contacts, wealthy friends, supposedly in the name of charity so the magazines would come and publish pictures of the supposedly great and the supposedly good gathered together under my father's roof. He knew I was here in town, with you, so we had to go, no question. I was still under his spell, even with you.

I was scared to tell you because I knew when I did you would not understand. You could not understand. How could you accept that I had tried to be someone else, pretended to be someone else, when in reality I had all this and one day the house, the money, the art, books, music, jewellery, the clothes, the cars, would all be mine?

You would never have been able to accept that, not when I told you where the money came from, how he, how we, got the money. That is why I did not. It felt like the biggest lie I had ever told, the biggest lie I had never told. I never did tell you, did I, my love?

So, I tell you now. Industry, exploitation, Mafia connections, corruption, everything wrong you can think of my father did it to walk over people, land, planning, the law, for his own ends, but he will never understand, even now, that anything he ever did was wrong.

The Camorra from Napoli, well he says he did not mean to get involved, he was never really a part of it, but they came for him, his father too, and he did what they asked, what they said. Not the drugs, not the counterfeit money, at least I don't think so, but they would come here and disappear into the big rooms for long conversations. My mother and I, we knew not to ask.

We were not a large family, so we were not big shots, but we had money and the industrialists, the politicians, they all pay up for the protection, the tax evasion. Then ten, maybe fifteen years ago came the family disputes, the murders, and arrests of those at the top of the tree, and I think then they left my father alone. Probably even forgot about him.

For his part, he would say the Camorra helped the poor as well as the rich, but others paid the consequences because of people like him and so we live in the big house on the hill.

He says he did it for me, my mother and I, like his father did it for him, but he did it for himself, for his ego. That is why he lives in the house from where he overlooks the town, the harbour, the shops, the people; he looks down on it all. King of his castle.

I always said I would reject it, but I am beyond forty-years-old now Michael and what prospects do I have? What purpose do I serve? I have not made my own way in life. I have failed and what does life hold for me now?

My father and I, we do not talk about how we feel, so we do not know how each other feels. He is not interested in what I want from life. Sometimes I think I should give away most of what I have but the one time I tried to discuss this with him he simply laughed in my face and walked away. Everything he did was for my mother and I, everything he does is for me, that is all he says over and over again. I have tried to talk to him, but he does not speak.

He has not spoken to me, not properly, since mother died. His Sofia, or so he thought. He lost control of her, for that is what it is all about for him, control of people, control of everyone and everything that surrounds him. Then he did not have it anymore.

The only person who properly fully rejected him and she had to take her own life to do so. I fear, and I hate to say this, that one day I may do the same. I will have to do the same. Like mother, like daughter, as the saying goes.

He thought she had rejected him before and he never let that go. He found out about a man, Roberto, who courted my mother just before she met him and who he was convinced was my father. I was born early, you know. Poor Roberto. My mother told my father time after time that it was simply not the case, but he found him and has hounded him ever since. Again, control.

I try to run from all this, to escape, but I never can. I love being in England with you, but I cannot stay there, pretending to be something, someone I am not. I love Padria, but I cannot stay here, pretending to be something or someone I am not to people who know where I come from, know who I am. For that reason, I hate Padria and I hate myself.

I love the way you talk to me, I love the way you listen to me, I love the way you write, I love your compassion, I love your generosity of spirit, I love your anger so well contained and so well aimed, I love how you taught me with patience in your lectures and tutorials, and you did not judge, me a mature student still finding her way in life, looking for a change of direction, a mature student who had worked in restaurants and kitchens but wanted something different. Yes, I wanted something different, for I had never done any of that, never really lived that life. That was a lie? How could I lie to you? How could I lie to myself?

You did not judge me until I told you the truth. After that I could not expect you not to judge me. For as long as I am on this earth I will never go unjudged and maybe I deserve that. I cannot keep running, trying to escape, or searching for something I no longer believe is there.

I will always be lonely, maybe not always alone, but certainly lonely.

People write love songs, love letters to the lonely, but they do not want to be with them, for they too then become lonely. It is understandable. It makes sense.

Again, I miss you so much, you lovely, lovely man, but I know we cannot be together. Not now, not really then, not ever.

Please do not be sad for me. Please remember the good times that we shared; however brief they were. Please continue to write your heartfelt, thoughtful words and please keep searching for whatever it is you want to find. Please continue to be the patron saint of lost causes.

Please continue to walk the streets of weeping cities, but walk with purpose, walk with intent to find something better, someone better, something you want, someone you want, the light you so desperately need, without compromise. Walk with a smile. You deserve that at the very least.

Yours never and forever,

Marianna x

***

The message on his phone had informed him that a number of boxes had been shipped from England and were in storage in Naples, ready to be delivered. The text contained a number for him to ring, and, after a stuttering conversation with a man who spoke little English, he ascertained enough information to agree that the shipment would be dropped off that day and he should wait in for it.

He grabbed a copy of la Repubblica, which he purchased on a regular basis alongside La Stampa in an attempt to improve his Italian. He had, however, in more than a year largely failed in his quest to learn the language, due in part to his friends' excellent grasp of English and endlessly looking up translations becoming much more of a chore than a pleasure.

Morrison had planned to read his paper while sipping a beer at a pavement café, but that would not now be possible and at around 1pm a driver rang to say he was around twenty minutes away. Waiting in the Piazza San Marco, he directed the man to the entrance down the narrow street leading away from the square.

The containers were heavy and large, bulkier than he had expected. Luigi came out of the tabacchi to see what was going on and from outside his bar Tommaso, caught casting a curious look in his direction, offered a brief wave before hastily retreating inside.

He knew what the boxes contained. The largest, a wooden crate - for which the driver waited while he emptied it - was packed tight with books, vinyl and CDs and was thus far heavier than the others. Another housed diaries and notebooks, the third held photograph albums and pieces of nostalgia such as his mother's birth certificate, old birthday and Christmas cards that meant something to him, and the final one was stuffed with magazines, newspapers and articles he had kept or cut out either because he found them interesting or had thought they would at some point come in useful with his writing.

He dealt with some of the contents immediately, ordered his books, including copies of his own, into sections - genres, authors etc - and added them to those that had been shipped prior to his move and were already in his library bookcase.

He did the same with his music and put the box files containing his magazines and articles, as well as his notebooks, into a storage cabinet next to his computer desk. The diaries were placed in the same cupboard along with the likes of old birthday and Christmas cards he reasoned he was unlikely to look through at any point in the near future.

Before closing the cupboard, he remembered there would be a number of cards and notes from Marianna, so, removing these, he added them to the box of photographs, which he decided to sort through later.

As he came across magazine cuttings and printouts he had saved he remembered the rush of nervous excitement, almost sickness, he had felt when his publisher rang him to say *The Patron Saint of Lost Causes* was due to be reviewed in four literary papers, magazines and websites over the coming weekend.

The reviews, he would discover, were good; they praised his writing style, the depth of his characters, his recognition of the importance of minutiae in the lives of those who made up his story of people whose existences on the surface appeared to be geared to little more than making ends meet.

The first one was a print of an email forwarded by his publisher and had the words "Great Review - more to come" in the subject line. Pasted in there was a four hundred to five hundred-word piece from the Northern Literary Review, a publication he was familiar with and had picked up on a semi-regular basis when he had found himself in a newsagent large enough to stock such a niche paper.

He felt an emergence, almost a surge, of pride as he sat at his desk and read the piece, written by Gina Waterhouse, who was pictured under the headline The Search For Those Who Need Finding.

The Patron Saint of Lost Causes by Michael Morrison
Hexagon Books
Fiction, £7.99

IF you have never heard of Michael Morrison, there is a very good reason - he did not make it easy for you to discover him.

The liner notes of this fascinating tragedy, which in turn steals your belief, offers hope and immediately rips it away from your grasp, tell you that the author viewed himself as one of the lost causes this enriching tale of failure, success, failure again and probably more than anything else desire and a lack of such, focuses on.

Morrison does not possess the descriptive prowess to make beautiful the downtrodden, those of doubtful mind, the faded glamour or the humdrum that the likes of William Trevor or Colm Tóibín have in spades, but he more than makes up for this in a yarn that carries along with it such waves of empathy to make the patron saint of the written word commit the sin of jealousy.

He sipped his coffee and moved on to read the other pieces he had saved from the Yorkshire Arts Review, the London Conversation and a website called It's All Literal.

Quotes he had long forgotten now stirred emotions ranging from pride at his achievements and wonderment as to where the words they described came from right through to the regret that he no longer produced such work and the incipient nagging doubt as to whether or not he could again.

"Morrison is one to watch for the future, a writer who can twist desperation into joy, ugliness into beauty and back again in a single paragraph."

"Michael Morrison is no lost cause, and this debut novel recognises the patron saint, the guiding spirit that got him over the line and pushes many of us through the invisible barriers that stop us, not necessarily reaching our goal, but simply taking control of the wheel and driving ourselves to a better place."

"One of those rare things of beauty; a novel that is not driven by plot but by character, feeling, emotion, the senses that govern the decisions that all of us make and that form the path of our lives and bring us together and tear us apart in extraordinary and polar circumstances."

"If you try out just one new author this year, make it Michael Morrison. If this book does not bring you to tears, you have no heart. Where has he been all our lives?"

Where had he been all their lives? That was the comment that stuck with Morrison; words that once had him considering how he might have to adjust his life, a new life, a new "extraordinary circumstance" that he had not anticipated but had hoped for when he wrote his novel.

He picked up one of the few copies of the book he possessed - he had actually bought three to replace the ones he had received from his publisher but given away - and looked at the cover, a simple affair which featured a drawing of a solitary figure, pictured from behind, walking away to who knows where, perhaps disappearing altogether. He liked the cover and recalled a lyric from a song by one of his favourite bands, Belle and Sebastian, which noted: "I only buy a book for the way it looks."

The stab of pleasure he felt when he first saw a finished copy returned, a level of jubilation that quickly gave way to the usual nagging, gnawing feeling of discontent. What if the actual readers, were there to be any, hated it? There were whole sections in charity shops and stalls at village fetes packed with forgotten and unwanted books, and recycling facilities returning many unloved, left on the shelf novels to pulp. All of this could mean nothing but more disappointment.

Indeed. Where had he been all their lives?

Most authors started in their twenties or thirties and weren't celebrating the publication of their first novel at forty four. Charles Dickens had completed *The Pickwick Papers* by twenty four, Dostoyevsky had written *Poor Folk* by twenty five, Emily Bronte had both written and published *Wuthering Heights* by twenty nine, Charlotte Bronte had composed *Jane Eyre* by thirty one, George Orwell *Down and Out in Paris and London* by thirty, James Joyce was thirty four when he wrote *A Portrait of the Artist as a Young Man*. Morrison, in comparison, had reached the age of forty four when *The Patron Saint of Lost Causes* finally hit the shops. Forty four. Forty bloody four.

Where had he been? What had he been doing? Mostly the things that everyone did; living his life, going to work, doing the shopping, the housework, watching TV, spending time in the pub - what you do when nothing really seems to happen. Only for Morrison with added bitterness, jealousy and anger that his life and his background had not afforded him the sort of opportunities that other novelists had been gifted through being born into families with connections that offered the breaks he had had to work so hard for. Marianna had been gifted those opportunities but did nothing with them.

Here he was years later accompanied by the same thoughts but living a different life, one away from his Yorkshire flat which had overlooked a narrow lane, an alleyway, a dirty, scruffy alleyway, to be accurate, in which a solitary streetlight shone the way to the main route into the ugly beautiful awful wonderful empathetic cruel dark nasty traumatised wounded lovely compassionate city in which he had lived most of his life. Yes, a different, new life afforded by his success. Yes, he could call it that. To a degree.

A purring Romeo trampled over his papers and he realised he needed a break. Feeling unable to tackle the emotive stuff yet, he visited the supermercato, walking the long way round so he could take in some sea air and do his shopping on the route back, buying wine, tea, coffee pods, milk, bread, butter and cheese and, at the last minute, a rarity for him these days, a bottle of single malt whisky.

Turning right past Tommaso's, he looked in but caught no sight of the owner, a straightforward, honest man whom he had come to know reasonably well, and, as it had started to rain, he quickened his speed as he neared home and made the decision to, for a change, stay in that evening and work his way through his newly returned possessions.

His haste was tempered by a familiar snappy voice.

"Hey, hey mister, how is my cat?

"You mean my cat?"

"Yes, your cat. What do you call him?"

"Romeo," Morrison said somewhat curtly, eager to escape the rain and return to his examination of the contents of the boxes he had received.

"Romeo? I called him Romeo."

"Yes, I figured he would not want a new name. He had got used to it. It's not such a bad name and maybe he will eventually find his Juliet."

"Juliet? What Juliet?"

"As in Romeo and Juliet, the Shakespeare play. Surely you know that."

"Of course I know that. What do you think I am, a fucking idiot? I wouldn't name him after some nonsense written by your stupid playwright."

"Simmer down man, for heaven's sake. I never said you were an idiot. You said what Juliet so I... anyway, never mind, calm down please, it simply doesn't matter. So why is he called Romeo?"

"After Romeo Benetti of course, you fool."

"Ah, the dirty Italian footballer of the 1970s."

"A true animal, always ready to roar, that's what his opponents said. Only the English would call a player with his passion and tenacity dirty. Stick to your bloody cricket, tennis or the bloody boat race if you can't take the heat of a real game."

"You bite too easily my friend. Romeo, he doesn't bite."

"No, he's soft like an Englishman. He sleeps, purrs and when he is awake he just demands things, loudly. Rude and arrogant, just like an Englishman. He does not go out and get anything for himself, does not defend his territory, just simply waits for everything to be put on a plate for him. A bit like your Gary Lineker."

"A winner then."

"He wouldn't be winning if he was still with me, but everyone wins against an arrogant stupid Englishman. You come to the greatest country on Earth and still act like you rule the world, when actually it is we who give you everything, invent everything good you have in your crappy, miserable country."

"What, like the wheel or are you talking more pizza or lasagne?"

"Everything, everything Morrison. Italy, the foundation of western society, you clown. The jeans you wear, the newspapers you read. All that you enjoy. Ice cream! You English think you've gave the world all of that but no, no, we Italians were right there at the beginning."

"Ice cream? That may well have been the Chinese, even the Americans, but who cares? I think you may well find it was the Greeks at what you refer to as the beginning. Or was it Adam and Eve? Greece, the Cradle of Western Civilisation, you ignoramus. Democracy? You would barely know about that, I suppose. The alphabet, maps, poetry, philosophy. The Olympics. Anything else you want from them? And how about the Inca, the Aztecs? Did you not go to school? First year stuff. Egyptians, Mesopotamians, probably the Aboriginals."

"The bloody Greeks, what do they know? What do they know about... no, no, no, I am sorry, I'm sorry, I always go too far. You know I have been lonely since the death of my wife and I adopted Romeo in the hope he would provide me with some company, but it did not work out and my impatience and frustration at living alone mean I did not always treat him and do not always treat other people with the respect they deserve."

"Yes, you said in your note. That is a sad situation to find yourself in."

"I wrote you a note?"

"You pushed it under my door. About Romeo, after we argued."

"Ah, yes, that note. I do remember. Anyway, how is my cat... your cat?"

"He's doing just fine. We get along well. Pop in to see him sometime if you like."

"Thank you. I apologise to you and maybe I will come and apologise to him."

"Ha ha, ok, he will hold you to that. Enjoy your day."

"Goodbye Mr Morrison."

"You know my name?"

"Of course I do. It says it on the red post box at the bottom of the stairs. Mr Michael Morrison, apartment two. I saw it as soon as you moved in. Only an imbecile or a fool would not take note of the name of someone living in the same building as them. Anyway, they talk about you in the bar, in Franco's, and they say your name."

"Hey, just a minute, while you are here, you have lived here a long time I take it. What do you know about the house on the hill, the big house overlooking the harbour?"

"Where the girl, the woman died?" Rossi's face took on a serious look and he folded his arms.

"You know about that?"

"Yes, I remember it well, I know because it was the same date as my wife died. Not the same date as in the same year, but the day and month, July 17. My wife has been gone more than ten years now. Anyway, anyway, what do you want to know Mr Morrison?" he added, appearing genuinely concerned, if not a mite flustered.

"What happened to the house after she died? I know it is abandoned and I have been meaning to go look. I will tell you why some other time."

"The man, the owner, a terrible man who treats people like shit, he packed up and left almost straight away. Didn't even lock up, so the paper said. Left all his art, music, furniture, everything. Just went. Of course, the thieves moved in first and emptied the fucking place. They must have made a fortune. Then there were the squatters. Then the police or the authorities fenced it off to stop people entering, but you can still go in. People have broken the fence down and there are ways into the house.

"It was his daughter, she hanged herself in there, you know. But did you know his wife did the same many years ago? No-one knows why but they say he couldn't stand to live there anymore, with all the memories, so he moved into a small place up in the hills. Just left everything behind, so they say. A sad tale all right."

"Yes, a very sad tale indeed. Thank you. Thank you, Mr... er..."

"Rossi. Roberto Rossi. It says it on the red post box at the bottom of the stairs. Mr Roberto Rossi, apartment one."

"Yes, I knew that. I saw it when I moved in and it was written on Romeo's vet's details. Only an imbecile or a fool would not take note of the name of a person living in the same building as them. Thank you Mr Rossi. Goodbye."

"Ha ha, very good, very good. For an Englishman anyway. Goodbye Mr Morrison. Enjoy the rest of your day. Hey, hey, Mr Morrison, before you go, I must confess I lied about knowing you from your name being on the post box. I know you and your writing, but I think that and a few other matters are for another time. That and why you ask about the house on the hill and that bastard Stefano Bianchi."

"And you can tell me what you meant last time we met when you said you can do what you want in your own building anyway. Goodbye for now Roberto Rossi."

***

Some of the photo albums were from well before his own birth, black and white pictures of his mother and father's wedding, shots of their parents, old family gatherings. Grainy pictures protected by plastic sheets, many out of focus, blurred, ruined by an unwanted flash, night shots which never came out on which were placed white circular stickers with "No charge for this photograph" typed across them. He wondered why they hadn't been thrown away but made no attempt to do that himself.

Moving into the mid-seventies, many were glossy, line-up shots, when he was a child, pictured with his younger brother, sometimes his mother, on the odd occasion his father who was averse to being photographed and was usually behind the camera.

Some pictures made him smile, the odd one laugh, some brought about minor waves of nostalgia, others he could not even conjure up when or where they may have been taken, and on some he did not recognise certain individuals. All of them made him wonder about life, its purpose, where it had gone and what happens after it disappears.

Affected by all these memories, he made a mental note to invite his brother to stay for a few days.

Beginning to think of the pictures he should have taken in his life, he laughed aloud as he recalled the images snapped in his mind that he never committed to camera. A chubby young man, resplendent in too-tight replica Manchester United shirt with the single word "Rooney" written on the back above the number ten, standing in the doorway of a church in County Clare, southern Ireland, talking to the priest; two elderly gentlemen in Australia who had parked up their mobility scooters and were passing the time of day, behind them a boarded-up sex shop.

The collection in front of him displayed little in the way of such humour.

He lost himself in thought, the pictures coming alive as he commentated to himself: "Us four at Christmas, two round a table raising a glass, my brother and me on the floor playing with toys; me in a scruffy back yard, head stooped, thinking far too deeply for a child of that age; all of us on holiday in Bridlington, my brother on a donkey on the sand at Blackpool, both of us with ice-creams on Scarborough sea-front; both of us in the identical bottle green jumpers mum knitted for us - him smiling, pleased, me looking not pleased in the slightest - me with a monkey in front of the tower in Blackpool; me in my first cricket whites, bat in hand; all of us at grandma and grandads, Christmas hats on, pulling crackers at the table, all of us at grandma and grandads, Christmas hats on, pulling crackers at the table, but grandma no longer there; all of us with Christmas hats on, pulling crackers at a table at our house, because there was no grandma and grandad..."

The images brought back associated memories, unfulfilled dreams; standing proudly in a new Leeds United football strip as a child, still able to fantasise that one day he might play for the team, a shot of him playing cricket, aged around fourteen, hoping he may one day make it into the Yorkshire side, an earlier one of him playing a table football game, another sitting at an old second-hand typewriter bought for him one Christmas, believing this was the first step towards him being a journalist or maybe even a writer.

He had informed the careers officer at school that was what he wanted to be, only to be told he was better at maths than English and a job in the bank was the route to explore.

He smiled at the clothes he wore as he moved through his late teens and into his twenties, his first wages affording him several impulsively purchased designer shirts, and he remembered the increasing amount of time he would take to prepare for a night out. In the hope of what, he was no longer really sure.

Those identical bottle green jumpers knitted by his mother for himself and his brother came to mind again, as did the intense sadness that surrounded him at the time, at home, at school, at play, when he could bring himself to play. Bottle green jumpers, two bottle green jumpers. "If one of the people in a bottle green jumper should accidentally fall…"

The 1970s' wallpaper in their terraced house survived well into the eighties - way longer than those jumpers - as did the brown sofa he was pictured on with a black and white cat they had for many years on his lap. It had been a long time since he had thought about the early decor of the house they lived in for three decades and he shook his head at the passing of so much time.

There were shots from work parties. He looked happy but unwell, gaunt, almost haunted. There were colleagues he loved, that when he moved on he said he would keep in touch with, but invariably did not. There were colleagues he despised and some he barely remembered, their names and minor impact on his life prompted only by the pictures.

How quickly time goes. How quickly we go through time, he thought. He could hear his father telling him that the years fly by as you get older, his response one of laughter and contempt as the concept appeared ridiculous. It no longer did so.

It also now seemed that time moved at different speeds. He could recall almost word for word a conversation he had with a fellow primary school pupil before they posed for a school photo more than forty years ago with no idea what life had in store for them and the thought that so many hours, days, months and years had disappeared since then caused him to shiver.

He was not sure whether the music he had chosen to play was deliberately relevant or accidentally so, but he briefly stopped what he was doing as the singer poignantly revealed that the faces on the pictures he had been looking through now meant nothing to him.

Travelling through the years the images became sparse as the people on them passed away, he reached his self-conscious teens, no longer wanting to be photographed, and then, apart from the odd holiday snap, did not bother with a camera for years, eventually only having one on his phone.

Although he never made notes on his phone he was reasonably adept with the camera functions - and with all his pictures now digital they would be wiped from history forever at some point in the future when he was no more.

He would be erased too, leaving behind little evidence of his own existence. Maybe it was time to do something about that.

Likewise, these shots in celluloid, in albums and loose, would eventually be found and tossed away, whole lives dispensed with in an instant. Instant pictures from an instant camera, instantly disposed of. No memories. That thought briefly saddened him, until suddenly he visualised the photograph of the Bianchi family outside their house.

Then he saw the letter. He had received it around two weeks after his return from Padria and it was the only contact he had from her after the party. He picked it up with some hesitation and as he held it, both hands, his arms and his torso shook. His chest heaved as it dawned on him he was touching something her fingers had left imprints on, something she had poured her heart into writing, something that had brought tears to his eyes when he first read it. Something to which he had not replied.

His mind flashed back to that precise moment, when he found out, found out for certain what had happened to her.

He had fervently clung to the hope that she would return. That on his first day back lecturing at university after the summer break spent worrying, fretting, panicking, she would be sitting there smiling, hanging on to his every word as if nothing had happened, taking notes as he spoke, texting him as the session ended, asking to meet for a drink or a bite to eat, and they would simply carry on as normal. As normal - what would that be? What could that be?

When the call came that the principal had bad news, he intuitively knew what it was. Of course he knew. One of the students, Marianna Bianchi, who he was aware some of the staff had taught in their tutorial groups, had died back home in Italy. She had, in fact, it was believed, taken her own life.

The news must be broken to the other students in tutorials, lectures and discussion groups and... and... and... and... Morrison heard no more.

All hope had gone. Did he really have any hope anyway? He had known, if truth be told, he would not see her again, but he had never imagined that this would be the reason.

Committed suicide? Killed herself? Because of him. No, no, no, he must not make this about himself, it was about her, not him.

In his heart he knew the reason why, but surely he should have had some clue that this could happen. Had she said anything to him? Given him any idea? Why had no one, her father, contacted him?

The late summer had been ripped out of his life and he had moved straight to winter, skipping the beautiful colours of autumn altogether, and he remembered thinking it was November forever from now on.

He recalled musing that it had been unusual to receive a proper handwritten letter, but Marianna was that sort of person; old-fashioned in many more ways than he had realised, with a considered style of handwriting and one that contained a confidence and skill, particularly as she was writing in a second language and at a time of extreme sadness and pain. Not many possessed that anymore, most people now communicating through e-mail or dreadful, truncated text-speak peppered with ridiculous emoticons.

He had feared there would be something obvious in its contents, something that would tell him what she was going to do, and he had blindly, wilfully even, stupidly missed it.

Now here he was again, hands clasping his cheeks, going over and over situations he could not change. After the party, the next morning he had called her, of course he had, three times, five times, ten, twenty times. He texted her, of course he texted her, frantically and repeatedly, and with more desperation each time. He emailed her too, but nothing came by way of return.

That afternoon he stuffed her belongings into the holdall, a large red and white striped affair she had excitedly pulled down from the overhead storage as the plane landed in Naples. Having handed it to the concerned looking woman at reception, he explained they would be leaving separately and Marianna would call for it when she was ready. He should have gone to find her before flying home, cancelled his flight maybe, flown back over to Padria even, but he didn't, he did nothing.

After so many drawn-out weeks in the summer break with hope receding and no further communication from her, before he knew the horrible truth in his heart he accepted it was over between them. He had gone to her flat on the outskirts of the city, a tiny place, beautifully furnished, showing all the hallmarks of what money can buy.

He had originally thought the furnishings to be those of the owner from whom she had rented the place but was no longer sure. He wondered if it had all been provided for her. Maybe she owned it, or her father did. He went there several times more, asking neighbours, searching for the slightest sign that she may have been there. There was none and he knew it was over, completely over. But no word?

Was the letter her word? Was that the clue? If so, he could have saved her. Saved them both. The more he thought about it, the clues were evident. Obvious, even.

They had not known each other for long, but she had made a serious and lasting impression on him. As a mature student attending his lectures, she appeared confident, clever, eager to learn and she gave him goose-bumps. He had misjudged her as someone, like his own mother, who had never had the opportunities others were afforded to follow their educational desires. But in an entirely different way, maybe she hadn't.

They had enjoyed what amounted to an old-fashioned courtship, first a coffee, then a pub, swanky wine bar and a restaurant, their attraction growing each time they met. He loved her Italian spirit, her passion, her liveliness, her noise, music, cooking and smell, but had he crushed some of her individuality? He would never know.

He grimaced as the all-consuming sadness of Marianna's life gripped his whole being, the lack of a purpose that he had never noticed before, never considered and one that had ended in a rejection of life itself.

He had been wrong, badly so, in believing that money makes you happy. It doesn't, not as a lone entity anyway. Maybe it helps improve the lives of more than it damages, but it must come with love, acceptance, understanding, a moral base and a desire to do good.

It wasn't his fault though. How could it be? She had known him for just a quarter of a year and sold him a lie. But do we not all do that? Are we really one hundred per cent the person we tell ourselves we are, so much so that we tell others and ultimately believe our own lies until something happens, or someone comes along to smash the mask and reveal our true selves?

Yes, it was his fault after all. How could it not be? His lie, his personality, the way he portrayed himself, had brought about her lie. His lie had become her lie and her lie his. Maybe then the fault of both of them.

He thought of Tennyson's despondent Mariana - "I am aweary, aweary, O God, that I were dead!" - and noted the difference in the spelling of the name before immediately chastising himself for the unnecessary pedantry. Sometimes he really did despise himself.

Snapping back into the present, he poured himself a large glass of Lacryma Christi from the bottle chilling in the fridge. He downed it rather too quickly and reached for the notes and cards - no photos of her, save for the one he had printed from his phone and still carried around - he had received from Marianna.

The postcard at the top of the pile - pile was an exaggeration as it contained just one letter, a few cards, and some hand-written notes - was sent from Padria a few weeks before they went there together, which seemed strange as he was now reading it in an apartment in her hometown.

Dearest Michael, how wonderful the past few months have been, you have taught me things I did not know about - brilliant writers, brilliant people and the brilliance of the world we live in. You have truly inspired me, and I am missing you so much. Next time I come here you will be with me. Wish You Were Here, your Marianna xx

Morrison did not miss the irony of the last line. He closed his eyes and momentarily lost himself in past conversations: "Oh Michael, I have finished The Story of Lucy Gault and it was truly amazing, so clever... These books on Ireland have awakened a desire in me to go there, maybe we can do so together. Can we Michael, please? The Blackwater Lightship. What is this about? Can I borrow this...?"

Her energy, almost childlike, had stirred a range of feelings in him from embarrassment at his own diminishing interest in life, inspiration at her eagerness and guilt at what he felt was his inability to reciprocate. It suddenly hit him that she had realised this and was gently teasing out of him a rebirth of positivity he had not believed possible.

Can I? Can we? We will... you will... that's what she had said. She must have still believed. But they never did any of the things they talked about and it was too late for next times now.

The notes were mostly of minimal content, thanking him for books and nights out, which transported him back to the joyful, funny evening on which he attempted to cook proper Italian food for her in his flat and the night he took her out round some real ale pubs to introduce her to the joys of British beer, largely without success and with consequences to her health the next day. She had laughed at his attempt at making a vegetarian crespelle, though it was well-intentioned and she was clearly flattered.

Pouring a whisky, he winced as he thought back to his day of poring over cookbooks before the clumsy construction of that supposed Italian meal, prepared for a person of Italian descent who was desperate to escape her background and probably did not want reminding of it at every turn.

In the pubs she had initially appeared somewhat bemused at the Yorkshire characters drinking local brews, their strong accents occasionally making her chuckle. She told him she was shocked at the amount of beer they managed to consume and the bad language they used, but she liked the pub culture, though it was somewhat alien to her.

"It does not offend me, it is funny, I will get used to it, I want to get used to it," she told Morrison, which pleased him. It had made him feel, at the time, they just might have a future together.

They went to the theatre in Leeds to see Arthur Miller's *Death of a Salesman* and both agreed what a fine production it was. A note expressed her delight at an evening throughout which he had not felt so relaxed in years.

Morrison laughed as he was reminded that, despite his aversion to the cinema, he even agreed to see an arty French film at an independent picture house - he would never have gone to a huge multi-screen complex with people chomping away on buckets of popcorn.

He remained still with the note in hand, again lost in recollection of the Padrian trip that in retrospect should not have ruined everything and, if he was being selfish about it, had not ruined everything for him, before taking the little collection and placing it with the photographs in a drawer under the wooden cabinet in the main room.

He picked up the letter again, sat back and put his head in his hands, rocking slowly. He felt as though every emotion had been wrung out of him. He could not even cry.

Then his eye caught the line: *He found out about a man, Roberto, who courted my mother just before she met him and who he was convinced was my father. I was born early you know. Poor Roberto. My mother told my father time after time that it was simply not the case, but he found him and has hounded him ever since.*

9

Friend And Foe

The sound of cheering and whooping captured his attention as he walked alongside the football ground and saw a man at a gate taking money in exchange for tickets and programmes.

"Excuse me, who is playing, please?"

The man seemed taken aback at being asked a question in English and Morrison noticed a poster advertising the match, a local derby between Padria and Calcio San Marco, which probably explained the sizeable crowd. He smiled at him and paid the €3 admission.

Perhaps surprised to see a foreigner in attendance at a match, the man put the money in a pouch and handed him a ticket, singing loudly at him: "Padria, Padria, the greatest football team the world has ever seen."

Morrison smiled back, fairly certain this would not be the case, but was impressed to see a small stand, floodlights and an astroturf pitch, as well as a raised bar on the other side of the ground, outside which a substantial number of people were enjoying drinks in the sun.

As the teams ran out, the home side in red and white stripes, San Marco in blue top and white shorts, he found himself clapping enthusiastically along with what he estimated to be around three hundred, maybe three hundred and fifty fans.

The game was reasonably entertaining with both teams working hard, which made up for a lack of skill and in the case of some players, fitness, though the heat of the early afternoon sun may have played its part in the general exhaustion.

At half-time he took a stroll round the ground in the direction of the bar and stood behind one of the goals for the second half, and as he joined in the applause for the victorious home team at the end of the game, decided he would venture in for a drink.

As he reached the bottom of the stairs and looked up towards the balcony he saw Roberto Rossi sitting at a table with another man he recognised as "that bastard" Stefano Bianchi.

***

Turning swiftly, he walked away from the ground thinking about how much his life had changed. Measured as if a heartbeat, most people's would simply register a straight line, but his would resemble a mountain range of peaks and troughs, its spikes more numerous since the publication of *The Patron Saint of Lost Causes* and particularly after the writing of *Walks Through Weeping Cities*. But maybe it hadn't changed as much as he thought... he had walked those streets in pursuit of the words for his second novel, lived their lives, and it was just, well, they were different streets he walked now, with sights, sounds and smells that combined to lift him out of the mire he had willingly jumped into.

Franco's was bustling with people enjoying a post-match beer after walking back to San Marco, cooled by the refreshing breeze and noisily discussing the game. Morrison, however, remained alone and quiet, watching the traffic go by, people rushing along to wherever they were going, shopkeepers lingering in doorways, taking advantage of a lull in custom to breathe in some fresh air.

He wondered about their lives and how they came to be doing what they were, but he mostly wondered why Roberto Rossi was at the game with Stefano Bianchi.

Maybe he had simply bumped into him, maybe they attended all Padria's home matches, or could he be an actual friend of Rossi's? The fact that Rossi had called him "that bastard" made this somewhat unlikely. But where were they now? Were they still together, plotting and planning?

Franco and Pino were both busy, so he could not ask - what would he say anyway? What could they say? Maybe he was just being paranoid after all, he contemplated, and his thoughts drifted.

He considered the life of the artist across the square, whose shop never closed before 9pm, chasing a late sale, head moving left to right, right to left, hope in his heart, as he looked up and down in search of the approach of a potential customer, then, when none was forthcoming, picking up his canvases and hauling them inside for the night.

Would he just continue to paint in the belief that someone would eventually turn up and buy the lot? Where did he keep them all? Surely at some point he would run out of space. He looked around fifty five to sixty years of age so, given the speed at which he seemed to work, say he had been in the shop for twenty five years, that would amount to around eight thousand paintings, say six thousand five hundred allowing for breaks, holidays and illness.

And what about the man who sold "frutta e verdura" opening seven days a week way before Morrison rose and closing well after 10pm? At times, watching from Franco's, he was cheered when a customer entered the store and made the final purchase he was surely only still there in the hope of securing.

The fruiterer - standing in front of his produce, hands together behind his back, rocking to and fro, greeting passers-by with a few words and a smile - and the artist and his gallery were flanked by hardware stores, pharmacies, antique and cake shops, a place that sold gas and various convenience stores, all working hard deep into the night.

The clear ring of the basilica bell just sixty or seventy metres away would tell Morrison it was now 10pm and still these shops remained open, the work ethic massively different to England, their owners' families, if they had them, waiting patiently for their return.

He wondered about Luigi in the tabacchi. Luigi, chubby, lacking height, hunched shoulders, nervous facial twitch which seemed to change gear depending on the stress of a situation, happy to take a back seat in conversations.

A clean, tidy man, always dressed in black trousers and a white shirt, his establishment was pristine and well kept. The light brown walls were dotted with pictures of the town from long ago, as well as portraits and candid shots of what Morrison presumed to be Luigi and his late wife - they could only have been in their early thirties, he thought. No children, he noted. Luigi seemed to be a happy man despite the death of his wife and that gave Morrison hope.

A fridge was stocked with soft drinks and small wine racks were artfully arranged on the walls. His best seller, Morrison had noted, seemed to be the local Falanghina, also sold by Franco at the same price.

The wines on the wall racks were far more expensive: "For the Americans who stay in the posh hotels, Mr Morrison."

Mostly though, Luigi's custom came through the extensive range of cigarettes he sold, displayed in a huge rack on the wall behind the counter, though these days that was simply not enough to sustain the business of any retail tobacconist, even in Italy, where it seemed to Morrison the majority of people still smoked an inordinate amount.

The introduction of a Lotto machine, he said, had boosted custom, the old men of San Marco coming in three times a week to buy a ticket and, as in England, making the same joke that this one was a winner, returning days later to check their fortune and commenting "Ah well, another week at work then," even though most had surely long since retired.

But did the tabacchi really attract enough trade for it to be a viable business? Surely not. Maybe Luigi had private income, an inheritance?

Luigi had smiled when he told him how, around six years ago he had upset his good friend Franco. Finding himself up against new competition from supermarkets, the internet, and more modern cafes, he had brought in a glass case and filled it with cakes and pastries, followed by a small container in which he placed slices of pizza.

"I started to sell drinks, just coffees and soft drinks at first, but then bottles of beer, a local draught and some wines, paid someone to design a price list and fancy menu," he laughed as he spoke with Morrison one afternoon, rocking back and forth while hugging his considerable stomach.

"I bought five small round tables, these here, and two benches outside for those who wished to take in some fresh air or, more likely, enjoy a smoke.

"He was very annoyed. More than annoyed. I had never seen him like that," he said, nodding over towards Franco's.

Luigi, an unassuming man, explained he had not deliberately aimed to push himself as competition for Franco and, as such, had not informed his friend of the changes, intending them as more of a surprise.

This was a misjudgement as the surprise was that the normally laid-back Franco had been displeased at first, then angry with his friend, and eventually confronted him. The two, after heated discussions, thrashed out a solution in which Franco acknowledged Luigi's need for new custom and Luigi accepted that his new approach could hit Franco's takings.

"In the end we agreed that he would supply the pastries and snacks to me and the profit would be split, which was fair enough, and I agreed to reduce my beer and wine selection and for him to supply them also," he said, adding that he now closed the tabacchi earlier to minimise the effect this may have on his friend's night trade.

"We moved on from the fall-out and we laugh about it now. I saw you looking at the pictures of my wife and me. Those pictures make me sad, but they also make me happy. Life, for those of us left behind, goes on and we make what we can of it. We go on, we carry on, whatever it throws at us. There's always a way. You should know that by now Mr Morrison."

Morrison had initially and perhaps harshly thought Luigi had the appearance of a bedraggled old bloodhound, not given much to conversation, happy listening and observing, but had gradually learned that, particularly around closing time after a glass of red wine, he was quite an amenable chap, who, as on this occasion, had, in his own pleasant unassuming way told him a home truth.

One night he surprised Morrison by expressing worry over his health, bringing him a gift of a pot of honey to soothe a lingering sore throat.

The next day, with Morrison taking on a somewhat healthier appearance, Luigi astounded him by taking him to the small courtyard garden between the apartments.

"Come, come, Mr Morrison, I have something special I think you will like. Look, look, my beehives," he said, before displaying a deftness of touch and love towards the small creatures, gently talking, almost cooing to them, illustrating to Morrison a whole new side to the man.

"Treat them well Mr Morrison and they will treat you well too. That is why my honey will look after you and make you better."

It made Morrison happy to discover there was far more to Luigi's life than working in the tabacchi every day and dwelling on the better times when his wife was alive.

On learning of Luigi and Franco's brief fall-out, Morrison had imagined the former's appearance to have become even more crestfallen, his facial tick and hunched shoulders ever-more pronounced, and he wondered if he could work an embroidered version of Luigi the beekeeper into a story he was half-heartedly cobbling together. He was pleased relations between the two were good again.

Morrison grew to like Luigi and would often call in for a drink and sometimes a small lunchtime pastry.

Even though he was no longer officially a writer, he still carried a pen and paper and would use his time in the tabacchi to make sense of the notes he had made on his recent wanderings before perhaps typing them up on his computer back in his apartment later in the day. Sometimes he simply wrote down what he had seen while he was there, often wondering what the other customers thought he was doing - writing a review for

TripAdvisor, perhaps. Luigi knew not to disturb Morrison when he began to put pen to paper.

The customers were largely local, the elderly men - almost always men, almost always elderly - smartly dressed in short-sleeved shirts and belted chinos reminding Morrison of an England long gone as they trekked to the shop every morning for their paper, leaving with it rolled up, tucked under one arm as they sauntered back home to devour the contents, perhaps with an espresso for company. Occasionally they would stop for a short rest, reading a story that had suddenly caught their interest before continuing away from the square.

"The new England doesn't read newspapers, Luigi. You know, the thrill of seeing someone buy a paper and read a story with my name on it never left me. It was just gradually replaced by the disappointment of them not doing so."

Luigi merely nodded and grinned, leaving Morrison to write in his notebook as he took inspiration from the tourists, particularly the Americans complaining about the distance from their hotel to the main town and the difficult conditions underfoot at Pompeii or Herculaneum - what did they expect, new pathways to be laid down for their convenience, a taxi to take them round the ruins?

On top of that of course, there were the oft-repeated mantras regarding the standard of food in their hotels; too much pasta, not enough burgers. Cheese and grapes for dessert? Ridiculous. Where were the huge slabs of gateau they so craved?

Then there was quiet Tommaso - laid-back, not given to emotion - round the corner from the square, who had a down at heel look similar to that of Luigi, although taller, a stumbling gait which saw him lurch from side to side as he made his way between tables and from customers to the till and back again, multi-tasking not being his strong suit.

He generally dressed in a too tight maroon cardigan over a buttoned-up shirt of a colour which did not match or complement, with a slightly strange lop-sided carefree smile, a facial expression that implied curiosity, bemusement or disbelief that Morrison took to mean the story behind his demeanour was not a dark one.

His bar, no doubt run without much change over the decades, was inherited and came with sizeable apartments above, so there were no worries about providing housing for his family should they wish to stay in the business, and Morrison figured his life could not be so bad. Maybe that is why his skin, brown through more than sixty five years of Italian sunshine, did not wear the wrinkles of his contemporaries. Again though, there could be more to the story. Much more.

He had counted down the days to his winter break. "Twenty Mr Morrison, nineteen to go Mr Morrison, I cannot wait," he would say while Franco would remain open as much as he could, which suggested different financial situations or levels of love for what they did.

Tommaso had told him the Irish drank the most and stayed out the latest, sometimes into the early hours, but rarely bought food.

Morrison laughed as he was informed: "They enjoy a drink and sing-song, raising the ding-dong, they say, raising the ding-dong, just like in the films. The Scottish the same. The English want to eat as well, except when the football is on, then it is full concentration and 'Eng-er-land, Eng-er-land' all the way through the game. The Scots and Irish, they always end with spirits, the English and Americans just wine and beer, the Germans lots of beer and, well, the Russians who come here now, anything at all, with a fair few vodkas thrown in for good measure."

As he spoke his smile almost formed a straight left to right diagonal across the bottom half of his face, his brown eyes twinkling.

Morrison pondered how long the businesses here would remain, what the buildings used to be. How long would Luigi, Tommaso, Franco, the gallery owner, the grocer, continue trading in Padria and what would take their places when they moved on? It was the way of life.

Everything is the same but everything changes, sometimes for the good, but often not. Pockets of sadness the world over. Minor changes that history, aside from maybe a local writer, never records. Cafés, restaurants, bars, shops all closing, mostly greeted by a casual shrug, but behind the scenes families arguing, rows, tears, trauma, worries and doubt; was I such a bad barman, the clothes I tried to sell so terrible, my cooking so poor?

When change happened and everything seemed lost, there was always a different dance to fill the floor. At this moment, however, everything appeared settled in this little part of the world that Morrison had, on the surface, got to know and love so quickly and so well. Except for the issue of Marianna and her father, which was the real reason he had come here. Sort that out and maybe there will be another dance for me, he thought.

Oh, and Roberto Rossi. Who was he? Friend or foe? What exactly was he up to?

Morrison's extended period of contemplation - how long had he been sitting in silence, just watching, staring, thinking? - was interrupted by one of the subjects of his consideration, Tommaso. Dressed in his customary maroon cardigan over a vivid green shirt, he had wandered over to Franco's from his own bar, his tendency to lean to the left when setting off occasionally making it appear as if he was heading in a different direction than the one he intended.

Always eager to share his not inconsiderable knowledge of Padria, in a manner very similar to Luigi, over a beer he told Morrison all about how the quaint streets of his hometown had been quiet in the very different days when his father owned the business and he was but a child before the tourists arrived.

"Before then it was only the wealthy that visited and then only to the big town and the posh hotels, Mr Morrison. Those with money did not like it when the airlines for the masses brought ordinary people to the new and cheaper hotels and tourists spilled out into what was a village but would eventually become a town, with streams of coaches, minibuses and taxis adding to the local traffic and extending the season," he said, adding that he was fine with this but many still did not approve.

That night, later than usual, Morrison, having bid Tommaso goodbye, walked home along Via Cappuccini and almost fell, twisting his ankle on a raised cobble stone, which caused him to limp back to his apartment.

He was spared embarrassment as, to his knowledge, no one saw his minor accident, and as he observed the choreography of the shadows jumping ghost-like on and off the walls that lined this narrow street he thought of the residents, shopkeepers, those who ran bars and restaurants for decades and had passed away, their memories gradually fading but perhaps their shadows always remaining. One day, of course, he would join them.

Pouring a brandy to help ease the pain of his swelling ankle, he looked across the square to where Franco was turning out the lights and recalled the advice he had imparted to Pino to: "Seize the day before it is too late, seize the opportunity while you can and enjoy it. It came too late for me and I did not enjoy it as I could and should have done, or rather I did not take it early enough to allow myself to enjoy it. People who sit in these bars and walk these streets often leave no imprint. Many have no wish to. I hope I did. I hope, if it is what you want, that you do that too."

He had not thought much about it since and hoped his comments would have no negative effect on Pino and, as a result, Franco.

His peace, his period of contemplation, was shattered when he heard the downstairs entrance slam, followed around twenty seconds later by the opening and closing of Roberto Rossi's door, and a dark thought crossed his mind.

10

Think Too Much And You'll Miss The Sunshine

He enjoyed sitting and watching people swimming, listening and smiling as their initial cries at the cold hit on entering the sea gave way to screams of joy when their bodies adjusted to the temperature.

It was clear from their reactions that it could not be too cold, but Morrison never ventured in himself, partly because he was no fan of water but also the hassle of changing before getting in and again on leaving, drying himself and carrying wet swimwear and towels home seemed too much for a few minutes of possible pleasure.

Rather than swimming - he found even the public baths cold so assumed the sea would chill his bones if not freeze them - he sat mute and alone, making notes, occasionally glancing up to take in what was happening around him.

The late afternoon had been a hot one, but the slight breeze had rendered it cool enough for him to walk the route around town via the old harbour, the narrowness of the streets and the towering buildings providing adequate defence from the sun.

Twice he had been sure he had seen Roberto Rossi, but he had hastily disappeared from sight and as he turned to look back from the harbour there he was again.

"Rossi, Rossi," he shouted, but there was no reply, so he continued on his way, albeit suspicious and on alert for further sightings.

"That bloody man," he muttered to himself.

Most of his days panned out similarly - a stroll, a rest, some reading, a drink or two - unless the weather was bad, when he would stay in and from his window seat watch one of the storms that punctuated lengthy periods of perfect summer.

This became a real treat, watching intently as enormous black clouds came rolling in across the square, witnessing the rain becoming a torrent, cascading down the walls of the shops and bars of the square, thunder and lightning adding to the atmosphere. Romeo, far from being scared, would simply curl up on his lap, purring fondly, content simply to be with his flatmate.

He had found the weather muggy throughout the summer, occasionally oppressive, sometimes leaving him slightly irritable and at a loss as to what to do. As his first year passed though he bought clothes more suitable, even shorts, became less conscious of the heat and would often walk in high temperatures before resting at a midway point.

Reflecting on his progress he realised he felt more positive and on the whole as happy to be alive as he ever had been. If slight vexation due to the heat was the price to pay, then so be it. It wasn't the only price, of course, it never could be, but that's not for now.

He was genuinely surprised at the amount of interest people in the area expressed in the weather, a supposed British obsession.

The self-professed meteorologist, who also worked as a waiter in the small side street bar where Morrison sometimes stopped on his way to the bench, was the third person to have told him about the ongoing changes and forthcoming developments in the world of weather.

Franco, while pleased at the extension of the tourist season the ongoing heat had brought about, was concerned it resulted from irreversible environmental changes. Luigi said if the temperature increased at the same rate year by year it would be unbearable: "like living in Africa", while the waiter gave Morrison the benefit of his detailed knowledge of the climate across Europe.

"I know your weather sir, I study the patterns. I know of your hot summer of 1976, and this year has been the hottest since. In a few years you will not need to come here. England, especially the south, will be like living in the Mediterranean. In Italy, France and Portugal it will be too hot, so maybe we will come to you to experience the warmth of Italy as it used to be."

"I doubt you would want to do that," Morrison said, his mind momentarily flitting back to the rain, fog and mists of the Bradford streets he trudged. "But I am no expert. I have not examined the changes like you. I just take each day as it comes."

Luigi told him how the weather affected his bees and Tommaso, also inclined to talk about the elements, eventually also gave Morrison the benefit of his observations.

"I am sixty three years now Mr Morrison, sixty three years, can you believe that? Sixty-three years and I have never seen the snow like you have in England. I have seen the ice when the cold makes the rain freeze and everyone slips, and we have the big rain when the clouds burst and the next day it is not so hot as the day before, but not the big white sheets, the snow covering the streets. Only on top of the mountains and on the ski slopes, but not here, not here in Padria."

"Ah, it's not all it's cracked up to be Tommaso. Especially driving in the bloody stuff. For most it just means struggling to get to work, slipping and sliding, battling through the sludge, but you keep that beautiful snowy white image in your mind, a picture so much nicer than the reality."

He briefly considered that as a metaphor for his failed relationship with Marianna.

Looking up the temperatures later that evening, he discovered that the area was, despite the concerns of the locals regarding increasing heat, still not as hot as he thought it might have been, with only June to September containing an average daily high above 81°F. He was happy to find that for the majority of the year, cloud or wind, or a combination of both would cool the air.

Conversely, he discovered that the cooler season lasted from late November to late March and rain fell throughout the year, which was something he had not expected, but accounted for how verdant the place was, he supposed.

He found too that the smells of the streets changed as the year progressed and he would learn to love the individuality of the seasons, particularly appreciating the beautiful aromas of the orange blossoms of the spring and the liquorice-like oregano which told him he was almost home as he passed under the small bridge near the square.

He felt that by breathing in these scents he was somehow replacing the poison that had for years infected his body and mind, heightening his appreciation of his senses, making him feel alive again.

In that first year in Padria he also discovered that the surprisingly cold and wet winter was considerably more bearable than that of northern England, and the tourists had largely disappeared by then, which had both benefits and disadvantages as far as Morrison was concerned.

He appreciated the summer's different mix of people, the cultures and personalities that arrived along with the re-awakening of much of the town, which he thought of as hibernating between November and February as folk snuggled around wood burners in bars and eschewed chilled pints of lager, dripping condensation, for glasses of warm red wine or pints of Guinness. In contrast, he loved the space that winter allowed, added to the slight smugness brought about by feeling part of a real local scene, akin to a secret kept from visitors.

By late March, the temperatures were creeping up again and expectation would grow. He could feel it in the air. People would stay out later, the bars would re-open their outside areas, Franco would start to operate within the perimeters of the weather, staying open into the warm dry evenings and closing early when the rain threatened.

"I'm playing it by ear, as the English say," he would tell Morrison with a grin while comedically tapping his ear.

Elderly couples would bring their chairs outside and sit watching the world go by, children would reappear in the streets and lanes from behind closed doors, people would tend their small gardens, allotments, pots and flower displays and the chatter would return. Early evening skies began to clear and a sense of optimism emerged as a blue sky dotted with clouds became less likely to signal rain.

His plan to re-read one or two stories in a William Trevor collection he had brought over from England was foiled by the noise created by the family already on his usual bench, sharing a picnic, so after exchanging friendly nods he sat nearby for a while, observing the scenes in the water and scribbling notes.

Having lost his earlier enthusiasm for reading, he wended his way back across town via the harbour, taking a small glass from the limoncello seller Gino and confirming that he had contacted his teacher daughter Angelina and arranged some lessons in basic Italian.

"I emphasise the basic," Morrison smiled, toasting the man with his refreshing limoncello, just the ticket in the current heat. "I don't want to look even more of a fool than I already do or will when I go back to the classroom by claiming I am an expert in linguistics."

"You will be fine, my friend. You will be fine. I will tell her not to be too strict, to go easy on you," Gino replied, visibly delighted at having brokered a deal on his daughter's behalf and regaling his customer with stories of some of her more characterful pupils. Morrison did not know then quite how much this conversation would one day mean.

***

Back in the square in the early evening, he had settled in his usual position at Franco's and ordered a glass of Lacryma Christi - it still amused him that the local version of why it was named the tears of Christ was because the man himself had apparently cried when he tasted it. To be fair, it was actually particularly good.

Franco and Pino were going about their typical business, the former in his everyday white apron atop smart shirt and black trousers, cooking in the small kitchen behind a hatch that opened out into the seated area just off the square across from the tabacchi and Morrison's flat.

Pino also sported black trousers with a striped waistcoat over a perfectly ironed white shirt. He was taking orders and serving breads, olives, small pizzas, pastries, wines and beers, chatting easily with the customers. Most were locals but with the odd tourist easily picked out due to the awkwardness with which they chose from the small menu, some at least attempting what they hoped sounded something akin to an Italian pronunciation.

Morrison alternated between reading his paper and losing himself in thought, smiling as he wondered about the Italian lessons he had booked and hoping they would at the very least enable him to order with rather more proficiency than some of those around him.

He smiled at the occasional drinker or diner, greeted others, swapped seats to allow a family to sit together, and had a brief but enjoyable conversation with a woman he recognised as being the owner of The Star of the Sea and who asked what he would recommend from Franco's menu.

Alone on the next table, casually dressed in a white blouse and light blue trousers, she smiled at him, her eyes warm and, he felt, understanding even. Of what he did not know.

"Erm, anything, everything really, something that will complement your mood, the atmosphere and what remains of the evening sunshine," he said, laughing aloud as he spoke, his attempt at a slightly teasing tone perhaps coming across as slightly pretentious.

"I am sorry, that came out all wrong. Basically, it's all good. Anything you choose will be fine. More than fine."

She smiled, leaned forward and said: "Maybe you over-think things, try too hard, which, may I say, I don't think you need to. Perhaps you are just taking the mickey out of me as you English say, but I like that. It will be white wine and a light pasta then."

Morrison, feeling relaxed in jeans and a salmon-coloured shirt, smiled back at her and, noting the amusement on her face, said: "I would never do that. I think this afternoon's sun has had a delayed effect on me. It has put me in a much too happy frame of mind. Either that or this."

He pointed to his wine and she smiled back.

The light-hearted chat lasted a minute or two more and Morrison deliberately made his answers shorter and less giving, though not terse or rude, because he did not wish to further intrude on the woman's evening.

He wondered if she was waiting for someone as she appeared a little on edge, checking her phone from time to time. She hadn't eaten after all but had consumed two large glasses of wine in less than an hour. Maybe a date hadn't turned up? Perhaps she had somewhere important to be?

She in turn took the hint that he perhaps also wished to be left alone, as was usually the case when he occasionally visited her bar down at the old harbour with his choice of paper, which today was La Gazzetta dello Sport. His reading of such newspapers had led to a gradual recognition of more words which enabled him to take part in basic conversation surrounding football and even basketball or cycling, which he had discovered were popular here.

On leaving Franco's, the woman patted him on the shoulder, making him jump slightly, gave him a warm smile, and said: "Don't sit on your own thinking too much. You cannot see when you are so deep in thought and you miss the sunshine, but maybe if it puts you in too good a mood that isn't such a bad thing, though you wouldn't want that now, would you? Be yourself, it is good enough, more than good enough, I can tell."

Morrison smiled back, taking in the fact that no-one had joined her. He nodded, aware that Pino had overheard and would later, along with Franco, either, as the woman had said, "take the mickey" or more likely use what they had seen to resume their undoubtedly well-meaning attempt to persuade him to relax and learn to enjoy life again.

In the event, Morrison left before any questioning could begin, but he knew this would only serve as a delaying tactic. So it proved the following afternoon, when too tired to bother giving much to the very hot day but wanting to escape the small confines of his living space, he found himself, newspaper in hand once more, ordering a quick pick-me-up drink, having almost forgotten his conversation with the woman.

Sure enough, Pino was quickly on the scene.

"That lady last night, Gabriella, a nice woman, she runs a bar in the harbour, The Star of the Sea, she took quite a shine to you. You not to her, my friend?"

"Ah, I know who she is, but did not know her name," Morrison said, adopting a quizzical look while twisting the spoon that came with the double espresso he had ordered to accompany his beer.

"I have been in that bar and seen her working there a time or two. She is nice, very nice, but it's not what I'm here for. She was friendly, it was just a chat. Nothing more, nothing less."

Morrison didn't mind that the questioning was generally one-way. If people wanted to know, they wanted to know, though he didn't volunteer information to those who didn't ask.

"But Mr Morrison, do you not want love? Was your love before so bad it has put you off for ever?"

Pino was persistent, he could be like this as the subject of his quizzing had discovered, but Morrison was again polite, almost amused by the waiter's observations, as the temperature slowly rose and he moved the table umbrella nearer to cool himself. There was no wind, the trees and plants around the piazza - which was now filling up with the late lunch custom that spilled out from the offices and shops, as well as the garages and service industries that populated the side streets splitting the side of the square heading away from town - stood still, the heat stealing the breath of the elderly and unfit.

"Maybe it is simply because if you don't love yourself, and by you I mean me, then surely you cannot love another.

"I don't know but honestly, Pino, no experience anyone put me through was so bad. It is just what I feel I maybe did to the other person or maybe didn't do, and ultimately, as a result, didn't do for myself, if that makes any sense at all. But I don't believe that is the reason why I remain alone.

"That is recent history and it still hurts. I will tell you all of it, but not today. There is something I must do first before that can happen."

Wide-eyed, Pino remained at his side, expecting more, so Morrison took a sip of his cold beer and continued: "At times Pino, you meet a person, you fall in love, they are perfect, you will be together forever and live happily ever after. Except you don't. It doesn't turn out like that.

"At first all is good; the nights out, the conversation, the lovemaking, everything works. You go for a romantic walk and the weather is good. You choose a restaurant and it is perfect. Then everything changes.

"You take that extra step and move in together. It is exciting. You re-decorate the house. You decide who does what; maybe you both cook, maybe one cleans, and one washes and irons. You choose a holiday to celebrate. You go away and nothing is ever the same afterwards.

"You hit a peak, then go over it and whatever you do, wherever you go from then on does not hit those heights. You begin to irritate each other. You discover the things you do not like about the other and the things you did like no longer seem quite so appealing. You begin to argue, and you start to deliberately behave in a way that annoys the other and discover you want different futures. Futures you never mentioned to each other. Marriage or no marriage, children or no children, to live in a place the other escaped from and would never go back to perhaps. From then on there is no recovery..."

"Slower, slower please." Pino emphasised his request with a repeated palms down gesture as Morrison again lost sight of the fact he was speaking almost passionately in a language relatively unfamiliar to the waiter, emphasised by an increasing lean towards northern pronunciation as he progressed.

By now breathing heavily due to his long monologue, he nodded, stopped, took a slug of his beer and continued: "Obviously Pino, I am not the only one whose life has taken these twists and turns, yet we mostly jump straight back in with another and try again in search of a perfection that is not there, though some swear it is. Then again, maybe I'm wrong and you will tell me how and why, but as humans we make the same mistakes repeatedly and always go back for more of the same. We live our lives in circles - everything comes around."

Pino left to serve a couple of customers who had arrived, but in between taking orders returned and whispered: "Everything, Mr Morrison, or just love, just relationships?"

"Everything Pino," Morrison exhaled loudly as the waiter reappeared at his side having slipped away to attend to a table, allowing him time to think of a suitable response.

"As a child I would cry at the sky, at the fact the sky would die and it wouldn't be the same one tomorrow. It would never return. Then for decades I cried about myself. Now I think once more about the sky and its beautiful striations that will never be the same again and about the sea, the land; things are going well, then look so perfect, then nature breaks your heart. I become upset about the same things as when I was young, because that is what happens, isn't it? Lives lived in circles."

Both remained silent for a few seconds before, the quiet making him uneasy, Morrison continued: "But come on my friend, what about you? Your father? The both of you? I feel you know so much about me, but I know so little about you, your family, your background, whether you are happy or sad, your lives away from here, before here and maybe after here. And never mind me, do you seek love?"

The weighty Franco, in his early sixties, perspiring with the outdoors offering little in the way of escape from the heat of the kitchen, appeared to have heard snippets of their conversation and came to stand behind Morrison's chair.

Patting him fondly on the shoulder, he smiled the friendly broad smile that only a child, yet to be introduced to the sometimes-tragic realities of life, or a secure in their knowledge older person whose lived-in face with wrinkles and eyes that told of sixty holidays, sixty Christmases and twenty thousand-odd days of worry could.

Rescuing Pino from having to answer Morrison's questions, Franco interjected: "But Mr Morrison, what is there to know? Like the barber, but not the taxi driver, I am paid to listen and maybe make suggestions. I am here to make your time better, to be of service to you, not to bore you with my life. I am the bar owner, the waiter, the cook, I am not three-dimensional and usually I stay that way, but today Mr Morrison you hook me in and I, as you say in England, will sing like a bird.

"I do this, I have done this for many years, my mother and father before me, here in this building, in this square, this square in Padria. It is what we do and what we are. No big dramas away from the usual family life."

His hands together behind his back, his mouth smiling but his eyes moving somewhere between sadness, love, happiness and regret - Morrison could not be sure - he continued: "My wife Patricia, she too was from Padria, 'pretty Patricia from Padria' they would say, but sadly she is...," he tailed off.

"Ah, she died, died from the cancer, almost ten years ago now... terrible, terrible... but you know this. Look, look here," he said pointing to a small, framed photograph on the kitchen wall from maybe twenty-twenty five years ago, picturing Franco, his arm around a small, slightly built, dark-haired woman with deep brown eyes.

"It is my favourite picture of her."

Morrison's mind snapped immediately to the picture of Marianna he always carried and he inwardly chastised himself for not giving Franco his whole attention.

"I do this now because she loved it here, this space, the customers who Pino, our only child, now serves. I hope one day when I get too old to work here, Pino will take over," Franco said, glancing over at his son but purposefully avoiding his gaze.

"But if he does not, it is the way of the world. Am I happy? Sad? As you might say Mr Morrison, happiness and sadness are not wholes, so the answer is probably bits of both, surrounding or surrounded by a larger slice of neither. Ha, I am beginning to sound like you now Michael. Your personality is, as the English say, rubbing off on me.

"I am happy to be here, happy to be here with my son and yourself and the lovely people who brighten my day and hopefully me theirs. Patricia still being here would, of course, make me so much happier, but I am happier than I would have been had I never have known her and maybe sometimes the sadder, as had I not known her I would never have lost her, but would not have Pino either."

He gazed fondly at his son.

"I would never want anybody else, could not... ah, but we go on Mr Morrison, we go on."

Pino, much thinner than Franco, way beyond the stage of young innocence but not yet crushed by repetition and hope unfulfilled, simply smiled back at his seemingly ever-cheerful father, looked across to Morrison and did the same.

Placing large beers in front of both, a signal that the kitchen had closed early, he said: "I have no idea what the future will bring. I spend my time here, too busy to meet someone other than the people who come here, but maybe one day, maybe one day this will be mine. If, of course, I want it to be and my father still wants me to have it."

Franco put a loving arm around his son and ruffled his hair.

A number of people wearing blue shirts with badges featuring a white letter 'N' inside a blue circle had entered the bar and excitement appeared to be mounting for what it transpired was a pre-season friendly game, even though this was not a venue in which people traditionally gathered to watch the bigger football matches.

Morrison - somewhat relieved that the conversation had ended - recalled as a youngster, maybe five-years-old, his excitement at being taken to watch his father play for the village team and his pride when he scored a goal on a mud-spattered council field in the arse-end of nowhere, the rain lashing down, the wind howling and the swear words shouted with impunity at team-mates, opposition players and the referee.

He remembered being taken to watch Burnley and Bradford City and then, finally, his father relenting and accompanying him to Elland Road to watch Leeds United versus Liverpool on his ninth birthday. Then, as he got older, there were games under floodlights and, when football became a global commodity beamed into homes and bars across the land, he would join the partisan pub crowds, fired up by a few pre-match beers.

"Mr Morrison," a voice said, interrupting his memories. It belonged to Franco.

"Are you okay? Do you want another beer to get you through the first half? It's time to get behind the boys."

"Yes, yes." He was okay, at least as okay as he ever was.

"Don't worry, I am fully behind the boys. Just remind me who they are again," he laughed, nudging Franco with his elbow.

The television, normally inside the kitchen but now outside, told the three of them the match was due to kick-off.

"If the weather is good I stop cooking and bring the TV out for the big games so we all can watch," Franco said, "and we debate the issues of Italian football, who is bribed, who is the briber, who is not and what should happen to these people. The usual things.

"Whatever happens though, we are Napoli forever and today you will be Napoli too. We have the passion to match the pride, and we do not, as you say, stick our noses in the air like Milan and Roma. Like Liverpool, we as people are working class underdogs and proud. Come on you Blues. Mr Morrison, you know it makes sense. Forza Gli Azzurri!"

Morrison nodded, repeating the phrase as best he could, and for that moment he knew that it did make sense. Blues forever, as in many ways it always had been.

I Know Who You Are And
I Know Him Too

The information he required had proved surprisingly easy to find and Morrison shuddered as he saw the newspaper headline: Figlia di un industriale multimilionario trovata morta in un palazzo. He had headed into the library, found a seat, Googled Marianna's name and searched for a translation website which converted the text into English.

The headline of the article dated July 18, 2022, read:

Daughter of multi-millionaire industrialist found dead in mansion.

THE daughter of industrial magnate Stefano Bianchi has been found dead in his palace overlooking Padria harbour.

It is believed Bianchi, thought to be in his mid to late sixties, phoned emergency services after he found his forty one-year-old daughter unconscious in the mansion, which contains more than thirty rooms. She was pronounced dead after ambulances arrived at the house shortly after 8pm last night.

It is understood she had only just returned to Padria to live with her father having spent time in Germany, France and the north of England. Investigations are currently taking place.

Bianchi's wife Sofia took her own life in the same building thirty years ago, also aged forty one.

Mr Bianchi did not respond to our requests for comment.

A second brief article only served to confirm Marianna's death by hanging. Morrison had hoped for more - maybe detail from the inquest, her father's evidence, possibly reference to a note that had been left behind, but there was nothing.

A third, recent piece, more of a feature, headlined Palace Of Tragedy Turned To Squalor, reported on the state of the abandoned and now vandalised house and was accompanied by photographs showing collapsed staircases, a littered dance hall with mirrors smashed, the library with books and music among scattered debris, graffitied walls, doors that had been broken down lying in the once grand reception area, a view from what had once been the main entrance through to the now overgrown and litter-strewn gardens.

Reading it, Morrison's heartbeat quickened as he pictured the desolation. How had this happened so quickly? Pure and simple vandalism? Opportunism? Decay? Protest?

The text concentrated on the original building of the palace, the life of Stefano Bianchi, the suicide of Sofia, his wife, and the apparent copycat hanging of Marianna.

It was written with some degree of empathy and sympathy, but to an outsider, one who had never visited the house, met any of the family, it surely served no purpose other than to act as a titillating tour guide through someone else's misery, someone's downfall, a building's misery and downfall, symbols of success kicked into the dirt.

Did the writer have no concern regarding the human element, the real people, Sofia, Marianna and even Bianchi himself? Morrison felt slightly nauseous.

IT was a palace built without consideration of expense, without understatement, without care for the thoughts of those outside the riches it contained inside, and ultimately it was a palace without love.

Controversial industrialist Stefano Bianchi's dream to live in a mansion comparable to those who made their money through Mafia activities in and around Napoli became reality when the house on the hill above Padria was sold to him by a Camorra contact more than thirty five years ago, after

Bianchi inherited a vast amount from his father Paulo, who was believed to have made his fortune through gangland contacts, though was often referred to as a metallurgist.

Behind its thick walls however, among the wealth, the lavish trappings and amidst the wild parties in the thirty-room building, the dream became a nightmare.

He read to the end, but oddly Morrison felt completely detached from the subjects of the articles and recalled a time back in England when he had headed into the city library to take shelter from a burst of spiteful rain.

He had learned from a newspaper article that Hungary had for some time reigned supreme at the top of the global league of suicides. Apparently though the transformation from communism to whatever passed for a supposedly better system had led to a boost in the morale of the country's people, so much so that in the late 1980s almost fifty per one hundred thousand Hungarians were taking their own lives every year, but that figure was now down by half. In Britain it was just seven.

The fact he found most interesting about a place he had only once briefly visited, clearly failing to notice the cloud of misery surrounding him, was that since being defeated in battle by the Hapsburgs in 1848 the people of Hungary still did not clink glasses because it reminded them of their conquerors. He resolved to raise a glass to that.

Processing these thoughts today, he opted to read no more but did print the pieces. Frustratingly he had no printer in his apartment and, making a mental note to rectify this situation, handed the library assistant a two Euro coin in exchange for the paperwork. He made his way back out to the main street, suddenly feeling unmoved, clear-headed and more akin to a private detective uncovering the details of a long-unsolved mystery.

Back home he poured a large amount of wine, but would not, could not raise a glass to Marianna.

***

Franco's cooking was carried out with love for his fellow human being. The man and his work were about genuine warmth and providing happiness, not about greed and attempting to fleece the tourists out of as much money as possible as many of the cafés and restaurants, at least in the main town, were most definitely guilty of.

It reflected the type of person Morrison had come to know him as: caring, considerate, without enemy, genuine, with a love for Padria and those who lived there.

When it was cold Franco, hands bronzed, scarred through years of moving over and around hot stoves and dotted with sun and age spots, would sometimes present him with a dish of potato, onions, garlic, chilli and tomatoes, cooked slowly in a frying pan, crisped under a grill and served with a hunk of bread.

He would tell him this was English food for an English person cooked by an Italian, or maybe Italian food for an English person cooked like an English person might. Refusing to accept any payment - "A gift to protect you from the chill, my friend" - he would do this to help Morrison feel at home when he believed he appeared lost or lonely. Franco, perceptive, always perceptive, intuitive even, didn't tell him this, but Morrison knew and he appreciated it.

With Pino, Morrison believed his work was merely that, an occupation that brought in money and one he was expected to follow because the family, in his lifetime and immediately before it, always had. He was friendly, attentive, took pride in serving the customers their food, wines, beers and coffees, but Morrison had always thought he was holding something back. He wanted to be someone else, somewhere else, but due to what was often talked about as being a typical Italian's love for and loyalty towards the family, he had done what was presumed of him.

There was no trace of bitterness, disappointment or protest, and there was obvious love and affection between father and son, but Pino perhaps had other unfulfilled plans, and maybe, deep down, deep in his heart, Franco knew this too.

In the depths of his second winter in Padria, Morrison felt that Franco, fearing a possible descent into loneliness for his English friend, as well as cooking him his special dish, only opened the bar for him.

There would be the usual lunchtime trade and maybe a few stragglers hanging around for a drink after work, for whatever reason delaying going home to their real lives. In the evenings though, sometimes there would just be Morrison, Franco, maybe Pino and the odd local out for a stroll who had decided to call in for conversation and to warm themselves around the old wood burner. This was especially true between Tuesday and Thursday when the weekend trade had retreated to its working week.

At this time of year, Morrison would spend the occasional afternoon in the Roman baths, which dated back centuries, but had been closed for a long time before being restored a number of years ago - a story familiar across the world.

The reopening had proved popular, and the baths were often busy but, if he went while most people were at work, this particular spa, which was away from the main tourist areas and not as ornate as many, was not too crowded.

The baths were mostly used by locals cleansing themselves after a hard day's work, as was the original intention, but a few tourists would usually be in there among the regulars, some of whom he would exchange the occasional word with.

Each time the receptionist would explain the rules and point to where the towels were kept and Morrison would go to the changing room which featured, to his relief, private booths.

He always smiled at the sign which explained that nudity was not permitted, presumably to protect the English and maybe the locals from the uninhibited Germans and Scandinavians, who were used to more relaxed regulations in their home countries.

There were several steam areas and saunas set at different temperatures and a freezing cold plunge pool, which Morrison was not keen on, but would use to cool down, feeling immediately invigorated on doing so.

This particular afternoon, he entered, looked around the first, less hot sauna and settled himself, immediately sighting Pino at the other end of the room. He was with a friend, a man unfamiliar to Morrison - or was he? - to whom he offered a perfunctory nod but decided not to bother them further. Pino barely responded other than with a furtive return nod and remained deep in conversation with his friend, who did greet Morrison's gesture with an understated wave.

Morrison would not have described Pino's reaction to him as icy, but it was clear from the speed at which he looked away, said a few hasty words to the man he was with and left his bench to walk towards the hotter sauna that he did not want to further engage.

He was not annoyed or slighted by this, but something about the brief interaction had made him feel uneasy and he believed he knew what it was.

Morrison decided to stay away from Pino and his friend - yes, he had definitely seen him somewhere before - and moved into one of the steam rooms, in which five or six other men and women were seated. Someone had added eucalyptus oil to the steam, which he felt provided a welcome medicinal touch and he remained, breathing deeply but quietly in the hope that it might protect him from the possibility of acquiring a cold.

Five minutes or so went by and through the steamed-up doors Morrison saw Pino and his friend leaving the baths and heading into the changing rooms.

He felt he had somehow stumbled upon a secret that Pino did not want to reveal or intruded on a place in which he felt he could go without people he knew seeing him, which seemed slightly strange given that it was a public facility and Pino would be reasonably well known through his work and the decades he had spent living in Padria.

Morrison's thoughts turned to other matters, in particular that of what to do about Roberto Rossi, who he felt sure had been following him. He was convinced he had witnessed the wretched man lurking in alleyways, cutting down back streets and dashing through shop doors.

Surely he could not be working for Bianchi? Had he been placed in the flat opposite to keep an eye on Morrison? Was the incident with Romeo pre-planned? Did this make him some kind of low-grade double agent? Could he even be dangerous? Rossi had looked nervous, tense even, when Morrison brought up the subject of the Bianchis, but had seemed convincing when expressing his dislike of Marianna's father.

After churning over these doubts for a considerable time he decided to visit Tommaso's bar which would mean he would not see Pino that evening, even though he did not want to appear to be avoiding his friend.

Around an hour later Morrison got changed and walked back to his apartment. He waved to Franco who was chatting with some customers. Pino, he noted, was not there, but had probably not yet had time to change into his work clothes after his visit to the baths or could simply be taking a rare day off.

Morrison sat for a while at his computer typing up notes while occasionally glancing out of his window. He played a selection of songs by Leonard Cohen to help him concentrate as he worked.

It was early evening now and the area was busy with people taking the opportunity to meet friends for a coffee or a beer before the light disappeared and it became too cold to sit, even inside the bars with their doors open to the square or at tables with free-standing overhead heaters.

Finding a burst of energy, he wrote at length about the walks he had recently undertaken, his visit to an art gallery in a town twenty miles or so away, some American tourists whose conversation he had listened to in a bar and his afternoon in the Roman baths.

He did not refer directly to Pino or anyone else he had seen or met, but he created a character that merged reality with fiction, though he was not sure why he had done this. Was it simply a means of filling in time or would he eventually use the person in a story? He briefly mused on which of his current scribblings his character would fit in to, as well as the possibility of undertaking a full, meticulously researched and constructed plotline.

The man in the baths had looked vaguely familiar and his mind kept returning to his features; his build, his stature, the way he had acknowledged Morrison with a half-wave and nod of his head. Was he in the crowd at Franco's watching the football that night? He was sure he had seen him chatting with Pino in the bar. Yes, yes, of course he had. Could he work the man and Pino into his tale?

He grinned contentedly as he recognised the signs that he was beginning to think about writing properly again. As if to stop him, Romeo jumped up onto the table and started to walk around the computer, which Morrison took as a sign to finish.

Rubbing Romeo's head and placing a few treats in his bowl to appease the cat, he saved his words, turned off the machine, grabbed his winter coat and wandered out into the square, this time turning left and heading into Tommaso's.

Given the chill in the air it seemed appropriate to order a glass of full-bodied red wine. There were five other customers in what was essentially a bar without frills and was the better for that.

Two looked like work colleagues passing time to avoid going back to whatever, whoever or wherever their evening was due to take them, a couple were clearly regulars given the tone Tommaso used when speaking with them, and the other was the testy Roberto Rossi, sitting alone, reading a newspaper and enjoying a beer, apparently minding his own business but clearly aware of all that was going on around him and everything that was being said.

Unprepared for this encounter, Morrison realised that he had visibly grimaced on seeing Rossi, but the two exchanged hellos and Rossi invited him to sit.

"No, no, I do not want to disturb you. You did not come out to talk with me. I will leave you alone," Morrison said, chastising himself for assuming Rossi would have been elsewhere.

"Disturb me. Do you really think I am reading this shit? I do not need this to tell me what is going on in this place. I already know what is going on. I pretend to read to avoid unwanted conversation and so as not to give off the appearance of someone who is desperate to gain attention, if you know what I mean."

"I do, I think, sort of, but I will only sit with you if you are sure," said Morrison, who would have preferred to remain alone, allowing him time to consider the approach he would make to the subject of Rossi and Stefano Bianchi.

"Of course I'm bloody sure, otherwise why would I have asked you to sit with me Morrison?"

"Okay, okay, calm down please. You did not want to speak with me when I saw you and shouted after you down in the harbour, so why would you now?"

"That is because I have not been to the harbour, you must have been mistaken. Why would I be down the bloody harbour like a fool, an idiot, with all the bloody tourists? I have better things to do. And stop telling me to calm down every time I disagree with you," he barked, rather louder than he may have wished.

"No, I'm sorry, I'm going on again," he added, his voice lowering. "I have been lonely since the death of my wife and I do not always treat other people with the respect they deserve."

"I know that now Rossi, you do not have to keep explaining yourself. Well, not about that anyway."

Hearing Morrison order, Rossi, obviously having missed the pointed nature of the last comment, bellowed at Tommaso to make it a bottle and two glasses. The initial tension between the two, who had gradually bonded after the argument over Romeo's name, subsided and they engaged in pleasantries before Morrison decided to ease his way into what would undoubtedly be a difficult subject by asking Rossi how he knew of his writing.

"You think I don't read, Morrison? You think I am a bloody idiot? I read your books and when Luigi mentioned the details sent to the agent it said you were a writer. Two and two in this case made four.

"You will not ask because you are a polite man and not given to seeking praise or attention, but I enjoyed your work and the critics were wrong, your second book was better than your first. I liked your passion, the politics; maybe your protagonist was partly Italian.

"The star of your first book, the main character, whatever, was a typical bloody Englishman, a goody two-shoes as you might say, like your, ha ha, Gary Lineker again - how can a footballer play with heart and soul for all those years and never get sent off, never receive a yellow card even? Frankly, your poetry was bloody awful, but what do I know? Maybe it was lost in the translation."

Morrison laughed, mostly at Rossi's honesty but partly out of relief that it was the poetry he had found unpalatable and not either of his novels, then he remembered Rossi's comments about being able to do as he wanted in his own building.

"So, if the whole apartment block is yours why do you choose to live in a small flat when you could surely have more space."

"Indeed, the whole building is mine. Not that I really care. The flats and the tabacchi below, the vegetable patches where Luigi keeps his bees and the flower gardens in the middle. I do not need them; I cannot be bothered. I just let people grow what they want and take what they want.

"Luigi is my cousin. I used to live up in the hills where I owned a large farm, which my family had run for seven generations, but when my wife died I took the spare apartment in this building. My son did not want the farm, he lives in Rome, he is a lawyer, he is different from me, so after around one hundred and fifty years the farm was sold and is no longer run by the family.

"It is a shame, but what can you do if your kids do not want to follow in the family tradition? Why would I need any more space? I took the cat for company, but he was an imbecile, he was mental, all cats are mental, and now you have him. Good."

As Rossi clinked Morrison's glass after sloshing in a large measure, the Englishman again laughed at the Padrian's bluntness, before, in a rushed and hushed tone, asking: "Rossi, quickly before anyone comes, what more do you know of Marianna Bianchi and her father? I remember you said you knew about the death, her father being an unpleasant character and you wanted to bring up some other matters with me."

He breathed deeply, awaiting a response. This was a start, but he was finding it difficult to ask the questions he really wanted answers to, instead of merely skirting round the edges.

Rossi sighed, took a large sip, and began: "Just one thing I need to tell you. I knew Bianchi for years. Stefano Bianchi. A son of a bitch. A son of a bitch even when he was a child. His family had money, a big villa in the centre of town, and sometimes his father would come to the farm, in the days when it was successful, and demand things from my father. Money I think, but I never really knew. I knew my father was scared of Bianchi's nasty bastard of a father though.

"Bianchi bullied me at school when we were children here in Padria, but as I became an older man I was not bothered by him anymore. Not bothered by his connections, what he did for money, the way he acted. Anyway, somehow he respected that, the stupid ignorant idiot of a man, and he no longer bullied me.

"When I took over the farm he never asked for money again and he became friendlier. We never mentioned what a bastard he had been to me. He took that to mean I had forgotten, and the imbecile came to believe that we were friends.

"He invited me to the party that night. The night you were there with his daughter. I had met her before, a few times, but only ever briefly and did not know her. I went, but I did not stay. I went just to be seen, so he would still consider us to be friends and there would be no problems.

"I do not need the sort of difficulties he could bring into my life, you understand? I saw you there Morrison. Lost and lonely. Out of place among those people, those horrible shallow people. I knew it was not for you. Bianchi said you were with his daughter, but it did not look like that. You had arrived with her, but you were with no-one. No-one at that party was really with anyone. They never are at Bianchi's dos."

"You were there? At the party? Surely I would have noticed you, dressed like a peasant, begging everyone for money," said Morrison, amazed at what he was hearing, his shock materialising in the genuine scorn with which he retorted.

"Shush, please. I was smart. In a suit. Anyway, anyway, let me finish. I asked your name. He told me, said you were a writer. 'A fucking writer or something,' he said. 'English as well.'

"I realised then that I knew who you were and when you applied for the apartment it all made sense. I had read your first novel, I looked you up and bought the other one and then the poetry. I wish I hadn't done that, what a waste of money," he added, grinning momentarily.

"I did not feel it was my place to tell you any of this at first, but I now realise you want to know, you need to know."

Rossi stopped abruptly, considered his choice of words and, wringing his hands, his voice breaking, mumbled: "There is more, but I cannot tell you now. About Sofia, my darling Sofia, Marianna's mother. I will tell you, I will tell you all about her, about how all this started, how it all... but not today, I cannot, not today."

"Marianna's mother, Sofia?" Morrison, shocked and slightly confused, repeated back to him. "You must tell me this Rossi. I need to know this. You and her? You and her, oh my gosh... of course, you must be the Roberto in Marianna's letter?"

Then, in a cracked whisper Morrison could barely hear, Rossi stammered: "The letter? What letter? Oh I, I must tell you everything. I will tell you it all. But not today, I cannot, not now, not today.

"Just give me a day or so, please Morrison. Oh, and one last thing, if you are thinking of seeing Bianchi, maybe confronting him, please watch your step. I think he is a changed man. I think what has happened has hit him hard and I am not sure where he stands now with regard to those who pull his strings. Just, well, you know..."

As Rossi finished he looked Morrison straight in the eye, his gaze unfaltering.

Morrison, in turn, puffed out his cheeks, drummed his finger on the table and said: "Look Roberto, I was hoping to avoid you tonight because I had already discovered something that meant I have awkward questions that need answering. I thank you for being honest, but... now this on top of what I already saw?"

With a widening of his eyes and holding up a hand, Rossi signalled for Morrison to stop. The conversation ended as Tommaso had finished serving the other customers and clattering clumsily into a chair on his way, came to join them at the table, from time to time getting up to greet new customers or to take payment from those leaving.

This was not too onerous a task as his establishment was not as busy as Franco's due to it not serving cooked food, although it did attract tourists because of its view over the cobbles to the side of the basilica.

Rossi immediately slipped seamlessly into his usual character, a cross between curmudgeon and joker, as he and Tommaso reminisced about the old days, their friendship as children when his father would come into town with his son and visit the bar, then owned by Tommaso's father, and the two children would play together, little or no thought ever given to the fact that they would one day inherit their businesses.

They talked about the deaths of their wives, Rossi's son not wanting the farm which was not making the money it used to and Tommaso's two children who had also moved away, though he still hoped that one day they would return to take over from him.

"If they don't, I expect they will sell it and that will take care of their futures," he said, screwing up the left side of his face in a gesture of resignation.

"It is the way of the world these days. You have your kids, you look after them, bring them up and they move away, want to do something else, something else they think is bigger with their lives. One day maybe they realise that what they had in little old Padria was not so bad after all and back they come."

Another bottle was opened, Tommaso was persuaded to partake of a glass and the talk switched to other long-established businesses which had been sold because of changing times, the internet, supermarkets, children not wanting to take them on, and eventually settled on Franco's.

Rossi, appearing visibly tense to Morrison, but maybe not to the others, said that Franco's family had been close and always taken pride in their restaurant. Pino was different, a nice lad, but much more serious than his father, more given to thinking, to dreaming.

Franco had always been happy with his place in the world, mainly in the kitchen, chatting with locals, having enough money to get by, enjoying a few drinks, an annual holiday, watching football and generally living his life. Pino worked hard too, was a highly efficient waiter but had shown little or no interest in developing the place or taking over from his father.

Tommaso stated that Pino definitely did not want the business, although it transpired that he had not actually said this, more hinted that he was undecided about his future, which Morrison already knew from the conversation in the bar some time ago.

Rossi said meeting a nice girl, getting married and settling down would sort him out, and Tommaso agreed but said it must be difficult with him having to spend so much time in the restaurant and there being no other staff to work there. He didn't seem to have any close friends, they concurred.

Morrison saw his chance, but opted not to say anything until, after finishing his wine, he informed them he was going to call in on Franco and bid his two friends goodnight. Rossi nodded at him and said they would speak soon, which suggested he was ready to answer his questions.

A sign had been hastily drawn up in Italian, English and French and placed outside the entrance to Franco's warning people there was a limited service in place for the next couple of days.

Morrison asked what had happened and Franco said: "I am worried, really worried that something has gone wrong. He went, just like that, leaving only a message saying he had to go away for a couple of days but would be back on Monday. I will have to manage on my own for the weekend and this will cost me money, but it cannot be helped.

"He does not normally let me down like this, but it has happened before, just the once and I thought he was okay after that, so it is probably nothing too serious and it is better anyway that such a thing should occur in the quieter months rather than in the summer."

Morrison decided to say nothing until he had seen Pino again and thought it better that he head back home when he had finished his drink rather than have more and risk speaking out of turn.

He put on a song that took him back to his favourite English city of Liverpool and inspired a brief ripple of nostalgia for the old country.

Spotting a note that had been pushed under his door, he read: "Stefano Bianchi, Via Garibaldi 13, Sant'Antonino. A bus leaves at twenty past the hour from 10.20am and returns at forty minutes past the hour until 6.40pm. The journey is forty minutes, but only fifteen kilometres. The village is up in the hills. You will find Marianna in the Cimitero Monumentale on the way to Sant'Antonino. She is in there with her mother. Take care, Rossi. PS: We will speak soon and I will answer all of the questions you have."

12

Here Is My Story... Every Single Word

The conversation with Roberto Rossi had given Morrison the focus and determination to face Marianna's father. He had been in Padria for around 18 months now and knew that if it was to become his permanent home he must get answers from the man.

Having made the decision that there was no better time than the present, he was stopped in his tracks by a knock on his door at which he was greeted by a stern-faced Rossi.

"I thought you would like these," said Rossi, dressed as usual in ill-fitting blue jeans and a red t-shirt, handing over a small package in the manner of a small child presenting homework to a teacher, before quickly correcting himself. "Well, maybe not like, but want, need even."

He was clearly nervous, displayed none of his usual bravado, fake or otherwise, and his skin lacked its usual colour, that of someone who spent a lot of time outdoors in the sunshine, instead displaying the pallor of a tired, beaten or unwell man.

Morrison stared at the smaller man, but said nothing, compelling Rossi to continue.

"Erm, they are notes of the work Bianchi had me do. All the time I wrote it down, every little thing. I have been up all night writing it all out in English, as best as I could. I wanted you to see all this so you would know that I was working against him, not for him. Never for him.

"At first I was scared of him and his cronies. For many years I lived in fear, but all that shit about owing him favours or else business stopped a long time ago, I just went along with what he said to appear as if I was on his side. I should not have done that, I know. I should have been braver, stronger and told the low-life shithouse to go where the sun doesn't shine. Somewhere like England," he said, managing only the weakest of smiles as he pointed at the two books and a note tied together with an elastic band.

"Oh, and in case you think I have altered the words in translation Morrison, you can keep the Italian version too and ask for it to be read in English by someone who can if that would ease your mind."

Seeing him look at the floor and begin to shuffle away, Morrison, surprised, caught off guard somewhat and friendlier than he had intended, eventually interjected: "Yes, yes, I will definitely read these. I was planning to visit the house today, visit him too, but instead I will read these, or at least the English version, and we will talk later. Oh, and thank you for Bianchi's address? How do you know it?"

Rossi looked away and did not answer, instead saying: "I am so tired. Tired of all of this and tired through being up all night. I will be okay after some sleep. Yes, yes, we will talk later. You will be shocked and you will be angry, but I hope you will understand. Come and see me after you have read everything and before you go to see Bianchi or do anything silly."

Morrison nodded solemnly, closed the door behind him, removed his shoes, made a coffee and took a seat at his desk, Rossi's books of notes in front of him.

***

Rossi's flat was a pokey, cluttered affair, more basic and blander than Morrison's just metres away. Dirty pots and pans were stacked in the small kitchen, suggesting he was capable of cooking for himself, but cleaning wasn't his domestic chore of choice. It was a place uncared for, off-white paint peeling off the walls, tatty flower-patterned rugs covering a tiled floor.

"I have been meaning to get this place sorted," Rossi said, embarrassed on reading the look on Morrison's face, indicating the mess in front of him with a sweep of his hand, a gold-coloured ring on his wedding finger and a small tattoo of a name and dates visible on his forearm.

"I haven't kept up with any of this sort of thing since my wife died and I left the farm. The place needs a good clear-out, painting, new furniture, but you have noticed that already, I can tell. Maybe I should just move, get away from here. Isabella would be shocked."

Morrison, the sting of the large whisky he had downed to calm himself now mellowing, noticed several pictures of Rossi's wife, a petite, pretty, smiling woman, almost as he imagined her, some with a young man, presumably their son, dotted around the place. There was not much else in the way of ornamentation, nostalgia or decoration, aside from two worn brown sofas and a basic dining table with one chair. No guests had ever come here, he thought.

"Doubtless she wouldn't have expected any different of you," he said, sarcastically. "You obviously had things on your mind, more serious matters, other than cleaning the house and washing up."

"Yes, yes... you have read my notes, I take it. I, I don't know what to say. Ask me anything you want and I will tell you. I owe you that at the very least, Morrison."

The basic wall clock - which had an annoyingly loud tick - said 6.20 and Morrison, sensing a long and difficult evening ahead, employed a business-like manner as he handed back the two books Rossi had given him and took out a wedge of paper on which he had made notes.

"Not quite one of your books Morrison or *The Diary of Samuel Pepys*, but it's all there, everything I did, all that I saw, all that I remember in the order that it happened."

Rossi was clearly on edge, moving from one foot to the other and scratching his arm and face. "Will you go to the police? Have you already done so?"

"The police?" Morrison said, genuinely surprised at being afforded an option he had not even considered. "Why on earth should I do that? I would imagine anything you witnessed that was on the wrong side of the law, anything you did that might have been on the wrong side of the law, they already knew about. They were probably involved in it as well as you already know, and I don't think they would welcome an Englishman sticking his oar in after all these years."

"Sticking his oar in? You have an oar?"

"It's just an expression, interfering in something when you are not wanted. That's all."

The silence that followed - tick, tick, tick - brought to mind those awkward minutes when a plane begins its descent to land, passengers slightly nervous, all idle chatter suspended.

Morrison cleared his throat: "Can we sit down Rossi? You are making me even more uneasy than I already was, hopping about, parading around."

"Yes, yes, sure, whatever, let's just get this over, shall we?"

There was no offer of a drink, no more pleasantries from Rossi, dressed in the same scruffy jeans and t-shirt as the day before.

Morrison, beginning to feel the heat as he sank into the larger of the two discoloured sofas, Rossi on the smaller one, stared down at his papers and almost fell into journalist mode, asking: "Tell me how did this all start? You have told me a bit about Bianchi and I have read Marianna's letter in which she says he thought you were her father, but..."

"I told you before, I knew him from being a child when he started to persecute my father, demand money from him. Then he left me alone, that is until he met Sofia, his future wife. This is what you really must know, what happened from the start.

"I did not tell you that he was angry that we had been together before they met, Sofia and me, and when Sofia got pregnant with Marianna shortly after they met, well, he went crazy, acted like a madman. Threatened to have me killed." Rossi was agitated, thrusting out his hands and arms left, right, up and down.

"Hold on there, what, you actually are Marianna's..." Morrison could not bring himself to finish the sentence.

"No, no, of course I'm not. I told him, no, no, no, she cannot be my child, nothing like that happened, it is not possible. Sofia, she was more than ten years older than me, but it made no difference to him. He told me he would finish me unless I did certain things for him. I said I would not, but then he threatened to do unmentionable things to my family, my friends and then, after I got married, my wife, my son and I could not live with that. Bastard... the bastard..."

Rossi, his face contorted, up and pacing again, stopped and sucked deeply, attempting to regulate his breathing to prevent himself from bursting into tears.

Morrison, more confident, still sitting, dressed in chinos and blue cashmere sweater, merely pointed to a shelf crowded with bottles and tins of oils, vegetables, condiments, spirits and wines, and indicated for him to pour two whiskies, which he did.

Morrison made to speak, but Rossi, now sitting again, elbows on his thighs, hands clasping his head, rocking slightly, lifted his right hand and motioned for him to stop.

Slower now, he said: "Please, please, let me tell you this story, this information. I must do so while I am able.

"I know I should have done more about what was happening, I know this, of course I know this. It has always been on my mind, has never left me because, yes, I have made money from all this, but it has also ruined things for me. I should have stopped it all, but I just continued to go along with everything, and instead of getting better it just got worse. The more I did the more he wanted from me, the more money he gave me, the deeper into it all I got.

"Isabella, she knew something was wrong, she said she had always felt, deep down, that something wasn't right, so I told her. Told her about

Sofia, what had happened, about his suspicions about Marianna, what Bianchi said and did, what I had been doing for him.

"She cried and cried. I cried and cried. She was shocked, said it was wrong, so wrong, all of it, criminal even, but she couldn't think of a way out of it. Not one that would leave us alive anyway.

"Eventually Isabella, she said she would have to leave me for the sake of the safety of her and our son, though thankfully she never did. I felt so ashamed, so weak, so helpless.

"Obviously, this bothered me so much, bothered Isabella so much. It was killing us. I had to do something so I went there, it must have been thirty years ago now, to the house. I crept up, hid in the woods, waited, waited, waited in the dark, in the trees, the cold, the rain... though I had no idea what I was going to do if Bianchi appeared.

"I didn't know why I had even gone there if I am honest; for, well, revenge perhaps, to finish him maybe, but I had been meaning to do something for years, been meaning to have it out with him, tell him what I thought of him, what everyone thought of him, fight with him, kill him or maybe be killed by him. All I knew is it had been eating away at me for such a long time.

"So, I'm there, waiting, in the dark, in the cold, but nothing, nothing, nothing. I don't know why I didn't go straight to the door, knock and confront him, but something stopped me.

"Then suddenly a small girl appeared, ten or eleven-years-old maybe, came out of the big door and just stood there, illuminated by the light from inside. She saw me, but just stood still, motionless, shone a torch in my face and stared. She said nothing. I said nothing and there was no sound coming from the house. It was like the entire world was silent just for those few seconds.

"The girl, she kept shining that torch into my face. I couldn't see properly, just like I couldn't hear, but I realised she had put her finger to her lips. She was still, no movement at all. No sound.

"I presumed she was telling me to be silent, but I was never going to say anything, never going to give myself away at that moment, not while she was there.

"Then she was gone. A man, possibly Bianchi, I couldn't be sure, appeared at the door and she ran inside and the door closed. I had missed my opportunity. Too cowardly to take it.

"I thought and thought about this for a long time, wondered, was she just telling me to keep quiet or did she recognise me and was there something she knew that she couldn't say or that I knew but shouldn't say?

"Eventually I realised she wasn't telling me to be quiet outside the house, but that I must always remain silent and so must she. She couldn't say anything about her life, their lives, what went on in that house, and neither must I and it must always be that way.

"I thought it at the time, but now I know for sure. That girl was Marianna and he thought she was my daughter. I, her father. I wondered if she ever knew of those rumours and now I know that of course she did.

"I think about all of this all of the time and it haunts me Morrison. Maybe that is why I am like I am. Marianna, Sofia, both now gone and Isabella too, yet you and I are both still here. Why is that? Is it because we did not act when our consciences told us to do so, did not have the courage and our cowardice saved us?"

"Your cowardice, Rossi, your cowardice, not my cowardice..." Morrison interjected loudly, up on his feet and almost jabbing Rossi in the face.

"No, no, not your cowardice, you are right, but if we had done something would it have made the whole situation worse? I don't know. I guess we will never know now."

He stopped, gulped again and went on: "When I tell you nothing terrible occurred because of me Morrison, in reality I do not know what happened to some of the people I worked on, but I do know it would not have ended well. It never ended well.

"Then it just went on and on, and my son moved away and that left Isabella and me, my darling Isabella, my childhood sweetheart right back to our schooldays together. Then she suddenly passed away and I sold the farm because it was too big, too much. It was lonely up there and people would come in the night with threats and jobs for me to do.

"Anyway, I moved down here with some of the money and to my eternal shame the money I would sometimes receive from Bianchi, with which I bought this apartment block. I used to help Luigi and others. I paid bills for people who were poorer than me, I tried to do good things, but it was still dirty money, I know that, I know..."

"Ah, the passion for gain Rossi, not too dissimilar to that of Bianchi's," Morrison said calmly, pointedly and with as much sarcasm as he could muster.

Rossi, shamed and red-faced now, blustered: "Yes and no, yes and no, Morrison. Anyway, eventually he did start to leave me alone. I don't really know why. I suppose Sofia was gone and he had other contacts, new people to work for him. I'm not sure he ever really did accept that I could not have been Marianna's father, though she looked nothing like me. Nor him, for that matter."

He stopped, took another long, deep breath, gathered his composure and continued: "I firmly suspect Marianna could have been... no, almost certainly was... fathered by a Camorra contact. She was not Bianchi's and the Camorra, well, they weren't above that and Sofia was such a pretty girl... such a pretty girl...

"Sofia... my darling Sofia, she would never have gone near that bloody man, but her father, well, Bianchi was leaning on him too and she was a loyal daughter, a lovely girl, and she could not risk things happening to him, so, well, the rest is... as it was, as it is."

Rossi stopped, spent several seconds staring at the floor, then raised his head, wiped away one of the tears that were now pouring down his face and, his voice cracked, blurted out: "I loved her Morrison. I loved her so much... so very much..."

Every emotion poured out of Rossi as he gesticulated wildly, his voice one second raised then rapidly descending to a hush as he spilled every detail of his life.

The passion with which he delivered his words meant Morrison paid no heed to the sound of the clock, only distracted in the brief silences when Rossi had to catch his breath or was overcome with feeling to the extent he had to swallow hard to regain composure.

It would have been easy for Morrison to fold here, allow sympathy to overwhelm him and let Rossi off the hook, but he needed to hear more, much more.

Another whisky each, then another as the evening moved on, twists and turns in conversation, tears and anger, love and hate, voices quiet then loud, then louder again, the language harsher, the tone more aggressive.

The clock showed 9.41 and Morrison, experiencing a sudden irritation, perhaps fuelled by the cheap whisky, stood up and raised his voice to drown out the tick, tick, ticking, the sadness enveloping them seeming to him disproportionate to the nothingness of the flat that encased the two main characters in this minor drama.

"That fucking clock Rossi, do you not hear it? Does it not irritate the shit out of you? Or maybe you do not hear anything. Maybe you choose not to see or to hear because if you did you would kill yourself through shame.

"You say all this, all these excuses, you play the victim, use the real victim Sofia as an excuse, yet you were still working for that shithouse at the fucking party and, I would imagine, keeping a watch on me. You know everything about me you bastard, and, I take it, so does Luigi and probably the bloody rest of them. Jesus, how the hell do you think this makes me feel?"

Rossi did not respond for some time, just bowed his head, slumping, now avoiding eye contact.

"Come on Rossi, you speak for the wolf, work for the wolf, now speak against him, work against him," Morrison, his face reddening, demanded.

Rossi's voice quietened, softened: "No, no, that was not what happened, not really. The party, well, I could have given the police the names of every corrupt bastard there, but what would that have achieved? I have all their names, but what do you do when the police are his friends? Not all of them, but many with power, and lawyers, judges, civic representatives, bankers, even journalists and writers like you Morrison, all fed and watered by Bianchi and his pals, but, like me, all with conditions attached. You do not win by suddenly playing for the other side. You have to be subtle, develop your tactics and even then it's a dangerous game.

"I could have gone to the police at any time, but if I had done that they, my wife, my son, the people I was watching for Bianchi, would have suffered more than him, so I did as he said. Nothing terrible, seriously, I promise you, please, please believe me, just getting information about people, spying almost, I suppose you could say. Basic things, silly things.

"I say this to you and it is all in my notes. He no longer asked me to do much by the time of the party and when he did they were low level jobs and I just went along with the pretence. Yes, I found out some things about you, even followed you on occasion, a little bit at the party if I am honest, but I never put you in danger. I would never have done that.

"Having this place after Marianna died, well it was safer for you; better for you than being on the other side of the town, near his house. He never comes round here, they never did, and here you have Franco, Pino, Luigi, Tommaso, and I have many other contacts, good people, so you are never alone.

"Luigi knows some of my past, Franco, Pino and Tommaso small parts too, but nothing really bad. They know because after some drinks I can't hold it in and I tell them bits, but I could never tell them everything. I told them nothing about you Morrison. If you believe nothing else I have written and said, please believe that. All they know about you is what you have told them, and Luigi, well, I just told him to look out for you. That was all."

Suddenly Morrison rose and grabbed a startled Rossi by the shoulders, shaking him, shouting: "But I saw you, I saw you with him at the fucking football, plotting with him, doing another deal for his money. I have seen you following me, heard you leaving your flat just after me and coming in just behind me... and, and Romeo, was that all planned?"

"No, no, that was not it," Rossi, startled by the sudden aggression from Morrison, pushed him away, causing him to fall back onto the settee.

"I, I just saw him there, I did not know he would be there. I had never seen him there before. He does not like football. I told him, I said to him 'No more Bianchi, you son of a bitch. We're finished. Do what you want to me, I no longer care.' All he said was: 'Just do what you feel, what you must, what you think is right' and he left, just like that.

"Nothing more. Not even a goodbye. I realised then he was a broken man. And Romeo... well, yes, I just wanted to force contact with you, but to be honest I did want rid of the bloody thing anyway, so you did me a favour there."

Rossi was properly weeping now, sobbing hard, and Morrison, against his better judgement, stood up and touched his arm in a friendly, conciliatory manner.

Rossi, repeatedly rubbing his arm to the point Morrison thought he might erase the small tattoo he had noticed, fell to his knees, having let out a stream of pent-up emotion, uncomfortable realities and previously unspoken truths he had held within him for the best part of his six decades.

As he eventually finished talking, Morrison nodded, still so far away from understanding Rossi's predicament or how the situation with Bianchi had panned out, but certainly having gained some comprehension of the goings-on he had read in his notes and now heard about. He was no longer devoid of sympathy either, which annoyed him. A failing familiar to him.

Without invitation, he got up, poured another whisky, slugged it, poured another, stared at the discoloured walls and the greasy mess in the kitchen, almost sneering, and said: "We've done the whole fucking bottle Rossi. I don't know what more there is to say or do. I really don't."

"I didn't kill anyone Morrison, please believe me," he pleaded.

"I know I did wrong, but most of what I did was to prevent further evil, stop more terrible things from happening. Two awful wrongs can never make a right, but if I was not involved, and please, often I protected the people Bianchi was after, everything could have been a whole lot worse. I am not a bad person. I did not mean any harm to come to anyone. I did not take part in any of that serious nasty shithousery, I was only on the edge, always on the edge, like a lot of people here.

"Yes I should have been stronger in the beginning, told him to go fuck himself, maybe persuaded Sofia away from him, then none of this would have happened. None of it…"

He stopped and Morrison, himself now welling up, his stomach heaving due in part to the speed at which he had necked the whisky, the tears blurring the golden liquid in his glass, said: "It would Roberto, it would. I do know that.

"Someone else would have worked for him, done his dirty deeds, the same as he was working for someone else, doing their dirty deeds, and they would more than likely have been far more ruthless than you. I suppose it's not so far removed from the class system back home that I am so obsessed about. Not really.

Rossi, all the while rocking, rocking, rocking, nodded, smiled and said: "Well, thank you for that at least."

Morrison, the alcohol now tiring him, his anger subsided, held up his hand indicating to Rossi to stop talking, and said: "Enough for now Roberto, enough for now. This has been way more civil than it could have been, maybe should have been, and I am genuinely glad of that. We are both tired. You need some sleep. We could probably go on for ever but we will carry this on some other time.

"Oh, but one more thing Rossi. No need to look so worried. What does your tattoo say, the one on your arm?"

Rossi clutched his arm, rubbed at it as he had done all evening, and said: "Ah, it is quite simple. It says 'Isabella Rossi, my love always'. That is all. What the hell was I thinking getting one of these stupid bloody things at my age?"

"No, no, it's a nice thing, a lovely thing. A good job it doesn't say Sofia's name anyway. Bye Roberto and thank you for being so honest with me," Morrison said with a sympathetic smile, at the final second rejecting the notion to engage in a departing hug.

"Will we... will we ever drink together again Morrison? Speak again? At Franco's? Or is that out of the question now? Is that all finished, all over?"

Without answering, Morrison merely shrugged as he picked up his notes and left.

13

Some Festive Cheer And A Little Hope

The scale of the festivities in the build-up to Christmas surprised Morrison. He had avoided taking part in the celebrations in his first year in Padria, spending most of the period indoors, inevitably wondering what he would have been doing if Marianna had been with him.

He fully intended to repeat that process but was caught out by an unexpected invitation from Franco to spend Christmas Eve and Day in the restaurant with himself, Pino, Tommaso, Luigi and Roberto Rossi. It was a generous offer, but one he almost declined.

He had thought he would maybe punctuate his day with a walk through the back streets to the main town and another by the sea into the harbour, where the twinkling lights, put up just two days ago on what he now knew to be the day of The Immaculate Conception of Mary, had already made him feel warm inside.

In addition, he was nervous as to how the dynamic between the group would pan out, the prolonged contact between himself and Rossi for the first time since the conversation in Rossi's flat uppermost in his mind. Berating himself inwardly, he accepted he could spend time alone any other day of the year and, after all, what price good companionship?

Franco, concern in his deep brown eyes, love and understanding in them too, always concern, love and understanding, noticed his hesitation in accepting the invitation and Morrison, observing his friend's look of disappointment, worry even, quickly raised a hand in defence and said: "Of course I would love to come. You just took me by surprise Franco. What would I be doing otherwise? Stuck inside talking to Romeo and feeding him his Christmas dinner."

"Mr Morrison my friend, I will not be offended if you have other plans, but I do not want to see you alone like you were last year. Bring your cat if you please. He will certainly enjoy the Christmas Eve fish feast I have planned and, of course, I shall cook something special that is vegetarian for you. Just bring yourself, your cat and a bottle and we shall eat, drink, maybe chat a little and hopefully be merry."

Despite himself, Morrison felt cheered by the installation of trees in the squares, the lights and decorations strung between apartments in the narrow side streets, and those which stretched from the main town to the Piazza San Marco.

There, a tree at the top end by the basilica was festooned with white lights while red and blue surrounded the rest of the area, which had flashing polar bears and penguins attached to the street lights at various intervals - not dissimilar to Blackpool but with at least a sprinkling of taste, Morrison thought. Most shop and bar owners had joined in by lighting up their stores and displaying festive messages.

The artist, who appeared to have extended his hours to stay open until around 11pm, advertised a Christmas sale in the hope of shifting a few of his works as presents and had hung a sign across his frontage wishing potential customers a "Buon Natale".

The fruiterer had placed lights of various colours over and around his signage and shutters, changing their settings over the course of the evening, with one allowing swathes of light to wash over the impressive selection of winter vegetables that would be snapped up for the traditional Christmas dinners prepared by the residents of the area.

The phone shop had made little effort, the pharmacy and antique shops had both frosted their windows, with the latter adding stencils of Father Christmas, known as Babbo Natale, and an elderly woman on a broomstick, who Morrison had discovered was named La Befana and traditionally brought children gifts on January 6, Epiphany, as she searched every house for Jesus. The badly behaved, he learned, supposedly received lumps of coal.

The cake shop was extensively decorated inside and out in a bid to attract people in to buy their festive snowmen and Santa biscuits and cakes. The most miserable efforts were not even those of the hardware and gas stores, both of which had merely placed tinsel on the inside of their windows, but that of the large supermercato, part of a chain, which had simply filled up on over-priced Christmas goods without any display of decorative goodwill.

Tommaso, a man not usually given to demonstration, to Morrison's amusement had installed a small tree and lit his wood-burning stove, as well as having introduced mulled wine to the list of drinks on offer. Luigi had tastefully decorated the tabacchi and made a more elaborate Vin Brule his star attraction too, advertising it outside.

He heated the wine up with the steam nozzle of his Gaggia coffee machine and, despite his somewhat cumbersome approach to movement, ladled it into mugs, careful not to spill any, adding raisins, flaked almonds and a splash of brandy as a final touch.

Morrison was extremely impressed with the sample he received.

Franco, meanwhile, had extended the restaurant's canopy out over the cobbles and set up see-through sections with sides to create the effect of a doorway, with coloured lights strung up in and around the makeshift marquee.

Inside was a brightly decorated tree and a somewhat out of place and tacky waving mechanical Father Christmas with a motion sensor inside causing it to loudly exclaim "Ho! Ho! Ho!" whenever anyone walked past. The phrase, thought Morrison, is obviously universal, though he questioned what the Italian translation might be.

Festive menus stood on each table advertising two courses for €18 and three for €23 leading up to December 24, when a special Feast of the Seven Fishes menu - including octopus salad, calamari, swordfish, tuna, salmon, spaghetti and clam sauce and the salted cod dish baccala - would be served with vegetarian and vegan options available at a very reasonable €35. Morrison noted there was nothing planned for New Year's Eve.

"I cannot be bothered with all that, as you English say, malarkey, so I close except maybe for drinks for a few hours in the early evening, and leave the food to the hotels and the bigger restaurants," Franco said, explaining to Morrison that a typical turn of the year menu would consist of a "huge faff" making the Capodanno feast of baked pastas, pork, lentils and a towering sweet bread panettone, which would be stuffed with citrus, oranges and raisins.

"Most people I know are fed up with it all by then, so they do not come here anyway," he added.

Franco said he would also close on Christmas Day so he could spend it with his friends rather than prepare lunches for customers, which he explained were generally made up of turkey with stuffing, mashed potatoes, gravy, cranberry sauce and various vegetables. Morrison suppressed a smile, as if this was something so radically different from that served in England.

Last year it had not occurred to him to decorate his apartment for Christmas, but with the spirit of the season capturing him now, he bought a small fake tree, a set of lights, baubles, red tinsel and a number of wooden characters to hang from the branches and felt quite pleased with his creation, later purchasing a small selection of ornaments to place around his room and kitchen area.

Romeo enjoyed tugging the decorations from the lower branches and playing with them. Morrison would generally return home to find a selection scattered across the floor, but he did not mind this and it pleased him that Romeo seemed such a happy, contented cat.

Rather than staying in, weighing up his life, his problems, the decisions he had to make, he filled his time walking between the square and the tourist areas and back again, enjoying piping hot cups of Vin Brule and the odd glass of the other seemingly popular Christmas drink Spumante, though he was less partial to this.

He stepped through the doors of churches and marvelled at the large nativity scenes lovingly created in such intricate detail, always lighting a candle, always pulling out his picture of Marianna and uttering a few words as he did so, and usually donating over the suggested amount. He had never understood religion, but he did now appreciate the awe surrounding some of these buildings, the intricacies and beauty of the designs created to fill you with a mix of wonder and fear. The best ones certainly succeeded in that.

He took in the smells of home-made cakes, sweets and nougats, and the sounds of children badgering their parents to buy them anything and everything from stalls unfamiliar, barely recalled from last year, the thrill of the Christmas season again new to them.

From his window he had watched intently as the market took shape and stalls were set up, the wooden cabins selling high quality baubles and colour-coordinated decorations that contrasted sharply with the tatty items with which the trees of his childhood had been swamped.

In the main town, the restaurants stayed open through the winter and the larger hotels had a Babbo Natale in residence, meaning parents had to find the money necessary to fund presents from him at Christmas and again from La Befana come the day of the Epiphany.

Franco told Morrison that a fast was observed during the day of Christmas Eve to help purify the body for the holiday period, but the fish feast in the evening ended this and it was all systems go until January 6, when the parties of the Carnivale season led the way into Lent, although he did not much go in for that "forty days of abstinence nonsense".

"Well, I couldn't do that, could I, not when I run a bar and restaurant? That would be even more hypocritical than when I serve food through Lent to the supposedly deeply religious. Obviously, people don't abstain altogether, otherwise they would die, but some don't cut down at all. They just carry on, live a lie in the name of religion. Then maybe we all live a lie."

Morrison said he was familiar with the concept and, not being religious, he too did not bother. He wondered how much Franco knew of the lie Roberto Rossi had lived.

Late one evening in Franco's bar after his first wander around the Christmas markets, he told Tommaso how he had enjoyed the experience. The older man screwed up his nose and said it was not like it used to be, with local people leaving and new ones arriving from out of town who did not make the effort.

"Anyway, surely it is not the same here for you as it is at home in England. I am sixty three years now Mr Morrison, sixty three years, can you believe that? Sixty-three years and I have never seen the snow like you have in England," he said, repeating a line almost word for word he had used in a previous conversation with Morrison.

Roberto Rossi, hands stretched out, shoulders shrugging, avoiding eye contact with Morrison, but not unfriendly, suggested he did not care either way, and said people could take part or not bother, he himself being of the latter persuasion.

Franco said he felt that the community still came together at this time of year. It was the same the world over - people leaving, new ones coming, all about money, but as long as people joined in, then what did it matter?

"You say you are not bothered Rossi, but no doubt you will be joining us for your free Christmas dinner," laughed Franco, teasing a smile from his friend.

The atmosphere was initially somewhat flat, with talk between Morrison and Rossi clipped and at a minimum, though the pair had exchanged minimal pleasantries over the past couple of days, but with no reference to Bianchi. Morrison felt an awkwardness in Rossi, a different awkwardness than he normally displayed, almost as if his spirit, confidence, arrogance even, had left him as he lowered his defences and emptied himself of secrets.

Morrison thought he would engage further with Rossi as the evening progressed, but he would not let him have too easy a passage back into his life.

His enthusiasm had been buoyed by the number of drinks he had taken through the late afternoon and early evening to warm himself against the December cold.

"January is colder, Mr Morrison, January is colder, but not like your January," Franco had told him. Morrison said he was looking forward to this Christmas more than any in years.

In fact, he said, he was already enjoying it very much. Roberto Rossi smiled but said nothing, resisting his natural urge to pat Morrison on the arm and offer a jibe along the lines of: "What the hell are you, some kind of daft child?"

He spent the next two weeks trawling the streets, buying drinks from the stalls, admiring the decorations, varying his walks so he could take in different areas, noting down details in case he could find use for them in the story he was progressing, which he was rather pleased with thus far.

Usually, he would reach his half-way point at the grand harbour in the early or mid-afternoon, but occasionally he would begin his descent of the steps as daylight was fading and the lights were beginning to twinkle along the shore and around the busy bars, giving the whole area a magical appearance. It wasn't really magical though. It could not change the past. It could not bring back those who had gone, not even for a day.

Briefly, he again contemplated what Marianna would have been doing if she was still alive. The realisation that they had never spent a Christmas together set him questioning once again what it would have been like if she was here, or even if they were back in England. But what good was all this thinking doing? He managed to wrestle the thought away instead of dwelling on it.

It was December 20, around 4.45pm and the sun was setting, the darkness and cold combining to give the harbour a spooky feeling, rendering the figures walking about near the sea's edge mere silhouettes, their arms waving, bodies twisting and turning, reflecting ghost-like in and in front of the water as they went about their tasks around their boats or preparing their restaurants for the evening.

The bars began to light up, mostly white, providing a sharp contrast between the immediate light and that in the distance, where coloured lights twinkled. Morrison zipped up his coat and put his hands in his pockets.

Carols were being played in a nearby bar, at least he thought they were until he realised these were not pre-recorded but were the high-pitched warming sounds of a children's choir. They were singing his favourite, which was also the one that made him most mournful.

"In the bleak mid-winter, Frosty wind made moan; Earth stood hard as iron, Water like a stone; Snow had fallen, snow on snow, Snow on snow, In the bleak mid-winter, Long ago," they sang in English, which surprised Morrison, who bowed his head as the sadness born from beauty gripped him.

His mind conjured up an image of a parade of ghostly figures, stooped, carrying lanterns in memory of lost close ones, the lights dimming as those holding them also faded and crossed over to be reunited with those they once knew and loved.

He barely heard another word until they finished: "What can I give him, Poor as I am? If I were a Shepherd I would bring a lamb; If I were a Wise Man I would do my part, Yet what I can I give him, Give my heart."

A young girl held out a collecting tin in front of him and, hoping she would not notice his watery eyes, he managed to produce a smile as he dropped a €2 coin into it.

It really felt like Christmas now, but he had only to cast his eyes above the harbour and up towards the decaying castle in the air from which no fairy lights twinkled and no angels sang to feel the punch of sadness once more. A near empty shell in which only badness and cruelty were captured, the only voices emerging from crushed souls the bitter ghosts of Christmases past, the only lights from the candles they carried to see their way along the cold corridors they walked.

Calling in at The Star of The Sea, Morrison decided he would have a glass of red, clapping his hands together to keep out the cold as he ordered from the woman, who was smiling at him, and almost he felt, recognising his emotion, his trauma.

"Ah, the quiet man I spoke to in Franco's bar one fine evening some time ago. A bit of a thinker, I recall. The shape of your face as the sadness overcame you just then gave you away as it always does when I see you, just like on the night when I told you that you cannot see when you are so deep in thought and you miss the sunshine."

Morrison recalled the conversation almost word for word but just nodded nervously, impressed by her quick assessment of him, but aware of a gentle teasing in her words and tone.

Now, what was her name? He thought Pino had called her Gabriella. In fact, he was sure he had, but decided he had better not use that name in case he was mistaken. She looked different. Older perhaps, thinner maybe, but still friendly-faced.

The waiter, a young man, returned with his drink and the woman raised hers across the bar as if to toast him. She remained talking to a customer and Morrison could not decide if she might like him in a special way - as had been suggested - or not and whether he would ever want that to happen to him again anyway.

People had said he was not bad looking, but the mirrors told him a different story. He had caught his reflection in windows and was unpleasantly surprised by what he saw; an older, slightly sturdier, more hunched man than he had believed himself to be. He had noticed t-shirts didn't look so good these days and he had to watch what he wore.

He had tried to take care of himself, even through the years of heavy drinking, using moisturisers and other skin products on a daily basis. He had less hair than he once had, there were lines on his forehead and around his blue eyes, which had lost some of their sparkle, but could on occasion smile. His face was friendly, even kind, he thought, but given to betraying his mood. People often said he looked sad, but mostly he was merely quiet.

It was the same for everyone, but he still didn't much care for it or the fact he had to work harder to make sure hair didn't take over his hands and feet and his eyebrows didn't grow wild.

Still, if that was the worst of it, he could cope and maybe the sun and pace of life here would slow down the process of mental and physical ageing, lesson his melancholy and allow him a cheerier demeanour.

Marianna hadn't minded his appearance or character and maybe the owner of The Star of the Sea didn't either.

He finished his drink, paid the waiter and waved goodbye to Gabriella, yes, that was definitely her name, who was deep in conversation with someone but noticed him leaving, hurried over and hugged him warmly - strange for a person he didn't really know - telling him to relax, enjoy Christmas and maybe share a drink with her early in the new year. He would do all of that, he promised.

At the very least, he would enjoy it more than anyone in the Bianchi household ever had, he thought but did not say.

***

Christmas Eve arrived and Morrison took in the wonder of the children at an experience he recalled fondly from his childhood when the following morning seemed an age away, and every year his father warned him that Santa Claus had seen him behaving badly and would not be delivering any presents.

The next morning would see his dad slowly leading the way down the stairs, his brother and himself behind, opening the door at the bottom, looking into the room and announcing that Santa had not been. Then the relief, when, of course, there was a pillowcase of presents there for each.

He sat with Tommaso for half an hour before the bar became busier and spent a while with Luigi in the low-lit tabacchi, complimenting him on the standard of his spicy Vin Brule, before heading to Franco's, where his friend had promised him a warming pasta bake on the house. It was getting busy, but Franco still greeted him enthusiastically, bringing him a glass of wine.

Pino was scurrying around serving customers with drinks and their specially prepared fish feasts. He smiled at Morrison and waved. He seemed much happier after his few days away following Morrison's sighting of him in the Roman Baths. He wondered if he would get the chance to broach the subject with him or whether it would be more tactful to not mention it.

Morrison thought he might have felt out of place alone in a classy restaurant - which is what Franco's place had become tonight, garlands of festive flowers adorning the marquee sides, mini poinsettias on each table and menus upgraded for the season - but he was happy at his tiny table in the bar area, sipping his wine, looking at the scores in the football section of an Italian newspaper.

"Do not read about the Napoli game, Mr Morrison. We were robbed," Franco, with a grin, shouted above the hubbub, keen to involve his friend in the evening's happenings.

"Luckily I can't translate much of it, so I'll just have to take your word for it Franco," he replied.

The place was full, but Franco, sporting a festive red waistcoat, busy yet still convivial, managed to find time for everyone, time to make them feel special, asking about their festive plans, while Pino rushed about preparing tables, putting food on tables, clearing tables, taking drinks orders from tables.

Almost every time he attempted to return to the kitchen someone called him over with a query, to which without exception he responded politely and efficiently. A proper professional, operating without fuss or panic despite the pressure, regarded with respect, not remotely how we treat the waiters in England, Morrison thought.

With extended canopy sides, Franco and Pino had managed to find space to accommodate between forty and fifty customers, around double the amount they normally catered for. Morrison hoped Franco had made a decent profit given how hard he had worked and felt heartened by the people enjoying their evening; many were couples, some were with groups of friends, a number were accompanied by children and Morrison realised he recognised quite a few of them.

It seemed almost everyone was enjoying the selection of fish and, as the only vegetarian, Morrison felt slightly out of place as he thanked Franco for his special dish.

"It is not a problem Mr Morrison, not one I am going to complain about anyway."

Christmas songs played and from where he sat Morrison could make out people buzzing about the square, moving between bars as the dance of the night quickened its tempo. At around 10pm he decided it was time to leave, caught Franco's eye and pushed some money into his hand, which he at first refused but then agreed to take as a contribution to the next day's food and drink.

As he turned the key in his lock he made the sudden decision to clear the air with Rossi, knocked on his door and invited him in for a couple of limoncellos which seemed an appropriate way to finish a Christmas Eve.

"We can't go on like this, Rossi, avoiding each other, not talking properly, you not having a go at me at every available opportunity," he said.

"People will wonder what has happened. We can't ruin their Christmas."

Rossi at first looked down at the ground, then raised his head, grinned and said: "What kind of a bloody inconsiderate neighbour wakes you up at this sort of time? An English one, of course."

14

The Best Christmas Ever?

People shouted, "Buon Natale signore, Buon Natale," and he replied as heartily as he felt he could.

Greetings were proffered with added enthusiasm, children were riding new bikes and scooters, families moving hastily from their homes to relatives or friends for the day and the bells of the basilica rang aloud.

His Christmas may have felt unfamiliar but the cold bite in the air, which made him pull his coat tighter, offered a harsh reminder of home.

He forgot about his muzzy head - probably caused by the half bottle of limoncello that had been consumed as Rossi and he put their differences aside - as he walked, turning back towards his apartment to pick up a bottle of whisky to take across to Franco's. Unwrapping Romeo's catnip-infused toy mouse, he smiled as the cat threw it in the air and kicked it around the room.

Tommaso was already deep in conversation with a tired looking but cheery Franco as Morrison arrived at noon as requested. Merry Christmases were exchanged and Morrison handed over the Old Pulteney single malt he had managed to source on the internet. It had been a favourite of his since a driving holiday in Scotland many years ago, which concluded at the distillery in Wick.

"The most mature in the whole of Scotland," he informed Franco with some pride.

"Please, don't open it today my friend. Keep it for yourself and raise a glass to me when you do open it," Franco said, admiring the bottle and placing it on the table.

Shaking his head vigorously in reply, Morrison said: "Absolutely not. It is a gift for you, my friend. Savour every mouthful."

Remembering how busy the restaurant had been the previous night, Morrison looked around, amazed to find the place immaculate.

"It is all so tidy, how on earth did you do it?"

"Well, we finished serving at 1am, much of the preparation had, of course, already been done for our dinner today, we clean and wash up until three, go to bed, get up later than usual, about 9.30am and here we are, ready for the big day. No problem, it's what we do. We are professionals or hadn't you noticed?" he laughed uproariously, grasping Morrison's right hand between both of his own and shaking it warmly.

Rossi and Luigi, his cousin, arrived together and Pino bustled through the door carrying a tray containing six glasses of Spumante, offering a formal reverential half-bow to each while handing them the fizz. Glasses were clinked and more glad tidings wished, with conversation mostly centred round the events of Christmas Eve.

Tommaso, today sporting a green jumper depicting a Christmas pudding, said he had enjoyed a reasonable night, his takings were good and he was pleasantly surprised at the amount of young people in his bar.

Luigi, a red-nosed reindeer knitted onto his blue jumper, had also fared well, considering the tabacchi was not typically somewhere that people would visit on their rounds, but he had experienced some success with people coming in for late presents of chocolates and bottles of spirits or wine and staying for a drink or two while they were there.

Roberto Rossi, in pale blue, but actually clean-looking, jeans topped with a distinctly non-festive thick brown sweater, had called in at both and, in his usual curmudgeonly way, described his evening as much the same as any other.

Morrison raised his eyes at this, resisted the urge to say something sarcastic and hastily looked away.

Franco and Pino, wearing Santa hats, had laid up a large table with white linen and when the first Spumantes had been consumed out came two bottles of wine, one Sauvignon Blanc and a Pinot Grigio. These were followed by an antipasti board containing Italian cheeses, cured meats, olives and sun-dried tomatoes, Morrison's served on a separate platter without the meats but with a small focaccia.

After an hour or so the assembled diners welcomed the turkey dinner previously mentioned by Franco, clapping raucously as the host bore the bronzed bird atop a silver platter into the room for carving. Morrison, in a grey cashmere jumper and dark blue jeans, at that moment wishing he had dressed a little more frivolously, was served an aubergine parmigiana with roasted cauliflower.

Taking their time over the food and enjoying several glasses of wine along the way - Luigi was asked to reveal the supplier of the magnificent Barolo which complemented the main course perfectly, and responded by tapping the side of his nose, causing much hilarity as everyone knew that Franco dealt with all purchases wine-related - they finished several hours later with a delicious palate-cleansing lemon panna cotta accompanied by a gorgeous dessert wine Moscato di Pantelleria.

Morrison said it was the best Christmas dinner he had ever eaten and asked, given that Franco was obviously a much more accomplished chef than his regular menu suggested, why his host did not regularly cook dishes such as the fish-based ones of the previous night in his restaurant.

"Because Mr Morrison, others do this kind of thing. Traditional Italian here, traditional Italian there, traditional Italian everywhere. If I did the same I would not win that battle, so I do my own thing, keep it low key, do not try to compete and I get the custom of those who are fed up with stuffing their faces with three-course meals every day of their holiday and locals tired of going home and eating huge piles of food every evening. That's all. Simple."

"Actually, it's because he's a lazy so-and-so," said Roberto Rossi, cheerier now, his face distorted in an attempt at mock derision. Franco disappeared back indoors for more wine, returning with a bill to be paid in the region of €60 made out in the name of Roberto Rossi for "fine wine, food and excellent company", which caused much amusement.

Morrison, who had noticed the symmetry between his improving stomach condition and his happier demeanour through the festive season which had succeeded in distracting him from his problems, grinned at Rossi and widened his eyes as if to affirm their friendship, the Padrian lifting his glass towards him in response.

Franco, with typical generosity, then offered up a plate of chocolates with vintage port as an accompaniment and Rossi asked Morrison if he had been up to the big house yet.

His loose tongue immediately provoked interrogation from the others as to why Morrison would visit such a place and over a period of around half-an-hour the whole story spilled out in a loudly babbled manner with the others continually interjecting with questions.

Tommaso asked why he hadn't confronted Bianchi straight away, Pino why he was really in Padria, Franco would he leave Padria once he had seen Marianna's father, Luigi, his facial tick gathering pace, if such a meeting would really bring him peace, all of them shocked, asking why he hadn't mentioned it before.

Morrison, suddenly weary through the intensity of the quizzing, almost bamboozled by the level of interest in him, leaned back in his chair, hands on his head and sighed loudly, struggling with his stuttering responses.

"It's just that, it's just that...well, Marianna is really not the only reason I am here. I wanted to find a new life, still want to find a new life, maybe to become inspired again, to recover mentally, even write once more.

"I see no reason to leave Padria once I have met with Bianchi. I certainly do not want to return to England. Obviously, I do not know if this or anything else will ever bring me peace, though I feel so much closer to such a thing simply by being here."

He asked if any of them knew Marianna. Did they remember her death? He knew Rossi's answer was yes, but the others all shook their heads solemnly when he produced her picture, though Pino said he thought he may have seen her around and Franco that he had read of her suicide.

Rossi, opinionated as usual, again expressed his view of Stefano Bianchi: "That son of a bitch."

Pino remained quiet, deep in thought, Tommaso said seeing Marianna's father was the right thing to do and Franco agreed, saying he believed it would enable Morrison to move on and enjoy his life.

The subject was explored for a good while longer, with Morrison feeling obliged to share with them details of his relationship with Marianna, the night of the party, his reaction to what happened, Marianna's letter, his discovery of her death and his decision to return to Padria.

Feeling under pressure, facing a sea of concerned faces, weighing up and trying to properly deliver his answers to their questions, he cupped his hands around his mouth and nose, let out a deep breath, the alcohol suddenly guiding an unfamiliar rising anger, and spat: "Come on, all of you, you all knew, all of you knew, you all fucking knew, you must have known, he must have told you."

He pointed directly at Rossi, who held his hands out and shook his head several times.

"No, no, Morrison, I have explained all of this..."

"You have, yes you have, but I need to know for certain from all of you. I need to be able to trust all of you and you need to be able to trust me. Yes, yes, you say you did not know her, did not know about her, but come on, please, you have all lived here for ever, who really knew about Marianna, who knew about Bianchi?"

His finger jabbing in Rossi's direction, he continued: "Who knew about what he has done for that terrible, dangerous arsehole of a man? All of you? Are you all against me, plotting against me?"

Franco stopped dead in his tracks, staring at the ground, shaking his head at this most unlikely of outbursts, Pino scuttled into the kitchen, Luigi and Tommaso merely sat, heads bowed in silence.

For what seemed like an eternity to Morrison, no-one spoke, then Rossi, meeting Morrison's fiery stare - which was accompanied by an aggressive jabbing of his forefinger - almost growled: "I have told you Morrison, I have apologised to you, you know the story but they don't. Let them speak. They will not deny you the truth. They are your friends, after all, or hadn't you noticed?."

Surprisingly, it was Pino, returning from the kitchen, who eventually plucked up the courage to speak, having put down a tray full of glasses of red wine, which was rattling as he shook with nerves.

"I think I told you, said to you, there was more to Roberto than he let on. Yes, yes we knew some things he had told us, but do we know everything? I have no idea. He has told us what he has told us, and we have never had a reason to disbelieve him."

Franco: "Roberto is a good person, Michael. He has been through a lot in his life. He will not mind me telling you that when he has had a few drinks he has sometimes said things he may rather have not, but nothing ever terrible. His situation is similar to a lot of people in this town and it is easy for you to come here and criticise, to judge, but not easy to avoid when you live in Padria. Please believe us, we are not bad people. We are your friends and we... we have come to love you."

Tommaso: "Michael, Michael, my friend, please believe us. Roberto told us he was looking after you, that Bianchi had put a watch on you, but you know nothing bad has occurred. You know you have settled here, made friends, wandered freely, and why? Because Roberto made that happen. If he wasn't involved you may well not have been here with us tonight."

Morrison grabbed a glass and gulped some wine. In disbelief at what he was hearing, he raised his eyes skyward, sighing loudly, but it was Luigi, looking over at Rossi with tears in his eyes, and speaking for the first time in a long while, who provided a timely interjection.

"Roberto, he is my cousin. We know each other well, he has looked after me over the years and he has told me he has spoken to you about the apartments, his money, my money, and yes, he has made mistakes, done some wrong, some bad things, but if he hadn't, someone else would have done them worse. He has only ever tried to limit the damage."

Looking directly into Morrison's eyes, he continued: "We are small people, Michael. We do not have the power to stop the likes of Bianchi and his bosses, but we come together as friends, we help each other as a community, and that is what we have done for most of our lives. Now we have tried to include you in this."

Morrison, silent for some time and now shaking as the tears welled up, a horrible sense that he had misjudged the situation and ruined the occasion, knowing he had disappointed his friends, who now believed he distrusted them, went to some lengths to convince them of his love of Padria and its people.

"I, I am sorry, I am so very sorry. I did not mean for this to happen, certainly not on Christmas Day.

"It has been so hard, trusting, not trusting, loving, hating, grieving, all those emotions.

"I have been here eighteen months now and for the first year did nothing about Marianna or Bianchi, except think about them. I could have done what I needed to do in barely a week. Just stayed in a hotel and got it over with, visited the house, gone to see her father, checked out and flown home, easy as that. But like I fell in love with Marianna, the first time I came here I fell in love with Padria, its people and its beauty and I do not want that love to end in the way the love between Marianna and I ended."

Rising to his feet, a gesture which seemed entirely appropriate, he took a step back, composed himself and, looking at each man in turn, said: "My friends, you have treated me as one of your own and I thank you all sincerely for that. I am truly sorry if you believe I have let you down. I believe I have treated Padria with the respect it deserves and I always will.

I feel so at home here and in some ways I am not even entirely sure it was only my love for Marianna that drew me back here."

Rossi went to speak but Morrison, now head in hands, continued slowly: "Three months I knew her, just three months, and even then I, I did not really know her. Why didn't I know her? I ask myself often. I didn't ask the questions that I should have. I was a journalist, I am, or at least I was, a writer and I should have been asking the questions my profession would have demanded, but I did not.

"She asked me lots but I just went along with falling in love with someone trying to make a life in England. Someone brave who had moved countries to follow what she believed in, but that wasn't the story at all, was it? I didn't know the story because I didn't ask. Eventually she just had to tell me, but not until the night of that dreadful party."

He crashed back heavily into his chair, fighting the tears as he remembered the conversation that took place as they sat on the bench, their bench.

"She told me they had a bank vault. A fucking bank vault," he positively screamed out the phrase with vitriol, and then: "Who the hell has their own bank vault?"

He took another large swig of his wine, swirled it round his mouth for a few seconds and, buying time, breathed heavily, then calmer, continued: "Please believe me all of you. I love this place. I have walked the streets of Padria and asked the questions that I should have asked Marianna and over the past few months in particular, due not in any small part to you, my wonderful friends, have come to realise I have found what I sincerely hope will be my forever home.

"I couldn't leave anyway. Romeo would never settle anywhere else; he wouldn't forgive me. He would have to go back to live at Roberto's and I could never do that to him."

He shrugged and grinned to attempt to lighten the mood and Franco, Pino, Tommaso, Luigi and Rossi all laughed, the latter for once moved enough to not offer a mocking response.

"Roberto, I am sorry. All of you, I am sincerely sorry," Morrison added, again looking at each of them in turn.

Tears, hugs and laughs followed, and a toast to friends by Franco, who then disappeared into the kitchen, returning with more Barolo.

Morrison puffed out his cheeks and exhaled, Rossi gave a sympathetic and almost apologetic smile, Pino, Luigi and Tommaso all stayed silent, their faces more relaxed as the tension subsided.

The Christmas spirit had dipped but the group had been won over by Morrison and Franco shed a tear as Morrison told more of Marianna, her father, her mother, the deaths and the dilapidated, rejected building.

"Mr Morrison, please, do not set me off, the woman in your picture, Marianna, she looks so beautiful, and this is a sad story that can have no happy ending, but you can gain some closure and that is what you must do before you can fully move on with your life and then you will be a true Padrian."

"To Mr Morrison and Padria," shouted Tommaso, unusually loud and effusive, more confident, his semi-permanent bemused expression almost unnoticeable, perhaps due in part to the alcohol he had consumed.

His raised glass was met with equally loud echoes of "Mr Morrison and Padria" from around the table and Pino brought out a bottle of port.

"We must all do what we believe Morrison and no-one would be-grudge you giving that arsehole Bianchi a piece of your mind and punching him square in the face," Rossi, his confidence returning, added.

It was early evening now and becoming chilly under the canopy. Rossi suggested they go inside the restaurant proper and maybe play some games. It seemed a sensible proposition and they all rose from their chairs, but Morrison's progress indoors was interrupted by Pino who said he had several questions he had been meaning to ask him and wanted to do so before he became too drunk.

Morrison sat down again and Pino positioned himself opposite him, saying: "I will make this quick Mr Morrison as I do not want the others thinking something is wrong and I do not wish to spoil Christmas for anyone.

"I know what you saw in the baths, and I also think you may have told my father. His attitude towards me has been different. I do not think he wants me here and I am not sure I want to be here any longer. If he cannot accept me for the way I am then he is no more my father than your Marianna's father was a real father to her.

"It hurts me because I love him, and I have worked so very hard to please him. I do this job in this place not because I really want to but because I feel I should. It is done out of love.

"Don't get me wrong, Mr Morrison, I enjoy it, sometimes I even love it. I like the people I serve and the joy we bring to them, but sometimes I just want some joy bringing to me. The joy doesn't come to me and that is why I must go out myself to seek it, but now it seems all I have brought is disappointment and maybe even disgust and I cannot face that."

Morrison held up his hand to stop Pino and, in almost headteacher-like manner, sternly informed him that he had said nothing to Franco.

Adding that he had not noticed any change in the dynamic between the two of them, he said: "If there has been a change it was perhaps sparked by the conversation in which you said you had no idea what the future would bring, you were too busy here to meet someone other than the people who come here, and you did not know if you wanted the business or if your father would want you to have it.

"Your father, he said if you did not want it, well that is the way of the world. He would be fine with whatever decision you made Pino and he will be okay with whatever you want to tell him. That, of course, is none of my business."

Lightly patting his arm, he looked into the younger man's eyes and added: "Pino, I consider you a good friend. I would never tell your father or anyone else anything that was not my concern. It is your concern and yours only, but for what it is worth, yes, he may dream of you having a wife and children and running the business, but I am guessing he would be fine if that was not possible. He loves you Pino, you are his son."

There followed a brief silence, after which Pino, his left eyelid visibly flickering through anxiety, apologised humbly for thinking Morrison would have imparted his secret to his father. Morrison, in turn, said he did not really know what the secret was, but could only guess.

"I believe that your guess would be right, Mr Morrison. Do you remember what you said during the very night to which you refer? You told me that as humans we always repeat our mistakes, we go back for more of what has already gone wrong in the hope that the next time it will work, or some words to that effect.

"I remember you asked 'How do you get up and face the day, the same day, every day, until something comes along and changes it, makes it worse even? To have the temperament to accept that what you have isn't perfect, but it's good enough to get by and be happy or happier than you might otherwise be.'

"Another thing you said, Mr Morrison, was that many people leave no imprint, and you said you hoped that if I wished to leave an imprint I would succeed in doing so. Well, I have made the decision that I do.

"Your words, they stayed with me and I could not shake them, the things they made me think about, and I shall walk through the gap you talked about and see what is on the other side. I hope I have already found some of what I desire, and I feel happier now, less anxious, but, as you say, it may not be as beautiful as I, at this moment, think."

Morrison would have hugged Pino, but the others were sitting inside and could see them and would surely ask questions as to what they had been talking about. Instead, they exchanged knowing smiles and went to join them.

"Good luck my friend, good luck. Be strong," Morrison said, looking over Pino's shoulder as the flickering lights across the square blurred through wet eyes.

"And to you Mr Morrison. Go to the house, remember the night of the party, reignite your anger, the reason you came here. Exorcise your demons and move on with your life."

15

Finding Out Means
Change Must Happen

What would he have been doing on a typical Boxing Day back in England? Recovering from a hangover alone? More enforced drinking with friends? Reading one of the many books people had bought him because they couldn't think of anything else? If things had been different would he and Marianna still be together, enjoying the festive period?

At about 9.30am he peered out on to the square feeling surprisingly lively considering the alcohol of the previous day and the rollercoaster of emotions he had experienced.

On seeing Franco, dressed in his usual white shirt and black trousers, sweeping the pavement, he thought he would wait until the early afternoon to venture over to thank him for the previous day and to test the water regarding Pino.

His recollections were hazy and he worried he may have said too much, Pino may have said too much, but then again perhaps neither had said anything much at all. He felt a dull pain in his head and took two tablets.

After today's festivities life would begin to quieten down, with the bus service back to normal, so he would do what he had come here for; visit

Marianna's grave, go to see Bianchi, walk up to the house, then get on with his life.

Various possibilities had crossed his mind as to what would happen - from Bianchi simply not being there, him being a thoroughly pleasant chap who was not to blame for what had happened, a fight breaking out or even one of them losing their temper and killing the other. He sighed and puffed out his cheeks as his thoughts darkened.

People were again criss-crossing the square to his left and right, on their way to family and friends or to bars and restaurants to celebrate Santo Stefano Day, most of the adults probably not feeling much like another day of over-indulgence, but the children, as always, ready for yet more treats.

Their existences will soon return to normality, Morrison thought as he sipped his coffee and watched lives unfold in front of his window - but what is normal?

He spent twenty minutes or so typing up thoughts about a man whose life was anything but normal because he had, deliberately or sub-consciously, placed himself in a situation that was anything but typical, with no knowledge as to what was really happening to those around him, seemingly going about their days as they generally would at this time of year.

He liked what he had written and decided he would stop there, settle and read a bit. He had not read as much as he felt he should during what was effectively a period of retirement, his collection of short stories by William Trevor carried around on walks and trips to bars, but too often undeservedly left unopened. An hour passed quickly as he completed three stories, impressed as always by the author's ability to build character and relationships and, most importantly, often without anything aston-ishing appearing to happen.

The writer clearly understood the mechanics of existence, the workings of the mind, the drama of the common man and woman, who appeared to live within bubbles, the action unfolding around them but not obviously involving them, which Trevor depicted beautifully.

Morrison admired Trevor's ability to write without exhibiting his own passions and being able to create emotion simply through human interaction, a skill he might even confess to being jealous of. He had been jealous at various points throughout his life but hated that emotion and had largely managed to push the feeling away. The result though had always been a surge of anger and injustice within him, rather than serenity or happiness.

He decided to take some exercise to clear his head as a minor hangover had crept up on him. It was just past midday and the streets away from the square were quieter than the previous day, people perhaps slower off the mark. It wasn't freezing, but he could see his breath in the chilly air, something that, incongruously, gave him a warm sensation.

As usual, he assumed position on his bench for a few minutes, recalling, as always, the moments he had spent there with Marianna when she told him of the party.

He thought about what an incredible thing life was that one minute you could be as happy as whatever the happiest thing in the world might be, the next that sensation has been crushed, a person dies, possibly as a result, or partly as a result of what happened, you move countries to the place you came to on holiday and are facing one of the most difficult and awkward confrontations of your life. On top of all that, you have unexpected new friends, the feeling that you may just want to write again, and it's Christmas.

Morrison looked across the harbour and up to the Bianchi house before continuing on his way as he was becoming cold. The smells of Christmas cooking dominated the narrower streets he traversed, accompanied by the noise of families, excited or exasperated.

He took a rare turn into the shopping area of the main town, its stores closed - back home many would now have re-opened for the Boxing Day sales - and only the occasional restaurant beginning to welcome those who had made reservations in an attempt to escape the drudgery of the kitchen or the confines of their own homes.

Choosing to head back, on approaching the square he noted the shuttered-up art shop, the pharmacy, the grocery and the antique store, the only tangible evidence of trade coming from the bars.

He could see a couple heading into Franco's, which was a good sign, so he followed them in, nodding at his busy friend, who returned the greeting, seemingly without much enthusiasm, yet managing to remain friendly and welcoming for his customers.

As Franco headed inside, Pino emerged into the outdoor seating area, handing out drinks to a family of four at another table. He too nodded at Morrison, who added a smile to his own nod.

Morrison thought there was something in the atmosphere, though he would not describe it as tense. He observed Franco and his son speaking, swapping instructions and directions and Pino held up a bottle of red in Morrison's direction, making a glass shape between thumb and fore-finger, to which Morrison again nodded.

Minutes later Pino brought over the large glass of Montepulciano d'Abruzzo and asked Morrison how he was. Morrison told him that in the early morning he had felt a little ropey after the excesses of yesterday but was more or less fine now, certainly nothing a good red wine would not cure. He considered attempting to explain the phrase "hair of the dog" but decided against it.

Morrison asked if he had spoken with his father and told him his intentions, to which a slightly evasive Pino said: "I must go as he will see we are speaking. We have talked. It was okay in the end. Well, sort of."

The two of them laughed to give the impression the conversation had been a light one and Morrison raised his glass to Pino, who headed off back towards the kitchen.

Franco came out and busied himself at a table near Morrison before moving over to ask if his friend was okay and explain how much he had enjoyed yesterday.

"I came to say thank you. I had the best Christmas ever. As Rossi would say, I sound like a child saying that, but I really enjoyed it, all of it.

Well, apart perhaps from my outburst for which I apologise wholeheartedly."

"No need my friend, no need. I am so very pleased you had a good day." A gap and then: "But you knew?"

"I knew what Franco?"

"About Pino. You knew?"

"It depends on what you think I knew or know."

"He has told me. He wants to move on, to leave the business. What else could it be?"

"I spoke to him yesterday, that is all, just briefly, and he said he had been thinking about it after the conversation we had. Remember? The one where you said if he didn't take the business on, then so be it. He said he had been doing a lot of thinking since then. It might not be for him. He just wants to explore other possibilities.

"It's natural to see if there is anything better out there and more often than not people end up returning to what they know. I told him it was not my place to let you know anything, it was his choice and he made that choice alone."

Franco, looking tired and concerned, agitated even, furrowed his brow, nodded and moved away to take care of an order.

Around an hour or so passed before custom died down and Franco and Pino joined him for bits and pieces of chat, interrupted by the occasional demand from drinkers and diners.

Eventually Morrison, aware that most of the conversation was directed from one or the other towards him rather than between father and son, crept away and headed back across San Marco.

He made himself a snack and began to read another short story, but the ringing of his doorbell interrupted him. He rarely had visitors, not even Rossi from across the corridor, and on answering the outside door discovered an out-of-breath, red-faced, visibly panicking Franco, who he invited upstairs.

"I have five minutes only," he told Morrison, almost breathlessly, before they were even half-way up the stairs. "I know his true secret. You know his true secret."

"I believe I know but he hasn't told me, and I don't think it should matter, not that it is really any of my business. It wouldn't matter to me, but I know there are reasons why it will or it could change things Franco, and Pino knows that too."

"Oh, it does not bother me, not in that way, well it does, but only because it is a shock. I was not expecting it. It never occurred to me; why would it? I just never thought of it, but looking back, well, you know, I suppose there was all the usual stuff, the typical signs and clues, but I just thought he hadn't had the time to meet a girl. Yes, it might change that he wants to come back to the business, but this will not change, will it Mr Morrison? It can't."

"It won't, you are right, it can't change, not really, but you still love him and he still loves you, yes? Have you told him? Where is he now?"

"He has gone for his break. There is no-one over at the restaurant. I have rushed over here to tell you. I did not, do not, know what to do."

"You are not opening for anything special tonight, you have no bookings, so close completely and talk to each other. Find out properly what he wants and make a decision as to what the future holds."

"I cannot run the business on my own Mr Morrison. I cannot cope. I do not know what I will do. I fear it is all over."

"Franco, you can find someone to help you, surely. You know everyone round here. You own the business, you are the chef, you just need a decent waiter. Calm down, think about things, take your time."

Franco, his gaze firm and sincere, nodded his understanding.

"It will not be the same, it could never be the same with someone who is not Pino, but you are right, I will close tonight and we shall talk. Talk about everything. It is always the best way. To keep no secrets. We have all learned that now."

16

The Moments Of Truth

He had been to Catholic burial grounds where some of the tombs were pure statements of wealth but discovered the Cimitero Monumentale to be sizeable yet modest and, having no idea where the Bianchi plot was, concluded it was within his reach to walk and search until he found it.

Many of the graves were simple affairs, little more than wooden crosses, a name and a small bunch of flowers, while others were grander family vaults. In some places graves were stacked vertically, like bricks in walls, step ladders placed nearby to enable visitors to make the climb to their loved ones.

The cemetery, just beyond the main part of town, back inland and up a small hill, was well kept with wide Tarmac-covered pathways, the grass mown short, benches at regular intervals. Relatives and friends of the dead had placed Christmas wreaths and flowers on many of the graves.

He had found it easily but knew locating the Bianchis would be much harder. So it proved as he walked up and down each row, approaching some of the showpiece vaults and looking through the railings that prevented entry to the inside. Some contained benches for relatives to sit on and many were filled with trinkets, cuddly toys, ballet shoes, floral tributes. Others had doors, a few of which he tried, but thankfully all were locked.

He could think of no reason why he should wish to enter a vault, other than out of sheer curiosity, the fear of what he might find inside enough to deter him after a couple of failed attempts.

He walked tentatively up to graves and tombs for around an hour, his legs feeling weaker than normal, possibly due to the cold or more probably through the apprehension he was feeling.

An overbearing stench of rotting flowers, stagnant water perhaps, overcame him and as he rubbed his nose he saw a large vault to the left of the entrance at the far end of the cemetery. It was a plain-looking concrete affair, a large stone cross above its iron gate, which stood under a slab on which the words "Fam Bianchi" were inscribed. Stones, gravestones, he presumed, were laid against the interior walls with one on the ground.

Breathing heavily, he felt his heart racing, his chest heaving and a sickness like a ball in the pit of his stomach - he really must visit a doctor - as he fixed his stare hard at the words, but try as he might he could not make out the names of all of them.

One he was able to read stated simply "Marianna Bianchi 24 ottobre 1980 – 17 luglio 2022" and on another, more worn, he could see the name Sofia Bianchi and the inscription 9 febbraio 1993, presumably the date of her passing.

There were other words he could not understand, but that was of little consequence. She was in there and he was almost with her, just a locked gate, cold stone and a few feet of earth separating them. Was he ever really with her or always only almost? He thought about their bodies, close to each other, at peace. What a ridiculously sad world it is when death is the easiest route to peace.

He also thought of Rossi and Sofia and questioned whether if they had remained together, left Padria maybe, Sofia would have still been alive. Then Rossi wouldn't have met Isabella and maybe such paths in people's lives are meant to be.

He asked himself if Marianna would have still been alive if he had not walked into that class that wonderful summer's day back in Bradford, and again he had no answer. Yet Bianchi, a mosquito in all their lives, biting, stinging, leaving behind nothing but disease and pain, was still able to walk among those whose lives he had tainted. Those who are still alive, that is.

"Sofia, Marianna, why, oh why? How did this come to happen? Who decided it was you who should die? If there is a God it must surely be a cruel God who has enabled this. Maybe you have moved on to live other lives, better lives I hope. I don't know any of this, but at least you are together again here in front of me. I wonder can you hear me? I do not hold the belief that you can, but just to let you know I loved you Marianna, I wish I had met you Sofia, and that I am sorry, so so sorry. Stefano Bianchi, will you tell me why this was allowed to happen? It is time I found out."

He uttered the words quietly, almost inaudibly, his hands together as if in prayer.

Morrison had dressed in blue jeans, striped blue and white shirt, navy jumper and waterproof coat as he felt strong in blue and realised he needed to be as he laid down a bunch of white roses on the slab by the entrance to the tomb with a note that said simply: "I know you are now free from the sadness that wrapped its arms around you. Love Michael."

He surprised himself by making the sign of the cross on his chest as he did so.

Morrison was aware the wider Bianchi family, for there must surely be one, would see this and maybe wonder who he was, but he aimed to make sure Stefano Bianchi knew the answer to that as soon as possible.

Feeling wretched but unable to cry, he again put his hands together as if in prayer and bowed, before walking backwards down the pathway and away from the burial vault.

As he did so he clutched the left-hand side of his stomach as a stabbing pain caused him to crouch, once more letting him know that whatever the problem was it hadn't gone away, like that of Bianchi.

He headed back to the front gate - past graves and vaults marked Famiglia Ruffini, Locatelli, Bellina, Moschini - through which he had entered the cemetery and left the eight or ten other people paying respects to their dearly departed, before following the directions to the bus stop that Rossi had given him.

Pleased to be on board the bus just minutes later, he was surprised at how suddenly calm he was and at the lack of any real emotion he had displayed, but nerves kicked in again at the thought of his encounter with Bianchi, which would be a deeply unpleasant one. At least he assumed it would be this way.

Soon he saw the sign for Sant'Antonino and left the bus, which had progressed through several villages, gradually ascending higher into the hills, a small number of other passengers entering and exiting at stops on the way.

He walked up the quiet road on which the bus had dropped him, which he eventually realised was the main street, comprising a convenience store, a pharmacy, an art studio and a bar which boasted panoramic views down the hill and out to the sea. Christmas lights were strung across the street and the few shops there were tastefully decorated.

He decided to go to the bar for a quick drink and to ask directions to the address which Rossi had provided him with for Stefano Bianchi. If Bianchi wasn't in he would either wait or would have to go back to Padria and return to Sant'Antonino at a later date.

Despite feeling the winter chill, he took a seat in the garden of the bar, ordered a beer and stared out across the hills and back down towards Padria. He could not see the town or the Bianchi house, reasoning it would be too far away. To his left he could make out hilltop settlements above country roads rich with farms and vineyards growing grapes, oranges, lemons, olives, verdant farmland towering above the glittering Mediterranean in front. He wondered if Rossi's old farm was nearby.

When the waiter returned with his beer, he asked him where Via Garibaldi was. The directions he was given told him it was only a three to five minutes' walk.

Morrison took a few seconds to check his feelings. He still felt some strength, but he was nervous, more nervous than he had been in years; as nervous as when he was a teenager in the minutes before he went out to bat at a vital passage in a cricket match, as apprehensive as the brief time just before approaching someone, a girl maybe, for a difficult conversation which could end in crippling rejection, that gut-wrenchingly acidic moment as you turn over an exam paper, the dread that the questions will not resemble any subject you may have spent months studying for, or the second your name is called in the doctor's reception room and you know the life or death result of a vital test is about to be relayed.

All these thoughts and more raced through Morrison's mind.

He gave himself a stern reminder that he must try hard to remain free of emotion during the initial few minutes of his chat with Marianna's father and, depending on Bianchi's response and tone, adapt his own tactics as the conversation developed.

He walked around one hundred metres along the main street and turned left as instructed, finding himself on a small lane, which at the corner began to rise uphill. He proceeded for another minute or so and took another left turn onto Via Garibaldi, a narrow and unremarkable street of whitewashed cottage-style houses, with no gardens to the front but gateways between the buildings that led to fields at the rear.

Most had colourful pots outside with plants spilling from them, some bedecked with festive additions, but number thirteen did not. He considered the possibility that the number thirteen meant the same in Italy as it did in England. He smiled as he thought of the word triskaidekaphobia, which had been the answer to a question he had set in quite a few quizzes that felt like a million years ago.

There was no car parked directly outside thirteen, though there were others on the street, and no obvious sign of life. Nothing on the outside said there had been a Christmas in this house. Morrison almost lost his nerve, but after walking past the house and to the top of the street turned around and made his way back to what Rossi had told him was now the home of Stefano Bianchi.

He knocked hard on the door. No answer. A second knock resulted in some audible movement and as Morrison heard the key in the lock turning he instinctively took a step back. The door opened to reveal Stefano Bianchi, clothed simply in brown cords and a burgundy jumper, smaller than Morrison remembered him, his face haunted, his chins hanging in folds of skin, nothing left of the fat smug smile of before, his body considerably thinner, eyes narrower and red-rimmed.

Sticking his chest out, he loudly proclaimed "Michael Morrison, I have been expecting you," beckoning him in and waving his visitor down a corridor which led into a small room decorated with dated flowery wallpaper and an old carpet, furnished with a settee and two wooden chairs, a couple of pictures hanging on the walls and a television in the corner. You would never have known it was the festive season. It could have been any day of the year.

"Sit down," Bianchi said, coldly, gesturing at one of the rickety chairs. Morrison did as he was instructed, while Bianchi settled on the brown settee. No drink was offered and Bianchi said nothing for a few moments before venturing: "I knew you would come here, that you would want to know about Marianna, what happened, what you think happened, to find out my side of the story or to tell me what you think I did wrong."

"Basically that," said Morrison, his eyes fixed on Bianchi. He felt as he spoke that all his good intentions to be calm had disappeared and he was suddenly close to bursting with anger.

"I have spent way more than a year building up to this moment, wondering where you were, what you were doing. You didn't even let me know about the fucking funeral. Come to think of it, you didn't even let me know she'd fucking died, so since you were not prepared to find me, I have found you. I have been to the grave you drove Marianna to, and Sofia too, and eventually I have found you."

As Morrison stopped, Bianchi looked him in the eye, smiled, a harsh, steely smile and laughed. Morrison continued: "Ha, yes, I have found you, found you here. Even this is too good for you, this shitty little place where you will never again hold one of your stupid grand parties."

Bianchi, still calm, held Morrison's stare.

"I did not let you know because she told me you were over, Morrison. It was finished. She told me. I have no need for that house, that place, anymore. My family worked hard for that and when I provide everything for my wife and daughter they... they..."

Looking down, he lost momentum, stuttered momentarily, the force of his delivery gone, his voice quieter: "They throw it back in my face. I could not understand it then, but I think I understand it better now, at least some of it."

"You did it for yourself Bianchi, not for them, and..."

"No, I did it for them as my father did it for me," Bianchi cut in, pointing his finger at Morrison, his temper rising.

"And they did not want it, any of it and now it is gone and they are gone too. All these years I have been alone. Sofia gone, Marianna away, and now gone too..."

Bianchi was becoming louder and banged his fist twice on the settee arm, finally displaying emotion, which Morrison had not been sure he was capable of.

"Oh, the loneliness of the accused, ha, isn't it always the way?"

"Don't you talk..."

"No, no, let me speak," interrupted Morrison - himself quieter now - who then, at more length than he had intended, told of the events of the day leading up to the party, what happened that night, the letter he received from Marianna, his discovery of her death, the visit to the grave. Bianchi had looked shocked at the revelation he had visited the cemetery, and more so when Morrison produced the letter Marianna had written to him.

Bianchi was silent for several minutes as he read the long, impassioned note Morrison had scoured repeatedly:

Dearest Michael,
... I am forced to use the money of my father... my mother... she left him, left this world, but she also left me... with a man I would grow to hate, but

also to pity... you cannot imagine the days I have spent in tears, the nights I have spent in tears, alone in my big room in that big house... wishing my mother was still here... the night we had before the party was... the best night I spent in Padria, truly the only night I could say I felt free of him... except I wasn't free... he has not spoken to me, not properly, since mother died... the only person who really ever rejected him and she had to take her own life to do so... one day I will do the same. I will have to do the same...

Yours never and forever, Marianna x

There were tears from both parties now. It would have been strange if there had not been. Morrison felt nauseous, bile rising in his throat.

Bianchi was breathing deeply as he struggled to speak.

"I, I do not know what you want me to say Michael Morrison. I do not know what I can say. Nothing will make it better. Nothing will make what happened disappear. You take a certain path in life and it works out right or it works out wrong. Usually, for most people, some bits right, some bits wrong.

"I still believe everything I did was for the greater good of the Bianchi family, but Sofia and Marianna were right, I did not listen. I should have listened to them. To both of them. I thought in the end they would grow to love what they had, appreciate it at the very least, but they did not.

"I would, however, like you to note that not everything I did was just because I am as selfish a bastard as you think.

"Do you really think I wanted to put on that stupid bullshit party just to show off to other wealthy people? Of course I didn't. Those people were not my friends. Some of them could well have had me killed if I didn't do what they said all these years. Had my wife and daughter killed."

He paused and drew a long breath: "In a way they did that anyway. Oh yes, I benefited from doing what they asked, made a lot of money, a fortune, bought things I could never have otherwise afforded, but it did me no good in the end. Sometimes these people would come to my house and threaten to take it all away. I got in too deep and there was no going back, but I should have had courage. I should have stood my ground. Instead, I pretended it was what I wanted, not what I was forced to do.

"The money became everything, it was everything, that and staying on the right side of these people. I should have done then what I have done now and maybe Sofia and Marianna would still be here. Now I have nothing but if I had done what I have just said then I would have had no money, no riches, but so much more in terms of life and so too Sofia and Marianna."

Morrison glared at him before almost spitting out the words: "You don't have my sympathy Bianchi. You will never have my sympathy. However, in some ways you do have my understanding. I do not know of the things you talk about, the damage that could have been done to you or your family, but could it have been any worse than the damage that has been done anyway? Your words are the same as those of Roberto Rossi. Forced to do what you didn't want to or else this would have happened, that would have happened, blah, blah, bloody blah."

On hearing Rossi's name, Bianchi looked slightly askance, biting his bottom lip, but Morrison continued: "I have forced myself into your skin, lived in both of your skins and I know I would not have done what either of you did."

He considered the impact of his next sentence, then slowly but authoritatively said: "The difference between you and Rossi is that you have death on your hands. You were higher up the food chain, far higher up; you were Stefano Bianchi, director of operations.

"To be like you I would have to renounce my whole belief system. Kill you because I do not agree with you. And don't think I haven't thought of it. Many times. How, where, when, over and over in my mind, but no, because that would make me no better than you."

Bianchi, softer voiced now: "No, I am no killer, never a killer and I was certainly not the director, directed maybe, and any directing I was doing was on behalf of others. Yes, yes, I sold my soul to these people, those nasty evil bastards. But it wasn't just them. So many others come crawling out of the woodwork wanting this and that, threatening the other if they did not get it.

"You have no idea. In your country maybe this does not happen. Here, everyone wants some of what you've got and you become suspicious of everyone who calls you, everyone who visits you, friend or foe. I was suspicious of you Morrison, I thought you wanted money, I thought that was why you were with Marianna.

"Most just want to see what you have got and try to use you, and you wave them off, but the others, the others are dangerous, so you swallow any pride you ever had and you just do as they say, do what you are told. Like a dog, you obey their orders and you get your reward. You do not obey and you take the consequences. A good kicking as you English say, yes? I was no different to Marianna in many ways though Michael Morrison, I..."

"Don't you ever say she was like you. Never say that. Never ever say that," Morrison almost screamed, half rising from his chair, blindly pushing away the tears cascading down his face, the picture of Marianna he carried flooding his memory. Bianchi got up and motioned for him to sit once more.

"Look, my friend..."

"No, do not call me your friend, Bianchi. Never call me your friend. Ever."

"Okay, okay. Look Morrison, hear me out, I don't mean she would have done what I did, but my father did it too and his father before him. I lived off the rewards and continued the whole stupid bloody game and she lived off the rewards too when I bought the house I had always set my sights on. What could she do? What could I do?

"We did not talk about it because in reality I too, like her, was ashamed. I've spent my whole life acting like a member of your royal fucking family and now look at me. No wife, no daughter, no house of my own, renting this shitty place in someone else's name just to escape, living a lie, but they will find me just like you found me. I am not hiding, merely waiting. Someone here who knows these people will realise who I am and then it will all be over. In some ways that will be a relief.

"Instead, I simply live in fear waiting for them. Why don't I just hand myself over? Leave, go somewhere else? I don't know, I don't know, I really do not know. Maybe I just don't have the heart."

Morrison had noticed a smell of whisky on his breath and Bianchi moved to pour them both a glass.

"Not for me, Bianchi. I cannot accept a drink from you."

"You accepted on the night of the party, so accept now," he responded, handing Morrison a large glass. Morrison nodded, almost humbly, and took a gulp.

"You see, you think I am asking for sympathy, but I am not. You think I am asking for forgiveness, but I am not. I am asking for some under-standing, but I don't expect that, not immediately, maybe not ever. I did not expect or want to end up like this Morrison, but I must live with the consequences of my actions, which were the actions others demanded. There were tough decisions to be made and I got them wrong. Have you never got anything wrong in your life, Michael Morrison?"

"I have got plenty wrong Bianchi, maybe just not that wrong," Morrison shot back, taking another large glug of his drink.

"Maybe I have been lucky in that I did not find myself in the situa-tions you did, but I know that I would not have been as greedy as yourself or your father. I know that I would have walked away, resisted all the temptations. In different circumstances, in another world, would I have been the executioner? The answer, Bianchi, is no I would not."

Bianchi's voice had become shrill now and his eyes appeared to bulge as he became animated, wildly flinging his arms around and shouting: "Very clever, very clever..."

"Not really, I stole the executioner quote, though I know not from where, but you justify your evil through some ridiculous false ideology. Ah, yes, Solzhenitsyn I think...

"What? I don't under..."

"The executioner... it doesn't matter, forget it, but to borrow some more, the line between good and evil cuts through us all Bianchi, but you chose to make the first move, to cut through it."

"You have lost me Morrison, but I am saying maybe you could not have walked away. Would not have been allowed to walk away. Maybe had you walked away your family, if you even fucking had one, would have ended up in the ground like mine and you would have had that on your conscience, just like I have.

"And could you have lived with that? Do you even vaguely understand the judgements I had to make? The decisions I had to make? I did not anticipate, could never have predicted what Sofia and Marianna did. I made the call that by continuing things as they were they would be safe. I was wrong, so wrong, but I know now that whatever I had decided it would have ended this way."

Morrison cut in: "But you could have talked to them, listened to them, tried to understand them..."

Staring at the wall, Bianchi was silent now, remaining so for almost a full minute - which Morrison found uncomfortable but resolutely did not offer him a way out - before, staring into his whisky, his voice quaking with sadness, regret, realisation, recognition of the truth, mumbling: "I know I could have dealt with it better, let them in, talked it through, but I shut everyone out.

"People say I played the big shot with all the trappings, but we were all trapped. I thought it better they did not know and that would keep them away from the horror, but there were other horrors and I did not see them, did not feel them, did not hear them. Both of them though, Morrison, both of them..."

Morrison went to speak, but as Bianchi refilled their glasses he raised his voice and continued: "Either of them, they could have walked away from me, walked away from it all, but they didn't. I trapped us in that house, with that lifestyle, but they could have left me behind. Look, look here..."

He pulled a large, framed photograph from an otherwise bare wall and thrust it towards Morrison, saying: "Here we are, Sofia, Marianna, me, all happy, smiling, a day trip to Capri, a normal family, the camera does not lie. It was not always bad. They came to places with me, stood by my side, they did not leave me."

"But they did," Morrison quietly interjected, almost without emotion, draining his second whisky.

"They did leave you. Maybe you are right in some ways. Maybe they did like the money you provided or grew so used to what it bought them, the freedom it appeared to buy them, they could not leave it behind.

"Marianna could not leave it behind. She relied on it. She said so in her letter. But that freedom was also her prison. One from which she never found a way to escape. There was no release other than the one she found."

He stood up, turned and made to leave, but Bianchi grabbed his arm.

"I too lost everything Morrison. Like I said, I am not expecting or asking for sympathy from you, but do not forget, I have lost my wife, my love, my Sofia, my freedom, my daughter and my life."

"Rossi's daughter more like, eh?" Morrison sniped, shrugging off Bianchi's grip. "Was she his, not yours, eh? Was that the problem?"

"Fuck you Morrison, fuck Rossi. How do I know? How will I ever know? That insignificant little bastard... None of that matters anyway now, does it? Who do I blame now? Rossi? Of course not. Who have I blamed all my life? My father for involving my mother and myself in all this mess. Who did he blame? His father for starting all of this. Who did Marianna blame? Her father, and yes that is me, not Rossi. Of course she did. Like mother like daughter, like father like daughter. Only she does not say that in the letter.

"Now it is finally all over. I have finished with it, but it is, of course, too late, for there is no-one left to hurt. I will not take myself away from the hurt because I must live with it.

"I deserve to live with it. I must live with it. I have killed everything I loved. Look..." He thrust a letter into Morrison's hand. It was from Marianna to her father, just a few lines, but written in Italian.

"I, I cannot read that," Morrison said, embarrassed. "I'm sorry Stefano."

He saw the look on Bianchi's face and realised the confusion.

"No, no, not because I won't, but because I can't. The language you see, I would need it translating."

Bianchi snatched it back and read aloud in broken English...

Dear Father,
These are my final words to you, not that we have shared many over the years. Not like most fathers and daughters.

You never did really talk to me, you were never interested. I was just a girl not worth bothering with and my mother just a woman whose opinions did not matter, and even after her death you still carried on in the same way.

As I grew older and I understood more I could not accept what you had done and what you continued to do even after mother died. She took her own life to escape you and still you did not change.

I am sorry, so sorry. Maybe I should have tried harder to talk to you, to understand you, but I do not believe I could live with the reality of why you are like you are. I did not want to know.

This will be the last you will hear from me for my duty is to make sure this continues no longer and the Bianchis will soon be no more.

Hopefully now you will realise what you have done and how you hurt me so much that this is the only solution I could consider.

Like mother, like daughter, Marianna x

Morrison could see Bianchi was shaking and the tears were cascading down his face as he uttered the last lines.

"You do not live with that Morrison. You cannot live with that. I found her, hanging there in that bloody dance hall and in that second I knew, I knew the reason why. I dropped to my knees and sobbed. Sobbed because she was no more and sobbed because I had always known the reason why, but I had not stopped to think for long enough that she might ever do such a thing.

"As I say, you cannot live with that and maybe you shouldn't. Like father, like daughter. In the end you see, we both wanted to stop this. My own daughter..."

Morrison stood for a second, nodded solemnly and said: "But would you have stopped it if this had not happened? Would you really have stopped it? Could you have stopped it?"

The two stared at each other for a few seconds, troubled faces locked in recognition of the horrific reality of what had occurred and how these terrible events had not unfolded in a matter of months, but had slowly developed over years, decades even.

Like global warming melting the ice, Morrison thought to himself later. You don't always recognise what is going on around you and, when it seems nothing is happening, a tragedy we have all been blind to for so long is slowly unfolding.

Morrison winced as the whisky bit into his stomach, forcing him to lean back against the wall.

"Are you okay? Mr Morrison..." Bianchi looked genuinely concerned.

Looking him in the face, eye to eye, striding towards the door, in an almost friendly tone, Morrison said only: "Yes, yes, nothing to worry about. Goodbye Stefano Bianchi."

Refusing the handshake offered by the defeated figure standing framed by a doorway to another unhappy house, he made his way to the exit.

"Goodbye Michael Morrison. You do not need to come here again. You will not see me again. I shall soon be gone from here, one way or another."

Checking himself and returning to the corridor, not having fully taken in Bianchi's words, Morrison remembered something: "Oh Bianchi, you never did say about the funeral. The funeral I did not know about. You know, I have no idea where it even took place."

"You knew she had died. You could have contacted me, Morrison. Anyway, it happened. It was quiet. Who would come? She had been away for years and didn't keep in touch with her friends when she returned.

"I was left on my own. I did not know what to do, who to invite, what hymns to play, so in the end I just did it. It was cold, without passion, without people. It had to be that way. I could not have faced it otherwise and there was no-one else to face it with me. What else could I do, Michael Morrison? Oh yes, it was the Basilica di Sant'Antonino."

He had been right. He knew it. He could picture it now. That huge, beautiful church, Marianna's lonely body, only her father to mourn her, consumed by guilt, fear, seeking or fighting denial.

His argumentative streak exhausted, Morrison could not bear to say that by the time he had been notified of her death she had already been in the ground for weeks.

Instead, choking back the tears, he shook his head, stood for a couple of seconds staring at Bianchi, turned and left the house, aware of Marianna's father still standing, still watching, still framed by the doorway, as he headed down Via Garibaldi, onto the Main Street and to the bus stop, the lurching in his stomach causing him to retch. Thankfully, there was no-one else there.

It was 5.35pm. There would be a bus in five minutes, but he would walk to the next stop or maybe the one after. Hopefully, it would relieve the physical pain he was in and allow him the time to think through what had just happened. How Stefano Bianchi, despite all Morrison's anger and resolve not to give in to him, had managed to elicit some degree of understanding, maybe even the sympathy he said he would never have, he could not figure out.

As he walked he felt mentally lighter, as if the mix of anger, frustration, blame and guilt he had offloaded had cleared his mind, but all day he had felt tension in the way he held his body, and knew he needed to relax, to calm down, to sleep.

He would have a glass of whisky when he got in. Just the one to enable him to sleep. Then in a day or two maybe, just maybe, if he had the energy, the nerve, he would take one last look around the Bianchi house.

17

When All The Parties Are Over

He swallowed hard and shuddered as he entered the once grand entrance and began to relive his only previous visit to the house - the cold recognition that passed between Marianna and her father and his obvious disdain for Morrison, who barely provoked an acknowledgement.

Despite the whisky he had not slept well and was exhausted, physically and mentally, his griping stomach and recollections of yesterday's discussion with Bianchi adding to his intense discomfort.

The words contained on the note Rossi had given him that morning - he had obviously seen Bianchi in the few hours since Morrison had met with him - played over and over in his mind: "Go to the house and you will find what you desire, what you need. Now we are together once more, Sofia, Marianna and me, and if God should forgive me and bless me with the opportunity I shall do all in the power he affords me to undo the horror I created. Stefano Bianchi."

He pictured the glittering chandeliers, the library that so mesmerised him, the dance hall, the balcony packed with guests effortlessly exuding an air of superiority, the elaborate furniture and overwhelming lack of love that chilled the whole building.

"I did not tell you because people judge Michael, you would have judged, you will judge," she had said to him, more confident now she was surrounded by friends and family than she had been when she informed him of the party.

And he did judge. How could he not? He had never been in such a place other than to write stories for the types of magazines whose envious readers sought detail about the wealthy and their homes.

The laughter of that night haunted him still, the deep, deep laughter booming out from within the core of those who filled the mirrored dance hall, their bodies, lithe from the time a privileged life can afford to dedicate to exercise and fat from the gluttony a privileged life can also afford, bulging out of fine but ill-fitting suits and dresses.

They were laughing. Truly laughing. Morrison had laughed as he stood alone in the ballroom that night, a cynical, sarcastic laugh as he realised he had no clue what the dance was. A foxtrot? A waltz? A tango? Where had their laughter gone now? As they left the party to take their carriages to plush buildings that were houses not homes, did that laughter continue? Were any of them laughing now? Marianna certainly wasn't. Her father wasn't.

He wondered how he could allow himself to be distracted by these questions at such a time and he remembered the pain that had resided within him through his final months in England and how it consumed him physically and mentally during the party. He had felt its presence intermittently since his move to Padria, though it was no longer permanent.

Even though he had been given warning of the carnage within, what he saw still shocked him, the place barely recognisable from what he had previously witnessed, save for the basic construction. He remembered Gabriella's warning as he passed her on his way to "please, please be careful" and to "call back for me if you need help".

The oak panelling had been torn from the walls, chandeliers ripped down and smashed glass, sheets of dust and plaster covered the floors where luxurious deep red carpets had once sat. Parts of the ceiling had collapsed, and he could see up to the roof where battens had been pulled down, missing slates letting in light.

The place smelled of dereliction, a thick dust hung all around him and the ashes of fires recently burned to keep warm whoever had wandered in here lay in piles beneath his feet.

What horror would he find here?

He thought of the pianist whose nimble fingers conjured up the music to welcome the guests, the pillared imperial staircases that spiralled up into the ornate gallery, where no evidence of glory remained.

The champagne-swilling swagger had disappeared, replaced by daubed simplistic slogans, some in Italian, one stating "Die Scum", another, the same red paint indicating the same hand, "Kill the Rich". Scrawled initials - people's or those of political parties or protest organisations - scruffily dominated walls once adorned with the finest flock wallpaper.

Almost all the doors had gone, enabling a partial view from one side of the house to the other, the space where the final door had been now affording an outlook over the harbour, the sprawling bay and to the hills beyond. Maybe it offered a way out, symbolised a better, brighter future, Morrison thought.

The only other light in the building came through the gaping holes where the windows once were and, through the roof, the December sun shining brightly on the revolution that had taken place in this palace of pain.

Wary that there may be squatters, perhaps people taking the opportunity to look round the house, he jumped as a bird flew over him and headed off to take up position on a banister at the top of the stairs. There were two young ginger and white cats, skinny and bedraggled, their protective mother, possibly the saddest-looking cat he had ever seen, standing in front of them. This was now their territory.

Morrison, with some fear and wearing inappropriate blue deck shoes, trod carefully, avoiding the glass and other debris - food packets, tins, bottles, cigarette ends, evidence of fires, syringes - and went up the stairs, down a corridor and through to where he remembered the library was situated.

A hacking cough had quickly manifested itself due to the concoction of unpleasant materials swirling round the rooms as the dancers once swirled.

The vast library shelving and cabinets had been ripped down and tipped over, the books, records and CDs liberated from their covers, smashed, pulled apart and left wherever they had landed.

Again, he became lost in memory, the proud stature of the room less than two years ago now seemingly impossible - the words of Dostoevsky, Conrad, Tolstoy and Kafka had lived alongside the music of Rossini, Puccini, Caruso and Corelli, but now they lay apart, silenced forever. The words, the sounds, were dead. Dead like Marianna.

The connection he made hit him hard and he found himself beginning to sob, not for the loss of those who were the custodians of all this room contained, but for those who had created these works - centuries of art in forms its authors could not imagine, left in pieces to rot, yet no more unloved now than it had been by those who had housed it.

Pictures that had been on the walls of the corridors had been left on the ground, frames and glass elsewhere, many of the photographs or works of art creased or ripped, those who once posed for portraits left literally in pieces, lives in dust, any evidence of their ever having been in this place rendered worthless.

And there it was, that picture - mother, father and Marianna, standing side by side in front of an outbuilding in the garden, not smiling, no obvious connection or love. He wondered who had taken it.

As he stared through a window he could see the building's remains, blocking the area in which the forest recommenced, its continuity broken by the clearing that accommodated this amazing structure whose thick walls did not prevent the escape of whatever love there had ever been. Exactly what he had thought at the party.

To Morrison, the building now resembled a disused hospital or former home for the mentally ill, seeing out its final days in a way its creators could never have imagined or wanted. It was a different place than he remembered, like its heart, if it had ever been allowed to beat naturally, had been ripped out.

It was no longer a house or a home and he imagined those with money eyeing up the development opportunity. Through a huge influx of capital, it could surely be made into swanky apartments or an exclusive hotel dominating the harbour, those able to afford to stay there again lording it over the locals.

A lyric contained in a popular Christmas song about loneliness and a house that was not a home popped into his head. Appropriate for the time of year, he supposed.

He pressed his hand to his chest, his heart beating so fast he thought he might collapse as he edged along to the dance hall, peering apprehensively round every corner, anticipating the discovery of someone or something, although he was unsure of exactly what.

As he scanned the ostentatious showpiece in whose mirrors he had seen his sorry self, shoulders drooping, standing at the edge of the floor, an outsider looking in on something he did not understand, a world he did not want to be in, he questioned whether Marianna had wanted to be in this world and concluded that despite her objections she clearly did.

She was perfectly at ease with these people so pleased with themselves, their lives, their circumstances, their surroundings; but he had seen the way they looked at each other as they swirled and twirled, still looking for someone else, a dalliance - is that what he was? A mere dalliance of the extraordinary with the ordinary? - still looking for something else, their eyes always seeking, always searching, their smiles for someone other than the person with whom they tripped the not so light fantastic.

He saw them and he heard them still. The ghosts of dancers, their shadows bouncing off the walls, moving up and down and across the floor. He heard the music and it gripped his whole being as it rose in pitch and volume, louder, louder, louder, to a crescendo and then a sudden stop as the ghosts slithered down the walls and made their way to the centre of the floor where they collapsed in a heap.

Marianna, choreographer of ghosts, was above them, curtseying to the applause of the ghost audience. Except now there was no music, no sound, no dancers for her to direct.

Then he saw it and let out a gasp, which became a sound he could not describe, something deeper, more guttural, a keening, a noise he had never made before. There it was. A piece of rope coiled on the floor. Above it a beam. It couldn't have been where... of course it couldn't have been where... They wouldn't have just left it there. It was simply a discarded bit of rope.

Morrison's whole upper body started to heave, his breath growing short but heavier as he processed his thoughts. He touched the rope, running his hands along a small section.

"Marianna, Marianna, please God, why oh why, my love?"

What was she thinking before she lost her will to continue, her will to fight? Could she not justify her life or the lives of those around her? Could she not see a way out of her situation? She could simply have walked away and left it all behind, returned to England with him, but she could never deny the tie to her family, whatever they had done to each other and to the people of this town. Maybe she feared the consequences of cutting herself off, but they could hardly have been worse than this.

There was dislike, distrust and disgust, but there was still love for her father, still that little bit of her - was it guilt? - grateful for the privileges she had been afforded by him and a belief that he really did love her. She had done nothing to fight to change her father, herself, their lives, to help the others her family had trodden on. Or maybe she had done good, good for others. There must be so much he had not known about her, had not been told or bothered to ask. He was struggling to think straight.

Was Morrison to blame? He had been through this so many times but still did not have any indisputable answer. He was part of a long chain of events and circumstances, certainly, but did not believe he was the cause of Marianna's death. Maybe he was just the final piece in her jigsaw, but if he hadn't been, then surely someone or something else would have come along and completed this sickeningly awful saga.

How did she go through with it? This was not cowardice. This took courage. When did the thought first occur? Before the party, before Morrison even, on the night of the party when she sent him away? Maybe she had tried before. How much physical strength and knowledge was needed to end a life this way?

Was she in tears as she tied the rope and prepared to go away forever with no final word? That split second after she had suspended herself, pushed downwards and the blood flow to her brain began to cease, did she regret it?

As she lost consciousness, but was still alive, did she ever drift back in and hope for rescue? Did she believe it would work or was it a cry for help? Her last thought, what could it have been? Did she fear the noose would fail? Worry that it would work? Did she think about those she would leave behind? All that she had left behind? Where has that all gone now - the knowledge, the soul? Surely it didn't just disappear when she died.

Incongruously, as he sat in despair, slumped, head in hands, brief waves of positivity began to flood him; lines that would not have been out of place in his first novel *The Patron Saint of Lost Causes*, thoughts and sentences that his character Jude may have mused on.

He knew it was his responsibility to ensure any good she did was not wasted and to ensure it outweighed the evil cast by others. Is that not true of all of us? You have to believe that, otherwise what is the point? Why make the effort? It can't only be through selfishness and vanity; it must not be that. It must be more than that, it has to be.

Now he was standing again, staring into the distance, for as long as a full minute, just thinking. He let the rope slip out of his hands, then at the end of the room he saw exactly what he had expected to see, but incredibly had not noticed before - a noose and alas what looked like a body, surely that of Stefano Bianchi, lit up by the winter sun streaming through the window.

Strangely, despite his long conversation with Bianchi, which had enabled him to understand more about the man and how he lived, he felt no happiness or sadness but pondered, was the death of Bianchi a good thing? Was it his fault or his victory? How had it come to pass so quickly? He could not bring himself to move any closer and he froze for several seconds, trembling, wondering how it had all come to this, before turning and exiting the room.

He only managed a couple of paces before reconsidering his actions. He could not, must not, just leave. Even Bianchi deserved more than that and, summoning all his strength, he entered the room again, looked up at the noose and its captive, hanging loose, framed by the window, and with a start, a lurch of his stomach, realised there was no body, no Bianchi, just a large plastic bag.

A note containing nothing aside from Morrison's name - indicating its contents were intended for him - was stuck to the black bin liner, dangling like a punch bag. He wrestled it down. It was cumbersome, packed tight, but not too heavy and he decided he would make his way home with it before inspecting the contents.

No body, yet he had seen a grey car outside. Bianchi's car? So where was the driver? Where the hell was Bianchi? He almost expected him to emerge from the shadows and wondered what he would do? If he was not here, then where was he? Had someone taken care of him, finished him off? Had he staged his own disappearance? Was the noose supposed to be some sort of sick joke? What had Bianchi left for him?

He collapsed and knelt among the debris for several minutes before his wailing subsided and he knew he could take no more. He checked himself in one of the cracked dance hall mirrors, heaved the bag on to his shoulder and headed back out into the corridor where he picked up the half-torn picture of Marianna with her mother and father, folded it around the tear and placed it in his trouser pocket, alongside the picture of her he always carried.

He recognised the sadness in Marianna. He recognised the sadness in her mother. He recognised the sadness in her father too. They swirl and they twirl no more, their dresses and suits unworn. Diamond girls and one diamond bastard now diamonds in the dirt.

Again he passed the graffiti that proclaimed "Die Scum" and "Kill the Rich" and, for what he believed would be the last time, exited the house, noticing but not stopping to investigate a freshly lit fire in what had once been the garden.

Exhausted, feeling dirty and dishevelled, griping acid in his stomach making him feel sick, the need, the desire, to be home and safe was accelerated. At the bottom of the pathway, near a dimly lit restaurant, he lurched into the main street and, almost breathless, hailed a passing cab, something he rarely did, generally preferring to walk and collect his thoughts. The driver, however, did not see him and Morrison decided he may as well continue on foot.

Progress was slow, the heavy bag sapping him of energy. He stopped regularly, pretending to take in the views so as not to appear exhausted. He wondered if people were suspicious of what he was carrying. Well, if they asked, which they didn't, even he didn't know.

He rested for a good five minutes on what he had always thought of as "their bench", again recalling that conversation - he could almost pick out every intonation in her voice - in which she told him about the party. It caused him to shiver.

Finally inside his flat, surrounded by familiar furniture and a purring Romeo, as he sank back into his armchair and felt a wave of calm wash over him, he pondered whether to call the police. Deciding against it as there was no body and nothing to report as such - well, except for the bag and its contents - he peered out and saw Roberto Rossi on the Via Sacra, quickening his pace to something in the region of urgent as if his destination was on the verge of disappearing or maybe simply to avoid the early evening light rain.

As he watched his unlikely friend - was that the correct description? - more probably on his way to Franco's restaurant to spread the news about Bianchi's apparent suicide note, he pondered the theory that life and death wasn't all about arrival and departure, searching and finding, as he had thought and hoped. Those were just the headlines, the distractions that bookended the swathes of normality that enveloped most people's existences.

Feeling grubby, he jumped in the shower and scrubbed furiously at himself. As the imaginary dirt disappeared down the plughole he thought about how much had changed in his life from working as a journalist in Yorkshire to becoming a novelist, falling out of love with words and life, being saved by Marianna and now this unexpected existence in Padria.

Suddenly the realisation hit him that in her own way she had changed everything. She had seen that she could only achieve in death what she could not in life and made the ultimate sacrifice to stop the suffering, not just of herself, her family, but Padria as a whole. She had walked away from all of it and brought Bianchi's empire tumbling down.

It was all over now, yet the sight of the beast's carcass, its Versailles, its Winter Palace, remained in full view of those who had fed off its evil and those whose lives it had ripped apart.

18

Just Once More To Say Goodbye

Torrential rain exploded off the concrete of the square and those with festive duties still to fulfil walked with quickened pace, umbrellas blown inside out, coats pulled tight as they bowed low to combat the accompanying wind. Morrison likened the scene to a Lowry painting set in Italy rather than northern England.

He was still trying to process his confrontation with Bianchi and the previous day's experience in the house.

Further consideration that morning had led to him giving in to his conscience and informing the police as to what he believed may have happened. Officers visited and found no-one present but confirmed the car outside did indeed belong to Bianchi, who appeared to have left the place in Sant'Antonino.

He did not inform them about the package Bianchi had left him. He could not do that, even though he recognised the hypocrisy in keeping its contents. Ah, the contents, what to do with those. He tried to remove the thought from his mind. There were other issues to consider first.

He asked himself again, had Bianchi taken his own life? Disappeared? Was he in hiding with someone protecting him? Had someone taken him, killed him even? When Morrison had confronted him he had possessed the demeanour of a beaten man, someone about to give in, not fight back.

Franco, Luigi, Tommaso and Rossi would doubtless be expecting every detail, but he felt it was all too raw to re-live for their entertainment so, despite the inclement weather, he decided to brave a trip out as he was desperate for some invigorating fresh air.

Earlier, strangely enthused, he had spent an hour writing, with the germ of a story which he had already named *A Town Called Jesus* forming in his head, but the thoughts and feelings he had experienced in the house were still uppermost in his mind. Could he turn the events into a positive, incorporate them in a story perhaps? Did he still have the skill to tackle a novel? Did he have the strength of mind, the inclination or the need? Was that even a consideration?

The beginnings of a cold were adding to a creeping feeling of being trapped inside his apartment with only his computer and a sleeping Romeo for company, so he put on a thick raincoat, barely previously removed from the wardrobe since his move to Padria and added a scarf and gloves for warmth.

As quietly as he could, he closed the door of his flat and then the downstairs exit to avoid alerting Rossi, put up his hood and drew it close in to avoid it blowing down, heading at some pace down the alley away from the square in the direction of the seafront.

Calling in at a convenience store, he bought some cough sweets, emerging hunched over, hands in pockets, just as the rain stepped up a gear, bouncing off its first point of contact, be that roof, window, wall, pavement, person or road, no prisoners taken.

Morrison lengthened his stride, moving away from the walls from which the guttering was depositing copious amounts of water, darkening the shadows, and towards buildings that were protected by canopies, awnings or covered walkways.

It would have been too easy to give in and return home but a steely determination to continue overtook him as he traversed the narrow streets and headed for the wider avenue that led to the seafront.

He stopped at a walkway to stare across the bay, the view of Vesuvius defeated by the sheets of rain, no boats braving the fast-moving waves that sped towards the shore and crashed against and over the rocks. He turned left and headed to the path that would eventually take him to the harbour.

Normally, as he passed the garden bar he occasionally used when the weather was nice and the views far-reaching, he could see the harbour and beyond to what used to be and, he assumed, still was in name, the Bianchi house, but today he could make out nothing save for the small church just twenty or thirty metres in front of him. He could have stopped there for shelter, but his mood was strong and his desire to complete his intended journey, for whatever reason, overrode the need to stay dry.

Eventually he reached the top of the harbour and stared down onto its cobbles, Christmas lights of different colours leaping and jumping in the rain, the water in his eyes blurring them, creating a sheen that blocked sight of the moored boats bobbing on the shoreline, the tarpaulins outside restaurants and bars all fighting a losing battle against harsh elements they were not used to.

The outline of the house - he never did know its title - could now just about be made out, the horrid afternoon giving it a more menacing appearance than defeat should afford it.

Instead of going down the steps, Morrison made an impulsive and incomprehensible decision to walk round the back of the harbour and up the incline to the building, a place that only one day ago he had vowed he would never visit again.

He made it to where there had once been a door that allowed entrance to this place that bellowed loud over Padria, displaying the power of its former inhabitants like a deluded head of a muster of peacocks with no right to be so proud. Inside, that power was non-existent, just a veneer that when it had crumbled revealed a mixture of pathetic cowardice, bullying, fear and loathing.

Morrison, noting the absence of a car and unclear as to what had compelled him to come here again, decided not to enter the house despite the protection from the weather it would offer, the irony of shelter given the horror it had let its residents be exposed to not lost on him.

He stared through the door, the entrance hall, up the stairs, over the balcony and into the beginnings of the corridor that had led to the library and dance hall, the room in which Marianna had taken her own life. With so much of the roof gone, the rain was dripping steadily in and forming puddles on the floor.

"Goodbye Marianna, I will leave you alone now, just as you left me," he said out loud before turning away.

"Like I turned away that night," he thought to himself.

"I turned away and left you to it. Left you to what remained of the wreck of your family life. Left you to die as you left me to live.

"But maybe not, maybe not... maybe this is me not turning away and leaving, but me coming back for you."

He knew now why he had gone back. He never did properly say goodbye. Not on the night of the party and not on his recent return to the house. And he also now knew how he could really say goodbye, say it properly. It was Marianna's story that he must write.

The tears were rolling down his face, racing the rain that was once again dimming his vision as he walked towards the fencing to look over the sea towards Padria. But he could not see Padria. The Bianchis never saw Padria, at least never for what it was. Not its beauty. Not its heart. Not its soul. It was just a place. It could have been any place. Any place to use and abuse.

She would see Padria differently in his story. How she would have seen it had she not been her father's daughter. Padria would view her differently too. She would make the changes she had never felt able to. He would free her up to do that.

It would definitely be the last time he would come here - he had thought this before, but now he knew for certain - and he took one final look at a house that had been brought down, its people surrendered, its place now firmly in the past. He felt little other than sorrow, the type he had felt back in England after the reaction to *Walks Through Weeping Cities* left him so badly scarred.

As he headed down into the harbour, suddenly the rain, as if in sympathy with him, ceased, its dominance over, the chill in the air now coming to the fore.

The area was quiet, not deserted, but not yet declaring itself open for any business, whatever form that might take in the days leading to New Year's Eve and the big Capodanno meal that would be followed by celebrations and fireworks parties. Then the piazzas would be packed with people, culminating in the Feast of the Epiphany when La Befana would distribute more gifts to children who had no doubt already become tired with or forgotten about the presents they had received on Christmas Day.

The idea of life returning to the humdrum for most people made Morrison's thoughts drift off into familiar territory he did not welcome, that of the futility of his and everyone else's existence. When he recovered from this sort of mood, he would always regret the nastiness his mind had conjured.

He would not, could not allow this to happen now and was saved on this occasion by a cheery wave from Gabriella, perched in the doorway of The Star of the Sea, the rain now having given way to shafts of weak unseasonal sun. He waved back and wandered over.

"What on earth are you doing trailing the streets on a terrible day like this? It is fit for no-one, certainly not for you. You look very cold, very wet and maybe a little bit unhappy," she said.

Morrison agreed he was all three of those things and consented to go inside.

She removed his soaking wet coat and put it over a chair next to a heater. Morrison estimated her age at forty five, younger than him and with a friendly, welcoming face, her deep brown eyes seeming to ask questions, to listen, to touch, taste and smell him as well as to see him.

Having brought them both a piping hot Vin Brule, Morrison discovered Gabriella had run the characterful little bar - oak-panelled, the walls decorated with old pictures of the harbour, the floor tiled - for twelve years, taking over the business after her father died, but working there with him for many years before.

"A familiar story," she said.

She asked him questions, lots of them, and at her behest he briefly outlined his life, from childhood to his move to Padria. She told him she knew the Bianchis and said it was terrible what had happened to them, and even had empathy for the father, despite the knowledge he was a ruthless man.

Morrison agreed he felt more sympathy than he had before his trip to see him and even hoped no harm had come to him.

He asked how familiar she was with Stefano Bianchi and she explained that everyone who owned a business or even lived in the harbour had paid money to him and his father or at least had it collected by them on behalf of others.

"Protection, really. Nothing more than that," she said, shrugging and smiling resignedly.

"That's how it was sold to my father, and we all know what happens if you do not pay.

"For some reason they never asked me for the money after my father died. Bianchi told me he had sorted it and I still don't know what he meant, but for that I was grateful. Marianna would occasionally walk through the harbour. She was beautiful and was not like her father, but still she did not mix with the locals. Maybe she just couldn't. My father used to say her mother was the same. Maybe it was the shame."

Almost two hours had passed by with only a small number of customers coming in and Morrison stated his intention to leave, feeling the effects of two large glasses of red wine and considered that maybe their conversation had become too heavy. He was not yet ready to tell her of his plans to write Marianna's story.

Gabriella hugged him and gave him her telephone number, asking him not to leave it so long before he called again.

"In fact, call round whenever you feel, as soon as you can. I would certainly like to see you again Michael Morrison, the writer."

Morrison, aware he had recoiled from her hug, felt himself blush slightly and answered: "I, I didn't mean to move away, it's just..."

She stopped him by placing her finger gently on his lips and after a second or two he continued: "Thank you Gabriella. Thank you for the shelter and a lovely afternoon. Oh, and yes, yes, I will see you soon, most definitely.

"Oh, and maybe now in a way Bianchi can finally pay you back for the money your family was forced to hand over to him. I cannot tell you about it now. I just haven't got the energy. It's complicated and I'm not sure I know what to do. There is a decision, many decisions, to be made. I would like your help, but that is for later."

After deflecting several of the inevitable questions from a quizzical Gabriella, Morrison left, feeling cheerier than he had earlier, his anger dissipating with the storm, his outlook having brightened the longer he spent with his new friend in the harbour upon which Marianna would have looked over from the garden outside the villa thousands of times in her life.

He did not want to read too much into the afternoon but could not help feel Gabriella had intuitively read his character and knew how to deal with it and him. He was aware though that due to her earlier concerns, conversation had largely centred on him and he needed to listen to her, to redress the balance, give something back. Yes, listen to her, something he had not done with Marianna.

Here he was again, thinking about a future which may not exist and comparing it with his past.

Morrison knew now that it would be unhelpful to simply keep losing himself in thought and memories of Marianna as he walked; her dark eyes searching, the questioning lilt in her voice, her uncertain exploring touch, the wonderful night they shared in Padria, the awful realisation that the party in the house on the hill really was their last dance. And then nothing. Just a gap, a vacant colourless space in his life where once, if only briefly, love had been.

Finally, he felt he could appreciate what they had together and genuinely believed that he could move on and experience love again.

Love for Marianna through telling her story as accurately as he could. Love for his new friends, love or friendship for Gabriella - it did not really matter which as he was now looking to a future he had previously not been able to countenance.

19

A Different Dance, A Better Dance?

Franco had not reopened after Boxing Day other than for a couple of hours one afternoon, and Morrison was worried following his friend's confused reaction to Pino's news and wanted to make sure he was okay.

He had taken advantage of the previous night's heavy rain by working until well after midnight on his possible novel with the occasional interruption from Romeo, through either his sonorous purr, the wafting of a paw for attention or his parading over the keyboard to remind him it was time for his meal.

Morrison would hastily grab a lump of cheese and some crisps for his own sustenance, fearing his inspiration may disappear in the time it would take him to cook something, with Romeo often rejecting his own food in favour of a piece of extra-mature Cheddar.

His relationship with the cat evicted by Rossi had grown over time, both winning each other's trust, Romeo now sleeping on the bed or sitting on the windowsill watching the happenings in the square, chittering at birds while Morrison worked.

Morrison sometimes wondered if Rossi regretted not treating Romeo with more kindness and patience. He would remember to ask him one day.

He found himself talking to Romeo more, about the book he had decided to attempt to write, his walks, the feral cats he had once seen living on the rocks by the sea in Cadiz and telling him how lucky he was to have this warm apartment. In return the cat showed no inclination to explore the outdoors despite Rossi's previous annoyance at his endless going in and out, for which Morrison was grateful.

Despite the best efforts of his pet, whose other contribution was to regularly knock over the few Christmas cards Morrison had received, the work was beginning to take shape and he believed it could eventually make a novel. If it was any good would anyone still want to publish his work? That was a question for later. There was much progress to be made before that issue needed to be tackled.

Having crossed the piazza, Morrison noticed a sign pinned to the door of Franco's, where the canopied outdoor area had been removed and taken inside and the shutters pulled down over the windows.

It read: "Momentaneamente chiuso. Ci scusiamo per l'inconveniente", which another man, also looking into the restaurant and recognising his failure to understand the notice, translated as "Temporarily closed. Apologies for the inconvenience".

Morrison thanked him and waited until the man had left before knocking on the door and then, when there was no answer, calling Franco's mobile and then the restaurant telephone number. Again, there was no response. He backed out further into the square, looked up and could see movement in the upstairs apartment.

He wondered whether Pino had left again, scribbled a quick note and pushed it through the letterbox as he did not want to intrude.

He wrote: "Just to say I hope you and Pino are okay. I do not want to bother you if you do not want to talk but you have been a great friend to me throughout my time in Padria, made me truly welcome, helped me feel at home in a place I did not really know, and if I can return the favour and help in any way, I would be more than delighted to do so. Take care, Michael."

Once more he thought he saw a figure peering through the upstairs window but did not acknowledge it as he had no desire to make his friend feel uncomfortable.

He went back to his apartment, stared at the contents he had removed from Bianchi's bag, breathed heavily and put on his coat with a scarf and gloves as the chill was bitter, but at least the rain had ceased and conditions were such that a walk at a brisk pace would warm him up quickly and hopefully help clear his thoughts.

When he reached the sea wall near the hotel overlooking the bay, one of the waiters spotted him and commented that he had not seen him for a month or so.

"This is my summer place. It is definitely not summer now," he said, but the waiter persuaded him in for a coffee and they discussed the difficulties the locals had in making ends meet through the winter months when the tourists had disappeared and the custom dropped off. Morrison enjoyed the man's company, said he understood and promised to visit more regularly.

On leaving, he stood outside and found the view over the bay more breathtaking than he perhaps had through the summer months; a beauty he had not previously observed caused by a mix of the low light, the slight red cutting through the oddly expansive variations of cloud colour, with the yellow-orange of the surprisingly bright sun breaking from behind and bouncing off the water.

Naples and Vesuvius appeared motionless across the stretch of sea from the distant harbour, its moored boats bobbing beneath the cliffs, their hotels resting atop after a hectic season.

His inertia allowed the cold to wrap itself around him and he shivered, but he was in a happy place, if slightly disturbed by the change of circumstance in the lives of some of his friends.

He thought for a while and concluded that Pino was doing the right thing by at least addressing his problems. Luigi and Tommaso lived their lives as they always did, the awkward situation with Rossi had sorted itself out, he was writing again and had met Gabriella. The only major difficulty at present was Franco and the restaurant.

Over the past few days Tommaso and Luigi had expressed concerns over Franco and Pino, and Rossi asked him about his trip to see Stefano Bianchi, loudly stating: "You should have shot the son of a bitch. It would be no more than he deserved, Morrison."

Rossi was surprised that Morrison had managed to bring Bianchi to the point of expressing regret over his actions and added that he was disappointed a fight had not broken out.

Morrison told him Bianchi seemed to have disappeared and asked if he knew anything about what had happened.

"Why the hell would I know? I tell you and tell you I do not speak to the man and he not to me. Someone has probably finished him off and good riddance too. Or maybe he has simply vanished, moved on, but if he was going to stage his death like you believe, well, he hasn't done a very good job, has he? An abandoned car is not nearly enough. I will ask questions though. Someone will know. However careful you are, someone always knows and they always find you."

"You gave me the note. Where did that come from then Rossi? Go on, tell me that."

"A message, a message left in the letterbox. Left by him, or by someone else, I do not know. I know nothing more."

Rossi also said he had caught sight of Franco, who either did not see him or pretended he hadn't and scuttled back into his restaurant.

Morrison thought about this as he walked. Some lives were changing in a positive way, others maybe not so. The actions of those involved could affect this to some extent, but in part it was just the way of the world. Nothing lasts forever.

He continued, slightly inland, taking the less picturesque route towards the harbour, past a few hotels, bars, shops, a petrol station and the football stadium in which the town team would disappoint around three hundred and fifty fans every two weeks or so, most locals choosing instead to support the big city side in Napoli.

As he neared the harbour he surprised himself by heading into a shop that described itself as an artisan chocolatier, emerging with a fancy-looking and more than fancily-priced milk and dark "Connoisseurs Collection".

He took the lengthier route, along the snaking cobbled lane lined with cute cottages, many with wreaths and other Christmas ephemera hung outside their doors and pots of winter flowers, red and orange, some adorned with brightly coloured lights. He thought it would be nice to live here but not as pleasant as it was before the advent of tourism, a common story these days as the secrets of the planet are spilled all over television and the internet, leaving nowhere exclusive and very little private.

Even Gabriella's flat above The Star of the Sea would have changed dramatically in the years she had lived there; the sounds of chatter replaced by piped music, the smells and tastes of fresh fish on the busy harbourside overhauled by that of fancy food cooked in tourist trap bars and restaurants, the view of the bay largely the same, only the house on the hill's rise and fall and the building of the big hotels making noticeable differences to the appearance of the marina.

Gabriella, highly visible in a long deep red dress, saw him as he approached The Star of the Sea and blew him a kiss. He responded in a less dramatic fashion, with a brief wave, not given to displaying affection or emotion in public. He also resisted the urge to tell her she looked nice. It was too soon for such a compliment and he knew his blushing face would doubtless have matched her dress.

"I knew you would come, Michael Morrison," she said, greeting him with a hug. Kissing her on both cheeks, he handed her the chocolates.

"I didn't think there would be much point in bringing wine to a bar," he shrugged sheepishly.

She looked at him for a moment, fondly, and said: "I will provide the wine. As long as you keep coming here I can do that. Well, obviously a few other customers would help. I can't expect you alone to drink enough to keep me going. Especially if you do not pay."

"But I will pay, obviously I will. I don't come here expecting a free drink. In fact, maybe I no longer need one," Morrison stammered and reddened - was now the time to tell her? - unsure of himself at that moment and slightly on edge in a situation he had not found himself in for some time.

Gabriella laughed heartily and said: "Lighten up please. Remember what I told you after I saw you that night in Franco's? Don't think too much. You cannot see when you are so deep in thought and you miss the sunshine. I will keep telling you this until you stop. Understand?"

Morrison nodded, smiled, nodded and smiled again. He understood, but said thinking came as part of his job, simultaneously remembering that last time he had not questioned her enough, had not really got to know her.

So, as they walked inside the bar together and Gabriella motioned him to a table, bringing a large glass of Aperol for each of them, he thought he would get in first and said: "I talked too much the last time I was here. This time it is all about you. Tell me everything about yourself. At least everything you want to."

She smiled, collected her thoughts, began to talk and almost an hour later was still telling her story. He had relaxed by then and liked what he heard. He already knew that her father had run the bar before she took it over and discovered that, like Morrison, she had never married and had no children.

A long-term partner left her heartbroken when, four years ago, she found out he was having an affair with a younger woman, a former waitress they had employed. Almost immediately upon the revelation of his infidelity, he moved out, set up home with the woman on the outskirts of Naples and Gabriella had not seen him since.

"Fourteen years together and over just like that, Michael. You share your life, everything, with someone for so long and then they just disappear. It is like you never saw or knew them in the first place. Maybe I never did know him. Not really," she said. "I have been alone since and just thrown myself into the business. It has kept me sane, if not exactly made me happy."

It was the first time Morrison had seen Gabriella display any sign of vulnerability and it saddened him, a mood change she quickly spotted.

"Hey, hey, don't get down. It is fine. We are here and happy at this moment." She touched his hand and curled the tips of her fingers around his, leaving them there for thirty seconds or so before withdrawing them to lift her glass.

She explained the bar had never been one of those that aimed to attract well-to-do tourists with money to spend, though some came, enough to make sure that along with the local custom that had stayed loyal to the bar over the years it had remained a tenable business.

"We never bothered with the expensive food, having people outside touting for custom, all that the other places round here do. We started out as a bar that existed in tandem with the harbour and what it stood for, mainly frequented by the fishermen, and we have done our best to remain that way while making the little changes you must in order to survive.

"I have the bar; we do basic snacks and I live in the apartment above. That is why I like the place your friend Franco owns. It is similar to here and he has not forgotten the locals."

Morrison liked her. She liked him too. He knew this now. He would be careful this time though and he suspected that would also be the case with Gabriella. She had been hurt, he had been hurt and, perhaps, unintentionally he had hurt another.

He was surprised to find that another hour had gone by and they had got on so well and talked so much that he had only drunk one glass of wine after the Aperol.

He briefly outlined the facts behind Franco's temporary closure, to which she said he must leave and see if his friend needed help. He said he would ring her tomorrow and they embraced before he went on his way, Gabriella telling him she would cook him a special meal one evening over the next week.

The Christmas lights around the harbour had regained their magic as the wind forced the wires they were suspended on to bounce and twist as the day gave up the ghost.

He walked up the steps and along the sea front, heading back towards the outskirts of Padria and wondered if Franco had responded to his note.

His phone made a pinging noise and he fished it out of his pocket to find a text message from Gabriella which read: "I forgot to thank you for the chocolates. A lovely surprise. I really enjoyed your company. I hope you enjoyed mine. See you VERY SOON I hope - and you still haven't told me whatever it was you couldn't the last time we were together! Gabriella xx."

Morrison was not given to spending much time on his phone but stopped to reply, first making sure he was not in anyone's way as this was a feature of modern life that greatly annoyed him.

"Enjoyed it very much and will be in touch ASAP. Just need to help my friend now, Michael."

A reply bounced back immediately: "Good luck, Gxx."

On reaching the square, Morrison cast a look across but saw no life in or above the restaurant and went back to his apartment, where he checked the post-box and found a solitary note that read: "Thank you for your words and your concern. You too are a great friend and deserve all the support and help you have received in Padria. I am so pleased you love our town and have settled here.

"I am going away to think about my future and that of the restaurant. I sincerely hope I and it both have one. I hope Pino does too. Do not worry though, Pino and I will be fine. We have spoken since I last saw you and we just need a little time apart to think things through.

"I am going to visit a cousin near Lake Como. I will return in the new year, after the quiet season. Pino, I am not so sure. I think he will eventually return but for the moment I must support and understand him so that we continue to have a good relationship. He is staying with a friend.

"Please accept my apologies for closing. I promise to be in contact soon, your good friend Franco."

For a few seconds Morrison felt sad, but quickly snapped out of the thought process that concentrated only on how this news would affect him and considered instead his friends, Franco and Pino.

He regretted that he would not be able to walk across the square as and when he chose to have a drink and a chat with them, but the good news was that Franco and Pino were working out their situation and it sounded as if Franco was at least planning on returning in the not-too-distant future. Hopefully, Pino too, Morrison thought, but realised he had again quickly slipped into selfish thought and internally corrected himself to add: "If it is best for him."

He instinctively felt the need to respond to Franco's note but realised there was no point. Franco would not be there and he did not have a forwarding address for him.

Instead, he called in to see Tommaso, who was chatting with Rossi and Luigi. A worried-looking Tommaso said he had seen Franco heading to the railway station and he had informed him of the situation regarding Pino. Tommaso, the stress of all that had happened rendering his movement more awkward, told Rossi who, in turn, passed on the news to Luigi, whose facial tick immediately became more pronounced. They all thought what had transpired was in the long-term for the best, for Franco as well as Pino.

The full story behind Pino's sudden departure was told and Morrison said he felt somewhat responsible due to seeing him in the baths and because of the conversations he had with him, but Tommaso said if this had not happened Pino would not have acted and the situation would have carried on forever not being talked about. Son would have grown bitter towards father and the ending may well have been an unhappy one.

"You are not preparing to leave too are you, Mr Morrison?" asked Tommaso.

"No my friend, I really do not think I am. It did feel suddenly as if things were reaching something of a natural conclusion, but maybe they are just beginning Tommaso, maybe they are just beginning. Who knows? Conclusions and new beginnings are rarely cut and dried."

"What the hell are you banging on about, you pretentious bastard?" yelled Rossi, attempting to lighten the mood.

"Well, since you have asked so politely, here I go. I concluded a life and began a new one, but I have been wondering what happened to all those people I knew, all of those people I met over all those years? Where did they go? What did they do? How many people who you meet play a significant role in a part of your life and then somewhere down the line disappear and you say you'll keep in touch but for whatever reason never see them again? You move on, start your life again and keep in touch with who you want, no fuss, no judgement, but some of your past always comes with you. Got it Rossi? You certainly should have."

There was silence around the table, even from Rossi, who still managed to comedically place his head in his hands and feign to bang it on the table.

Morrison ignored him and continued. "I'm fifty two, you're what, sixty two Rossi, you Tommaso, just older than that and you Luigi, maybe sixty five. Franco is over sixty and Pino in his thirties. Between us we must have spoken to hundreds of thousands of people and become very close to maybe one hundred of those, maybe a few for large parts of our lives, and close to a thousand for small parts of our lives.

"Us now, sitting here, at this moment, we are close to each other and important to each other, right? The role we play in each other's lives. But what happens next?

"Pino has disappeared. Will he come back? Will he make a new life. As the days turn into weeks, the weeks into months and the months into years his memories of us will fade and the significance we have to him be reduced to nothing or very little at the most. Perhaps he will occasionally think of us, Google us, maybe even search for us on Facebook and even send a friend request. This is life, this is movement and I think I have finally reached a point where I want it to stop. The movement that is, not the life."

"Fuck Facebook and all that other shit. I'm sixty one, you arsehole. Insignificant arsehole. You mean nothing to me any more Morrison," Rossi, properly back in character now, laughed uproariously as he emptied the remains of his large glass of red, his third, perhaps fourth of the evening.

"Each time you insult me you fade a little," he added, enthusiastically clapping his friend on the back to emphasise his lack of seriousness.

"Sixty three, Mr Morrison. You were correct. However, I think I may have told you my age before," nodded Tommaso, sagely. He was calmer now. "The friends I have had, the people I have met, have largely been here in Padria and we have stayed close.

"I have been content here, less so since my wife Elena passed away, but that was many years ago. When it happened I lost any oomph I had, any ambition for anything such as it ever was, but I am happy, I have my friends and I believe these to be my true friends, those who will not do me wrong and, God willing, will stay with me through my days."

"Sixty seven, Mr Morrison, so thank you," beamed Luigi. "I feel the same as Tommaso. We have been friends for life, we have known Franco for life, played together, grown up together, worked together, done business together, laughed and cried together. Now we wait to die together. My wife Donna, she died when she was young, just thirty five, and I did not meet... could not bring myself to meet another woman after that. We had plans, we would move, we would travel, we would have children, but none of this happened and it would have felt wrong to do any of that without her, so I just carried on as before, in the tabacchi, serving customers, sometimes modernising, small changes, nothing big, just living life because it was there to be lived.

"I love Padria, I love my friends, my garden, my bees and all those things that have kept me going up until this moment. I cannot speak for Franco, but I think he would allow me to say it is similar for him. He was far more driven than me after the death of Patricia, for he wanted to work through his grief and in doing so pass on a healthy business through generations. He did not want to be the one who was thought to have failed his family. For Pino, I do not know, and I do not know how Franco feels now."

A brief silence, then: "Have you never had a moment's happiness Morrison, you miserable English bastard? On and on you go, dragging us all down." It was Rossi again, clearly having chosen to offer nothing in the way of explanation of his own life, though Morrison thought that was maybe because he already felt he had revealed more than enough to him.

Still, he would cut him no slack.

"Yes, yes I have Roberto, now I come to think of it. Every time you open your mouth you make an ass of yourself and that makes me happy."

Luigi chuckled, Rossi grinned and asked: "What about when you are making love to a beautiful woman? Does that not at least make you smile? Maybe you never have Morrison, maybe you never have and that's the problem."

"Fleeting moments Rossi, that's all they are, fleeting moments. Like you say, making love, scoring the winning goal, that thirst-quenching beer or glass of wine on a hot day, the first shoots of spring, they all bring happiness, but they only bookend the day-to-day reality of our existences. The search for something better, the fear of... the fear of..."

"The fear of what Morrison? Get on with it man."

"Oh, it doesn't really matter Rossi, maybe it's not as important for some as it is for others. For some it's God, another person maybe, but for me it has always been failure and now I have to face up to the possibility that it is too late to act on that.

"The world is full of books and songs that remained unwritten, fragments of ideas, unresolved brilliance we should have all read and heard, and there are also those that should have stayed inside and remained just that, half-formed ideas. For me that's it, the nagging voice that says no, don't do it, keep it to yourself."

"It will be me you need to fear if you keep going on like this, you pitiful wretched Englishman. For God's sake Tommaso, get the man another drink before we all go under...."

Everyone laughed and eventually the conversation moved to football, with good-natured jibing about the standards of the Italian and English teams. Rossi, somewhat unnecessarily, made his allegiance clear, loudly slurring "Gli Azzurri".

When he eventually left, bidding his friends goodbye, Morrison smiled to himself, internally acknowledging Luigi's accuracy of thought, Tommaso's kindness and Rossi's way of stopping him from over-thinking a situation but somehow still cutting through the mess and conjuring up solutions to problems.

Franco, Luigi, Tommaso and Rossi; their strong bond perhaps forged because all four had lost their wives, unusual in a world in which the men in a partnership generally perish first. This, along with their shared love of Padria and businesses in and around the square, seemed to have strengthened that bond and turned it into something beyond friendship.

Franco was no longer here, but he, Michael Morrison, was and, for once, was enjoying life. He had become part of Padria and Padria was now part of him.

Was this happiness? Was it as good as it would ever get, perfection, the prize he had sought all his life? Or was it merely contentment, an acceptance that this was it? If it was, would it last? Time would tell and he hoped he at least had that on his side.

20

Walk These Streets, Smell The Flowers, Follow The Light

The cicada was unfamiliar to Morrison and to the best of his knowledge he had never seen one. Butterflies, bees, wasps, ladybirds, ants and, of course, mosquitoes, smaller here and with a less damaging bite than in some parts of Europe, were regular sights, but the noisy cicada remained hidden.

The constant noise they made surprised him as he walked past trees and bushes in the summer heat, compensating for their near invisibility, busily click, click, clicking without interval from morning until midnight, save for an early afternoon siesta timed, it seemed, to coincide with that taken by the locals. But this time of year? Maybe he simply hadn't previously noticed.

Morrison understood it wasn't a popular sound and could be, at the very least, mildly irritating, but something about its consistent rhythm, like that of a well-rehearsed but monotonous orchestra, gave him a sense of happiness, its volume increasing as the heat rose.

"Noisy, annoying bloody things," Rossi said as they convened over a lunchtime New Year's Eve beer in Tommaso's - Christmas decorations still up, mulled wine remaining on the menu - the owner of the eponymously-titled establishment busy with a healthy number of customers, presumably as a result of the closure of Franco's.

"A pointless, stupid creature that you never see - I have not set eyes on one in all my time in this damn place - working like a fool for nothing when the heat is unbearable, plaguing the hell out of everyone, not stopping all day and for what? To attract a mate? Surely one bloody cicada looks like every other bloody cicada, so why go to all the bother?"

"You must sympathise Rossi, for surely you are the human cicada, existing only to annoy, always chipping away, hoping to push someone over the edge and taking satisfaction when they bite. Anyway, as you in particular should know, it's not all about looks, and to be fair they do have a purpose and maybe it is to irritate people such as yourself," Morrison said, with a broad smile and a raised eyebrow. "Which is not a difficult thing to do. Perhaps it takes pleasure from that. I certainly would and indeed I do."

"That is because you are a typical Englishman who glories in other people's misfortunes. Like all Englishmen do. Worse still, a typical miserable Englishman from the north of that bloody country, yet still you have a sense of superiority justified only by tiny victories such as possessing the incredible talent and ability to rise above being pissed off by a small insect.

"Meanwhile, your insects, like the dull moth you bang on about, are common rubbish, reflecting your dour towns and cities, your downtrodden personalities, your people's bland pale skin colour determined by your dirty rain which makes you all so sodding miserable. No bloody wonder you left."

"As opposed to you Mr Rossi. The beautiful bay you see every day, the colourful, vibrant floral displays have turned you into a right happy-go-lucky jolly sort. I'm surprised you haven't burst into a rendition of Oh What A Beautiful Morning. Then again, maybe it's the volcano that has shaped your boiling hot temper, always ready to explode," Morrison retorted with a wide grin.

It made Morrison laugh when he considered his first impressions of Rossi as an ill-mannered, overly opinionated curmudgeon, the sort of person to whom he would have given a wide berth in a different place at a different time.

That negative opinion was, of course, at one point stretched to the extreme by Rossi's work for Bianchi – who Rossi had been told had now left the country, possibly for Scotland, where he was said to have visited family in the past – thoughts of which still troubled Morrison, not least due to some extremely unpleasant vivid dreams he had had since their meeting.

Morrison had learned to enjoy the sparring, which walked a tightrope between good natured, respectful banter and the trading of a level of insult that could sour a pleasant chat. He felt they were now at a stage of their relationship at which they knew and appreciated each other's boundaries.

Despite the occasional moment of tension between them, they had somehow managed to patch up a difficult situation and struck up a reasonably solid friendship, and Rossi's ability to sympathetically synopsize a complicated story sometimes surprised Morrison, given his friend's natural and preferred tendency towards sarcasm and cantankerousness.

They had even spent a pleasant few hours in Morrison's flat mulling over various topics while enjoying a few beers and a pizza.

Rossi had taken a somewhat unexpected interest in his book collection, especially the poetry, which surprised Morrison, not least his in-depth knowledge of the works of the likes of Byron, Keats and Coleridge.

They had bonded to the extent that he now felt able to share his concerns and dilemmas over the money and the dress that had been in the bag Bianchi had left him. He did not tell him about the picture of Stefano, Sofia and Marianna he had also acquired.

To his relief, Rossi was more amused than shocked, laughing uproariously at the revelation.

"Ha ha…ooh, ha ha ha," Rossi grabbed his side with both hands as he exaggerated his mirth.

"Ah, I knew we were not so different, Mr Morrison, we are not so different at all. Now, like everyone else, we have both got some of the bastard's money and don't you dare hand it in to the police. They already have enough of his cash, or whoever it belonged to before he got his grabbing hands on it," Rossi said, eyes bright, his swallowing of a mouthful of beer accompanied by a facial expression that suggested a forthcoming mischievousness which did not transpire.

"You are a good man, and this does not make you a bad person - and definitely keep that dress. Maybe gift it to Gabriella..."

"Erm, I somehow don't think she would appreciate that Rossi... not quite her style."

"Ah, maybe not. Well, perhaps you may even be able to find someone to wear it at another posh party one day! No, no, I am sorry. Before you floored me with the news that you too were now involved in what you would call the corruption, I was going to say it is all about how we react to what life throws at us.

"I am irritable and bad-tempered, but only since my wife died, though some might say that is not true, they might say I was always this way. You, you are a thinker, which causes people to assume you are miserable. I do not really think you are.

"You have made a difference to this place Michael Morrison. You have dealt with a difficult situation, turned on a light and I, for one, certainly would not want that light to go out. At least while I am still about and the cicadas are making their incessant row, of which the former will be, well, one more day, one year, a decade, two at the most, and the latter until the world comes to an end, never moving from the same bloody tree.

"Walk these streets and love their colours, sounds and smells. These streets are yours now Michael," he said, raising his beer to the man, before pausing for a second, pursing his lips and continuing: "Ah, I have finally used your first name alone... and these streets are yours to make of what you will. It is too late for me to change, I don't have it in me, but you, you can think your thoughts, write your words and learn to love again while you still can.

"You walk and talk like a character who wants to be written about, wants to be in a story, a stylish character, European, maybe Italian even, but you are not interesting enough, you do not have the looks or the personality to pull it off. So, write a different you into your own book, make yourself more readable, do things you are not capable of in real life. After all, is that not what books are for?"

Toasting his host with the drink Morrison had just poured, he continued with some emotion.

"And remember, these streets you walk now, they weep too, only you have to search harder for the sadness and when you find it you don't have to wait too long for the sunshine to dry your tears. Also, now you have money you are one wretched Englishman with the means to cheer yourself up."

Morrison, impressed by Rossi's words which straddled tragedy and comedy, life and death, complete, of course, with a fond nod to *Walks Through Weeping Cities*, shook his head, smiled at the man and clicked his fingers three times.

"I think there was a compliment in there somewhere and, if I am not mistaken in assuming so, I thank you Roberto. Yes, you are, of course, correct and, like the cicada, I will learn to call off the search for something or someone else, somewhere better.

"I have broken through those palisades – big word, eh, maybe you will look it up later – that denied me the life I wanted, the life I needed. Maybe I put up some of those walls myself, walking streets back home full of vicious ghosts, demolished dreams, hopes unrealised and lives wrecked, but those walls have come down now and I hope I will walk these streets untainted by destructive memory for a long time to come and I will do so with a smile on my face. I will dance my own dance."

"That's a step too far Morrison. No-one wants to see that. The English, they don't have rhythm, they don't have soul, music or romance. Just stick to your walking my friend."

"Who knows? Who knows? We'll see. But yes, yes, I will, I will stick to my walking and maybe in the next few weeks I will walk across to your flat in which I will find newly purchased paint and brushes, maybe some artwork, some furniture, and we will do up the shithole.

"You can't live like that. It's not right. Not for a man with your kind of money, a man of your standing. If you want to be friends and maybe have me over for the occasional drink accompanied by your obligatory rudeness, not just me of course, anyone, then we must make the place at least pleasant enough to sit in."

"Well maybe I will leave it just as it is, if that will stop you coming over," Rossi grinned.

"Well then, before I forget, I knew there was something else I had to tell you. I have taken on one of Luigi's vegetable patches, your vegetable patches or whoever owns them, and I intend to have a go at growing my own food, so maybe you can visit and help me out with that instead. You see, I am looking to the future Roberto."

"Mmm, on second thoughts maybe we will do up my place and you can provide the whisky this time now you have the money. The paint too. Anyway, what the hell are you going to grow on a vegetable patch, beans on toast? That's about as gourmet as the English get with food, isn't it?" Rossi laughed.

He proffered a firm, sincere hand to Morrison, who reciprocated, the two shaking and exchanging New Year's greetings, and as Morrison turned to leave Rossi shouted after him: "Oh and go to the bloody doctors' please. We have all noticed and we are all concerned, but the rest of them are too polite to say. We don't want the annoying Englishman dying on us now he can afford to buy the drinks."

Morrison nodded, smiled and waved goodbye, noting to himself once more that he still didn't know how much money Bianchi had left for him.

Suddenly though he recalled Bianchi's words – "Here we are, Sofia, Marianna, me, all happy, smiling, a day trip to Capri, a normal family, the camera does not lie. It was not always bad. They came to places with me, stood by my side, they did not leave me" – and the picture, the wretched, broken man's only evidence of family contentment, finally made sense.

He had left Morrison with money, a part of Marianna and an attempt at justification, maybe even redemption. It was all he had left.

***

Suffused with warmth through the relationships he had forged with Franco, Pino, Tommaso, Luigi and Rossi, and now with Gabriella, Morrison chose not to head straight back to the confines of his apartment but instead to walk over to The Star of The Sea before it became busy.

The bar was already lively with late afternoon drinkers, Gabriella slightly flustered, offering only a quick wave and raised eyebrows, her face flushing red as she looked after the twenty to twenty five customers who had already commenced their celebrations.

"Come on, let me help, you shouldn't be doing all this on your own," he offered.

"That would be great Michael, but what can you do? No offence, of course."

"Well," he pondered aloud, rubbing his chin in mock derision, and grinning at her before retorting: "I think I can manage to take drinks to tables, work your till and card machine, open a wine or beer bottle, pour spirits, make an Aperol Spritz and even, given a quick refresher, pull a decent pint. I have done the odd shift in a bar before you know."

"Fantastic, you are a man of many talents. You can start now by taking these to the table in the corner," she said, pointing to a tray of drinks and winking.

"I have help arriving in two hours and I will reward you with a glass or two at the end of your shift."

"You're a hard taskmaster," he said, "and yes, I will definitely take you up on the drinks."

"Oh, and here, you'd better put this on. You're bound to spill," she added, tossing an apron in his direction.

Morrison found he quite enjoyed the buzz of the bar as it kept up a steady stream of customers, all of whom were pleasant, spoke excellent English and were appreciative of his amateur but conscientious efforts to get their orders right.

Finally, assistance arrived in the shape of a woman, introduced as Giorgia, portly with a rosy face, who Morrison estimated to be in her late-forties and seemed to be on friendly terms with Gabriella, the pair hugging and whispering conspiratorially to each other on her entrance into The Star of The Sea.

She giggled almost childishly as she was introduced to Morrison and raised her eyebrows suggestively towards Gabriella, who studiously and tactically ignored her, simply pouring Morrison a glass of Spumante and saying: "You deserve a couple of these at the very least. Thank you so much Michael, I could not have coped without you. If you want some shifts, given that you are technically between jobs, then there is a position available. The pay may not be much, but the perks include plenty of subject matter for you to study and write about."

"Of course, I will gladly help whenever you need it. I shall demand a proper contract mind and will be joining the union," he said, causing the waitress to look at him and laugh again as he continued: "In fact, maybe now I can even afford to buy a part-share in this place and be able to help you out properly."

On Gabriella's look of consternation and slight bemusement, he added: "Look, I promise, I will tell you all about it tomorrow."

On finishing his second glass at around 6.15pm, Morrison indicated he would leave as the bar was now almost full and he felt he was taking up the seat of a potentially valuable customer.

"Come, come," said Gabriella, a nod of her head indicating movement towards the small kitchen area, in which she took hold of a slightly abashed Morrison, pulled him close to her and kissed him full on the lips.

Morrison blushed and turned a deeper shade of red when Giorgia, who had observed what was going on through the door, which had been left ajar, let out a loud "whoop whoop".

She bounced up and down, hopping from one foot to the other, clapping and cheering, quickly joined by a table of customers familiar to Gabriella, who put a hand over her mouth to curtail her laughter, while an abashed Morrison, in return, offered only a sheepish smile, held his hands up and shrugged his shoulders.

"Oh Michael, I have embarrassed you," Gabriella said, grabbing his right arm with both her hands. "I am so sorry."

"No, no, it's fine. I have been embarrassed before and I'm sure it will not be the last time," he said, making no move to free himself from her grasp.

"Go Michael, go, go, we are busy here and you will be happier back with your friends or with your little cat," she said, pushing him out of the kitchen and pointing towards the door, ushering him out, half laughing and half apologetic for the discomfort she had caused him.

Morrison smiled, looked down for a second, gathered himself, lightly touched her arm, and looking directly at her, uttered the words: "Goditi il resto della giornata. Ci vediamo l'anno prossimo. Oh, and, erm, Buon anno nuovo, Gabriella."

"Michael, where did you…? How on earth? You do not speak Italian…"

"Let's just say I took your advice Gabriella. I cannot say that in Italian or the fact that I have been seeing the daughter of the limoncello seller… not seeing her," he added quickly, "as in, you know what I mean… I have been seeing her to try to learn some Italian and she taught me those phrases. It took me ages, and it would have been easier to just tell you to enjoy the rest of the day and that I would see you next year, but… now I feel a little bit silly."

Morrison wondered how many times a person could blush in such a short space of time.

"Oh, you are such a sweetie, now get yourself off - and remember, tomorrow you will tell me all or else I shall ban you from my bar," Gabriella teased and once more waved Morrison, sporting yet another blush, out of the door of The Star of The Sea, shouting after him "oh, and happy new year to you too."

***

Morrison took off his coat, scarf and gloves, and fed Romeo, who had greeted him by rubbing round his legs and delivering a demanding yowl. He fondly rubbed his cat's ginger ears.

He put down a bowl of food for Rossi's feline nemesis and poured a large glass of red wine for himself, having warmed it up in the microwave, a process he frequently undertook although he knew it would be frowned upon by the experts and sommeliers. Toasting Romeo – "Cheers to a good few more years to come, my boy" – he took a seat at his computer and began to type.

The words flowed for he now knew the story he must write. It had been obvious all along, but somehow he had missed all the vital clues. In fiction as in fact, always missing the clues, he thought.

Despite the amount of alcohol he had consumed, Morrison's fingers moved across the keyboard faster than they had in years.

"The End.

Or was it?

Maybe it was only the beginning.

Or could it be the beginning of the end or the end of the beginning?

Whatever the answer, there would always be a new story to tell.

The writer was certain of that now."

He clutched his side as a pain sent him yet another reminder to write a note to call the doctor.

A collection of unthreatening fluffy white clouds danced playfully across the dying night as the year approached its final breath and he questioned whether the sunshine of Padria had enabled him to see his way through the darkness or simply blinded him to his fears and maybe even the truth.

Whatever the answer, like the moth he had chosen to fly towards the light and hope for change rather than simply sit in the dark.

Maybe someone or something would eventually flick the switch and dim his view of the way forward, but he was happy for now, like the moth enjoying the glow, and unlike the cicada, making noise from life's hidden corners where the light flickers on, off, on, off, fades and eventually dies.

He gazed over the Piazza San Marco, busy with revellers, and up to the basilica, half-closed his eyes and saw an army of shadows, leaping up, down and across the walls, in and out of the distorted illumination provided by the streetlights, a long and thin synchronised mass criss-crossing the centre of the square.

For a moment there was Marianna again, above the crowd, waving, smiling, her once sad brown eyes now sparkling and alive to the sound of freedom.

Then she was gone.

But not truly, he thought, not forever. Not really.

He smiled as he typed her name.

The choreographer of ghosts, still leading him a merry dance.

***

Acknowledgements

I didn't intend to write a novel. I was on holiday in Italy, sitting by the pool thinking about people and places, what they are doing and why they are there. What happens when they disappear behind closed doors.

I started punching out words on my iPad, was quite pleased with them, returned to England and forgot all about it.

Another holiday, this time in Greece, prompted me to look at what I had written, the ideas started flowing and then stopped just as abruptly. A couple of writing courses, eleven drafts, self-doubt and repeated thoughts of giving up, and a decade later here is *The Choreography of Ghosts*.

Would I do it all again if I had the chance? Yes, but I wouldn't make the beginners' mistake of writing without a plan. Ten years per book is not an effective use of time.

Along the way, many people made valuable contributions to *The Choreography of Ghosts*, mostly without their knowledge, so it's only right they are now recognised.

Firstly, my mum Jean for inspiring my love of words, my late father Derek for making sure I wasn't one of those lads who studied at the expense of sport and drinking, and my brother David for his encouragement, given despite not particularly being a book lover himself.

My partner Ness for putting up with my on/off obsession with writing this, reading every version from the first draft to last, pointing out errors, inconsistencies and making invaluable - though not always appreciated at the time - suggestions.

Matt Bird for his brilliant design and making sense of the road to publication.

Michele Vincent, a work colleague who charitably and typically volunteered to read one of the middle versions and offered valuable criticism not long before she died. I thank her wholeheartedly.

My much-loved cats Belle and Sebastian - both of whom recently passed away - for unknowingly helping me see the light when I didn't realise there was any.

Those on the various writing courses I have completed for giving me the confidence to carry on and, in many cases, putting up with my lack of reciprocation.

The people I have met throughout my life who I drew on to create the characters in the book as well as the residents of Sant'Agnello who were victims of my constant and surely suspicious observations and note-taking.

Oh, and whoever it was that abandoned the huge house on a Greek island and inspired the setting for the story twist, or the jeopardy as I understand they say in the game.

Finally, friends and colleagues who, when I finally had the confidence to tell them what I was doing and to take the advice of letting people know about it on social media, didn't laugh.

Sincere thanks to everyone and to the many I haven't mentioned.

I couldn't have done it without you.

About The Author

As a journalist for more than thirty years, people could be forgiven for assuming I have written plenty of fiction. I haven't. Well, not until now.

Aside from a short story - featured on my website if anyone's interested - published in a collection while I was working on the Craven Herald & Pioneer in Skipton in the early 1990s, it's been news, previews, reviews and features for papers, magazines and websites.

From Yorkshire to Devon (health reporter on the Express & Echo and music writer for various magazines) to Greater Manchester (features editor and assistant editor on the Bolton Evening News) and back to God's Own (well, South Yorkshire where I live with my partner Ness and, until recently, our cats Belle and Sebastian) to edit the Rotherham Advertiser, the fiction stayed inside my head.

Then inspiration struck on a holiday just outside Sorrento. It was far from being a complete idea and the true lightbulb moment came when I stumbled upon a dilapidated mansion on a Greek island.

As you will find out (and may have already done so), *The Choreography of Ghosts* is essentially a novel about loss, searching, finding and losing again - a life that, wherever it takes him, is never enough for sometimes successful novelist Michael Morrison. It could, if you want, also be about class, envy and how people's backgrounds shape their lives.

It's not about me, but safe to say I know how Mr Morrison feels. If he wasn't originally based on me, I have spent so long with him I now feel I may be based on him.

* For regular news, updates, free writing and more, check out my website at https://www.andrew-mosley.co.uk/ or contact me via Facebook, email, Twitter or Instagram.

Details are at the bottom of the homepage.